P9-ARM-988

THE
BOOKSTORE
ON
Amelia Island

SEVEN SISTERS
BOOK THREE

HOPE
HOLLOWAY

Hope Holloway

Seven Sisters Book 3

The Bookstore on Amelia Island

Copyright © 2023 Hope Holloway

This novel is a work of fiction. Any references to historical events, real people, or real locales are used fictitiously. Other names, characters, places, and incidents are the product of the author's imagination, and any resemblance to actual events or locales or persons, living or dead, is coincidental. All rights to reproduction of this work are reserved. No part of this publication may be reproduced, stored in or introduced into a retrieval system, or transmitted, in any form, or by any means (electronic, mechanical, photocopying, recording, or otherwise) without prior written permission from the copyright owner. Thank you for respecting the copyright. For permission or information on foreign, audio, or other rights, contact the author, hopehollowayauthor@gmail.com.

Cover designed by Sarah Brown (http://www.sarahdesigns.co/)

The Seven Daughters of Rex Wingate

Born to Charlotte Wingate

Madeline Wingate, age 49
Tori Wingate, age 45
Rose Wingate D'Angelo, age 43
Raina Wingate, age 43

Born to Susannah Wingate

Sadie Wingate, age 35
Grace Wingate Jenkins, age 33
Chloe Wingate, age 29

Chapter One

Raina

"Raina, there's someone down here to see you. Says it's a surprise."

As the receptionist's words came through the land-line she'd recently installed in her office at Wingate Properties, Raina practically leaped over her desk. Could it be Blake?

Please, *please* let it be Blake Youngblood, the assistant who'd disappeared without a trace a month earlier.

"On my way!" She hung up and darted out of her office and toward the wide marble stairs that led to the first floor of the Wingate Properties building.

She practically vibrated with anticipation, hoping she'd finally come face to face with the man she'd been looking for since the day she discovered he was the nephew she and her six sisters didn't even know they had.

Three times in the last few weeks, she could have sworn she'd seen Blake around Amelia Island, confirming her belief that he was still close by, but avoiding any and all Wingates. The other day, seated in the Riverfront Café, she thought she saw him walking along the wharf, gazing out at the Amelia River. Yesterday, when she was coming out of her sister's bookstore, she was certain she'd seen him across the street, right outside of this very building.

But a van had come down Wingate Way, blocked her view, and wham! He was gone. Her frustration was palpable.

Maybe today. Maybe she'd finally get the chance to thank him for helping her in her darkest hour. Even more important, she could tell him—a young man who'd been disowned by his father and had come to this island in search of his biological relatives—that he would be accepted and loved by the Wingate family.

Her heart plummeted when she saw the silhouette of a woman in the light. Not Blake. But when that woman turned, her heart rose again. Wrong assistant, but a great surprise.

"Dani!" Arms out, Raina rushed toward Danielle Alvarez, who'd been her right hand—and frequently her left—at her real estate firm in Miami. "What are you doing here?"

Dani broke into a smile, dark eyes dancing as she shook back some of the thick curls that never could be contained with elastic or clips.

"Surprise!" They met in the middle, throwing their arms around each other and giving a long, much-needed squeeze. "Oh, Raina Wingate, I've missed you more than words can say."

"Same, my friend." Raina drew back to look at her former assistant's familiar face, instantly seeing a rare sadness on the arresting features of the thirty-two-year-old dynamo. "What's wrong, Dani?"

The other woman grunted softly. "What's *right* would be a better question. I got canned from Wallace & Wingate."

Raina sucked in a shocked breath. "My own company? My own administrative assistant? Jack *fired* you? That's preposterous!"

But was it? Nothing Raina's soon-to-be-ex-husband did surprised her these days. She hadn't stepped foot in the office of their jointly-owned Miami real estate firm for months, and anything was possible.

But...*Dani*? Really? She was indispensable to their company.

"Jack didn't do the deed." Dani gave a tight smile. "Lisa *Dogfrey* fired me."

Raina almost laughed at the play on the name "God-frey" but nothing about this was funny.

"What? Why? When? And was anyone going to tell me?"

Although, to be fair, she hadn't talked to anyone at W&W except Dani since her last deal closed. Raina had come up to Amelia Island more than four months ago when her father had a stroke. Since then, she'd only gone back twice—once for an overnight attempt to get her marriage back on track, and another time to get some more clothes and belongings when she'd made her move here official.

Her life and work was on Amelia Island now. Her

work at the company she'd built was done, at least for the moment. And her marriage? Over.

"Was anyone going to *tell* you?" Dani scoffed. "You are *persona non grata*, Raina. Like, that woman won't let your name be spoken."

Raina felt her jaw loosen, hit by a bolt of distaste for her cheating husband and his mistress. They'd met when Jack had acquired—against Raina's wishes—Lisa Godfrey's up-and-coming real estate firm. It hadn't been long before Jack and Lisa merged more than their companies.

But Raina wasn't the loser in that painful situation, no matter how much it hurt to end a sixteen-year marriage. She had won the greatest of consolation prizes —two of them, as a matter of fact.

The twins growing inside her, a result of that desperate night when she tried to fix a broken marriage, brought Raina nothing but joy. The marriage may have died, but two new lives had been conceived, giving her the dream of motherhood she'd longed for.

"Why are you smiling?" Dani asked, reminding Raina that she hadn't told her about the babies, and she guessed Jack hadn't, either.

"Uh, I'm smiling because...she said you can't mention my name? My name is spoken every time someone answers the phone in that office, unless he's taken the *Wingate* out of Wallace & Wingate."

"We've all been instructed to call it W&W now, which is hard to say and so dumb." She rolled her eyes.

"Anyway, Lisa's cleaning house and I'm...the trash that got taken out."

"Stop it!" Raina gave her arm a light jab. "You're the best assistant in the real estate business."

Dani grinned, then looked from side to side. "Don't you have one here at Wingate Properties who might get offended by that? Or, I guess, your dad had one before he got sick and you stepped in for him."

"I did, but..." She sighed, anxious to tell Dani everything and already sensing this brilliant and resourceful woman could help her. "Come on up to my office, Dani. Let's talk."

Raina put her arm around the other woman and guided her up the stairs to the second floor of the transformed bank building, pausing at the top for dramatic effect. There they could look down on the marble-floored lobby and small work area where a few agents had desks when they weren't out in the field. Turning, she showed Dani the second floor, an open area with room for a few desks, and then double doors into the spacious office from which Raina's father once ruled the roost.

Since his stroke, the office had been Raina's, but she hadn't changed a thing. Dad might be seventy-five years old and recovering, but this was still his domain and she hoped he might come back to work at some point.

"Come in and sit down," she said, waving Dani into the office. "I have news. Big, fat, juicy news."

"Ooh, I like the sound of that." Dani stopped in the doorway, her gaze locked on the huge window behind the desk. It was a vista Raina never took for granted, with the sun almost always sparkling on the Amelia River behind the charming, quaint buildings across the street.

"Raina!" Dani exclaimed. "This place is even prettier than I imagined."

"Welcome to Wingate Way," Raina said, making a sweeping gesture toward the street that bore her family's name. "Home to Wingates and our businesses for a hundred years."

"Look! The wedding dress shop!" Dani pointed to the white stucco building adorned with breathtaking gowns in the window. "Madeline Wingate Designs?"

"Yep, that's my oldest sister's studio upstairs and the dress salon on the first floor. And over there is Coming Up Roses, my twin sister's flower shop. And see that brick house with the upstairs balcony?"

"Grace's bookstore?" Dani guessed correctly. "You've always talked about this street, but I never knew it was all so Adorable with a capital *A*."

Raina laughed, filled with pride for her hometown and her family's legacy, but also happy to have Dani right here. "And that's only part of it. Way down to the right? That beautiful Victorian?"

"I saw it on the way in—a literal gingerbread house."

"That's Wingate House, our inn," Raina told her. "And down there, at the other end, you can see the colorful awnings of the Riverfront Café, which my sister Tori is running this summer."

"Gosh, I didn't ask about your dad. Still doing well?" Dani's expression changed to true concern.

"He's recovering very nicely, thank you. Every day he

shows improvement. A stranger might not know he had a stroke," Raina said, "but his family can see that he's not quite the powerhouse that Rex Wingate once was."

"So you're taking over this business," Dani said, no question in her voice. "I bet that's your exciting news."

Raina tipped her head. "Nothing is official, but I think now that Wingate Properties is in my hands and running pretty smoothly, my dad is starting to enjoy life as a retiree."

"In other words, you're never coming back to the nightmare that is Miami." Dani threw her hands up, then turned to take in the office itself. "I guess this is the silver lining in the end of your marriage."

Raina gestured toward the sofa along the wall, considering how to best share her wonderful news as they both sat down.

"Silver...or maybe it's a pink or blue lining..." She lifted her brows and, at Dani's confused look, Raina placed a hand on her stomach. "Might be two boys, might be two girls, might be one of each."

Dani's jaw nearly hit the floor. "*What?*"

"I'm seventeen weeks, Aunt Dani. With twins. I've been waiting to tell you in person next time I went to Miami."

Raina could see the chills rising on Dani's arms as she tried to talk, but nothing came out, making Raina laugh.

"No! Oh, my goodness!" Dani lunged closer for a hug. "Twins? Well, that makes sense, since you're a twin. Seventeen weeks? After all you've been through, I can't believe it."

"Neither can I," she confessed, trying not to think of the three miscarriages she'd suffered in the past six years.

"How do you feel?" Dani asked, knowing Raina's history.

"So good. I had one scare..." She glanced at the doorway, remembering the evening she lay on the floor, bleeding, certain she was having her fourth miscarriage, until... Blake made sure she got help. "But it was fine and that's when I found out they're twins. Girl, I'll be kissin' fifty when my kids are in first grade, but I don't care. I will be there for every school play, awards ceremony, and birthday party."

Murmuring more congratulations through tears, Dani hugged her again. "I know how much you've wanted to be a mother. At the risk of being grossly out of line, how and when did it happen?"

"Based on my doctor's best guest and my last period, I think it was that one weekend after my dad's stroke when I went down to surprise Jack." Raina made a face, a little embarrassed that she'd practically seduced her husband that night. "Of course, I didn't know he was cheating on me, and only suspected the next day when I found some clues that she'd been in my house. I found out I was pregnant the day he told me he'd fallen in love with Lisa Godfrey."

Dani shuddered. "The things I could call that woman."

"Don't bother, because I don't care about her," Raina insisted. "The lawyers are hired, the divorce is in process, and I don't give a hoot if he gets the house, the business, or anything else we own. I've got Thing One and Thing Two."

Dani's eyes widened. "Does he know? Because he hasn't breathed a word of it at work."

"Oh, yes. He knows and...I guess he's happy for me. He said he wants to have a role in their lives, but since then, he's been completely distant." She swallowed, the words hurting her throat. "He's made his choice. And it's Lisa."

Dani looked skyward. "Sorry, but he's an idiot."

"Jack's a lot of things, but not dumb. It's okay, Dani. I have my babies. I have my family."

"All seven sisters together! Wait. Are they all here?"

"Five are. My baby sister Chloe moved to Los Angeles for a job in television and—"

"Oh, the runaway bride. I know Chloe. And Sadie's in Brussels, right? Working for a chocolate company?"

"She is," Raina confirmed. "Tori lives in Boston, but she and her two kids are here for the summer, which is beyond awesome. Stick around and you'll meet them all."

"I'd love to," Dani said, leaning closer. "In fact, I'd love to stick around for a long time."

"What do you mean? Can you stay for a while?"

"Define 'a while.'" Dani lifted her brows expectantly. "I mean, I got canned. My rent on the Brickell apartment went sky high. I'm thirty-two, single, and everything in Miami reminds me of my mom."

"Oh." Raina put a hand on Dani's arm, knowing the loss of her sweet Mami had broken this girl's heart.

"It's been two years and I still miss her so much,"

Dani admitted. "I actually think getting fired was a blessing so I could finally make a change and get out of South Florida. My dad's remarried and my brother's never around, so..."

"Would you move here?" Raina asked, almost afraid the answer would be no.

But Dani laughed. "Of course I would! Do you know someone who needs a decent admin?"

"Decent?" Raina choked. "Understatement alert. And 'someone' might be me."

"No! I thought you mentioned that you had an assistant, or Rex did. The kid you called Blake the Fake?"

Raina let out a sad groan thinking about how wrong she'd been. "He wasn't really a fake, he was..." How to explain it? The truth, she supposed. "He was—is—my nephew."

Dani started to respond, froze, and did a double-take. "Say *what*?"

"His name is Blake Youngblood, but he was born Blake Young and his father..." She grunted, furious just thinking about Bradley Young. "His father, we have discovered, is the love child between my father and a woman who worked for us for many years, but has passed away."

"*Stop!*" She slapped her hands on the sofa. "Rex had an affair?"

"No, no, no," Raina said quickly. "This all happened fifty-some years ago. Rex was in college and Doreen Parrish worked at Wingate House. When she died about a month ago, my sisters and Mom and I cleaned out her apartment at the inn. We found proof of the baby and, long story, we realized that baby was Blake's father. But..."

Dani inched closer when Raina's voice trailed off. "Yes?"

"He disappeared. I don't know where he went and his family is no help."

"Why did he leave? Did he not want you to find out the truth?"

"I don't know why he left," she admitted on a shrug. "He disappeared the night I had the scare and had to go to the ER. He called 911 and in the chaos, admitted he was the son of a man named Bradley Young—who had contacted my father, looking for money. Dad gave it to him, too."

She frowned. "But Blake..."

"Blake had no idea his father had been in touch with Rex. And he didn't tell me anything else. He called for an ambulance when I had bleeding and cramps and was gone when they got here."

Dani dropped back on the sofa, scowling. "But Rex knows, right? That's why he hired Blake."

She shook her head. "No. We haven't broken it to him, because after the stroke he sort of fell into a depression. We all had to move heaven and Earth to get him out of it. We have, but my mom is babying him."

"But what brought Blake here?"

"From what I can piece together, he broke off with his family in Iowa for personal reasons, after his father kicked him out. He sought out Rex, who he must have known was his biological grandfather, and got the job without telling him who he was. Before he could, my dad had a stroke."

Frowning, Dani considered the story. "Have you talked to Blake's family? Maybe he went back to Iowa."

"His father—who is technically my half-brother—must take after the *other* half, because he's apparently a Grade-A jerk. He won't even acknowledge Blake's existence."

"Why?"

Raina tipped her head. "Blake came out of the closet and his father couldn't handle it."

"Eesh. What about his mother?"

"She's a pushover who does what her husband tells her, or at least that's what I've determined from my conversations with her." They'd been brief, cold, and unsatisfactory. "I'm hoping he hasn't gone far, since I think his whole reason for coming here was to establish a rapport with my dad, and then me. Maybe all of us. Poor kid needs a family."

"Oh, Raina. What a mess." Dani reached for her hand. "And the divorce, too. You must be a wreck."

"I would be except I'm growing a couple of little angels in my body and nothing can make me unhappy," Raina assured her. "But I do want to find him. I've talked to people who know him, gone to his apartment, searched the internet. He could be anywhere now, but my gut says he's still around." She stood and walked to the window, rubbing her arms as she scanned the street. "I swear I've seen him a few times but that could be my imagination.

He has a really distinctive light blue hoodie with a round logo on the back and I thought I saw that jacket, but he escapes before I can get to him."

"How can I help?" Dani asked, in true Dani fashion. "Can I dig? Hire an investigator? Make calls? I can stalk his apartment, because he doesn't know my face. Good idea, huh?"

"I don't know." Raina's shoulders dropped as she turned from the window. "But I do need to find him, Dani. I *have* to."

"Are your sisters looking?"

"Yes, of course, but no one has a clue where to go or look next."

"We'll find him," Dani said confidently. "I think you remember I was an extraordinary assistant who could throw together an open house on a dime, reel in the most obnoxious builder, and spot a typo lurking in the corner of any sixteen-page contract." She gave a saucy smile. "And if you hire me again..."

"Done." Raina put her arms around Dani and squeezed. "When can you start?"

"Now. Please tell me you have a picture of this guy. Because we're going to find him and give Rex a surprise grandson to bring him joy. Then you know what's going to happen?"

Raina stared at her, feeling full of love and gratitude and amusement. "What's going to happen?"

"Then Blake Whatever He Calls Himself will have to arm wrestle me for his old job back." She added a smug smile.

"Then let's get started, Dani. Oh, where are you going to live?"

"I rented a studio apartment already." She grinned. "I was pretty sure you'd hire me."

Raina laughed. "Of course you were."

Chapter Two

Grace

A thread. That's what Grace Jenkins was hanging by these days—a thin, frayed, delicate thread that could break any day and her world would come crashing down. Work, life, family. Everything all seemed so tenuous, like one strong tug and...she would break.

She took a deep breath and tried to channel her inner Susannah Wingate. Her mother, the strongest person she knew, had been through hell and back these past few months and nary a blond hair was out of place. Mom kept it together, maintained her composure, never missed a beat, and inspired Grace every single day.

But today? Grace wasn't feeling like Susannah's daughter at all. She was...a mess. And so was this storage area.

She stood in the back of her bookstore, gaze on the five—oh, now it was six—boxes of books that had just come from different publishers. She had to shelve them today while Nikki Lou was spending the morning at a flower-arranging class at her Aunt Rose's flower shop.

She also had to open The Next Chapter in less than

ten minutes, help customers find the perfect book to accompany their Amelia Island vacations, return calls, and pay bills. If all that was accomplished by the time the afternoon manager showed up, then Grace could get Nikki Lou to a birthday party.

No, correction. First Grace had to get her daughter dressed for the party in the pink unicorn top she'd insisted she had to wear...but the applique scratched her tummy. So sometime between now and then, Grace would have to sew fabric on the inside to protect her baby's precious skin.

Oh, and her mother wanted Grace to stop by the beach house, because she hadn't seen her parents in days, and she'd promised Isaiah she'd help him with a project at the inn, and...there was something else floating around her lengthy to-do list, but she'd forgotten it.

All of that, every single thing, paled in comparison to the emotional rollercoaster of waiting for...the news.

Any day, any minute, she'd get a call from Dr. Amanda Alberino, a pediatric psychologist who had been spearheading her daughter's testing. Grace had taken Nikki Lou to three specialists now, all trying to determine if—and where —her little three-year-old fell on the spectrum for autism.

Since she'd started the process, Grace had gotten more and more comfortable with the likelihood that her daughter had far more serious issues than a case of profound shyness.

The doctors all referred to it as a "disorder," but Grace had spent enough time with Isaiah Kincaid, a new arrival in town who now managed the family's inn, to have an aversion to the word.

Isaiah said God didn't make anything out of order. Grace didn't know if she believed in God—certainly not one who'd left her a pregnant widow four years ago—but she liked what Isaiah had to say. She liked everything about Isaiah, if she was being honest.

Her phone rang in her pocket and she eased it out, kind of hoping it was Isaiah calling about...oh, no.

Not Isaiah. This was it.

Dr. Amanda Alberino.

She didn't move for a second, knowing this call would in essence dictate the rest of her life. Either Nikki Lou was far enough to one side of the spectrum that she could be mainstreamed...or she needed a more aggressive "treatment."

Whatever it was, Grace had to know, so she tapped the screen and took a deep breath.

"Hello, Dr. Alberino."

"Good morning, Grace. And once again, you can call me Amanda."

Grace smiled, picturing the auburn-haired psychologist, a woman in her early fifties with a tender manner and sharp brown eyes that managed to be both intelligent and kind. Wonderful with children and adults alike, Grace had grown to genuinely like Amanda and, more importantly, she trusted her.

And even more important than that? Nikki Lou liked "Doctor 'Manda," and trusted her as well.

"Do you have the final report?" Grace asked, too nervous for pleasantries.

"I do," the other woman said. "I'm not surprised by the results. As I strongly suspected, Nikki Lou has many of the classic markers of Level 1 Autism Spectrum Disorder, what we used to refer to as Asperger's Syndrome."

Grace closed her eyes and let that sink in, all the research she'd done spinning through her mind. "That's... treatable, right?"

"There's no drug or cure, but cognitive behavioral therapy, social skills training, and a massive adjustment in diet and nutrition can drastically reduce the challenges Nikki Lou is facing."

"Good, good," Grace said quickly, freakishly calm regardless of the news. "I don't want to change her, Amanda. I don't want to *fix* my beautiful daughter. She's bright and amazing and has the vocabulary of a child three times her age. I meant, how do we...help her get through life in the best way possible?"

She heard the other woman sigh. "Well, you start with that wonderful attitude, Grace. And I promise you, I have a plan."

"And I want to follow it," Grace assured her.

"I do want you to know that it won't always be easy," Amanda continued. "Nikki Lou might comprehend the most difficult subjects, like math or science or even esoteric humanities, and I do believe she has the type of intelligence that could manifest itself with that island of genius or special skill we talked about."

"That all sounds really good."

"But she still may struggle to navigate her way through a dinner party," Amanda added. "Or have a breakdown over something that, on the surface, makes no sense."

"Like a scratchy top or a flickering light," Grace said with a bittersweet smile, those most recent meltdowns fresh from last night.

"Precisely. So you won't be surprised to know that her learning process and her socialization will be entirely different from that of mainstream children."

"What exactly does that mean?" Grace pressed, vaguely aware of her heart hammering. Or maybe that was someone knocking at the front door of the store. "She won't be in a mainstream school? Not even by kindergarten in two years?"

"We'll see when we get there," Amanda said. "But she won't have a chance without intervention and preparation during the next two years. And I'm happy to tell you I have an idea for how to do that."

Grace dropped onto a box of books, glancing at her watch and wincing at the time. The bookstore should have opened two minutes ago, but this was more important.

"Go ahead," she said.

"I've been working with a local sociologist to put together a trial education and socialization program tailored to individual preschoolers. Nikki would be our first student, but the sociologist has another candidate as well, so your daughter would be in an experimental classroom of two."

"Okay," she said, drawing out the word. "What is the program?"

"Too complicated to explain in a call, but it will guide these children to participate much more than a standard early intervention class. Then, when they get to school at five, they have a better chance in the classroom."

A better chance? What mother didn't want that for her child? "I guess that's the right thing to do, then."

"If you're up for it," Amanda said. "I have to be honest and let you know that it will require you to do more hands-on work with her, backing up our work with an at-home program. In essence, Nikki Lou's program never ends, and the home learning is as important as what we'll do on-site."

"So I'd be homeschooling her?" Grace asked.

"Not exactly, but you are going to be involved. We will address Nikki Lou's challenges from every angle— emotional, intellectual, psychological, and physical. You'll put our findings to work in her life, and that will include exposing her to specific experiences, managing behavioral therapy at home, and helping her put into practice some tools she'll learn in the program. Oh, and you'll have to completely change her diet. I'm a stickler about sugar and processed foods affecting her."

Grace sucked in a breath, and could swear she heard her tenuous thread stretch a little more. "Amanda, I'm a single mom and I own my own business..." Her voice trailed off.

"Because Nikki Lou would be our inaugural student, I would propose to put her through this program at no cost. All we'd ask of you is a testimonial at the end. If this works the way I think it will, I'm hoping to roll this program out county, state, and nationwide."

"Oh!" Grace's eyes widened. "I wasn't thinking about the money, but that would be amazing. I want to have the time to make it work and do the at-home part to the best of my ability."

"You have a big family, Grace. Lean on them. This is really a chance to change Nikki Lou's life, and yours. Can we set up a time to discuss the details?"

"Yes, I—" She sat up straight at the definite sound of someone pounding on the front door. Who needed to buy a book that badly?

"Good, because I've already made arrangements for Dr. Grayson and his staff to come here on Thursday afternoon," Amanda said. "They will meet Nikki Lou and start creating a personalized daily program for her. It's the only day and time he's available, so please plan around that."

"Of course," she said, knowing in her gut that this program, no matter how complex or time-consuming, was an amazing opportunity for her daughter.

She also knew that Amanda was smart, kind, and came with the highest recommendations and superior credentials. Frankly, it was nothing short of a miracle that she had a practice on Amelia Island.

"My store manager is here on Thursdays, so you can count on us to be there," Grace said.

"Perfect. Thank you."

"Oh, no. Thank *you*, Amanda. I mean..." As it all hit

her, Grace was swamped with gratitude. "This is a godsend."

"We're so looking forward to working with your little girl," Amanda promised her.

As they finalized the appointment, the impatient customer banged on the door even harder, and Grace could hear a woman's voice calling, "Are you open yet?"

Jeez, lady. Relax.

She took a deep breath and decided to follow that advice herself. *Relax.* She had answers and good solutions. She'd get it all done, somehow. As long as no one threw any more curveballs her way.

TAKING a few moments to pull herself together before facing customers, Grace walked into the store to see the scowling face of Kitty Worthington, and instantly wished she'd stayed in the storage room.

"Grace!" Kitty peered through the glass pane as Grace unlocked the door. "Every business in Fernandina Beach is required to open at ten o'clock sharp, and you are well past the deadline. That is a rule of the Local Business Organization and you know it."

And no one took the rules of the Fernandina Beach LBO more seriously than this power-mad woman, who'd been president of the association for as long as Grace had owned this store.

She opened the door, breathless. "I'm sorry, I was on a—"

"We have *rules*, Grace," she said, breezing in without being asked. "I know your daddy is a bigshot and your maiden name is on the street sign, but that doesn't mean you get special dispensation, in my book."

Grace let out a breath and tucked the phone she still held into her pocket, regarding the other woman, whose cap of over-sprayed frosted hair did nothing to soften the lines on her face or the constant scowl she wore.

"I was in the storage room and time got away from me," Grace said politely. "What can I do for you, Kitty?"

"I need to see your presentation," she said, adjusting her gold-rimmed glasses to glance around the store. "I don't want any surprises on Thursday afternoon. I had to open my house to a crazy old lady on her deathbed and I'm in no mood for shenanigans."

"My...oh, *God*." The words slipped out with a whimper as she remembered exactly what that forgotten thing on her to-do list really was.

It was her turn to chair and manage the annual LBO fundraiser.

"Don't you 'oh, God' me, Grace Wingate Jenkins. Every business in town has to do this job once and this is your year. Point in fact, your year was three years ago but, under the circumstances of your husband's death and considering that you'd just taken over the bookstore, we moved it."

"Could we do that again?" she asked meekly.

"At the end of July? Ten *weeks* from kickoff?" she asked, her voice rising like Grace had asked to fly to the moon. "I will remind you that you agreed to chair this fundraiser and you are due to stand in front of my board on Thursday afternoon and tell them what you're doing, when you're doing it, and how much you're going to raise."

Well, that would be a short presentation, because the answers were she didn't know, she didn't care, and...nothing.

"I'm sorry, Kitty, but I can't be there on Thursday. My daughter has a—"

"You can't be there?" She straightened to her full height, which Grace would put at an easy five-foot-ten. With the helmet hair, broad shoulders, and nostrils that flared when she sucked in a breath, she looked like a giant gazing at Grace from behind her glasses with a burn of distaste and disgust.

Isaiah would call her Goliath, and he'd be right.

"My board meets on the last Thursday of every month and in July, there's one thing on the agenda and that is the Fall Fundraiser," Kitty informed her. "And in case you don't remember, that fundraiser is the only way the Local Business Organization can fund next year's special trips for the press and tourism events that keep customers in our shops."

"But my daughter—"

"Can be with a babysitter! And don't think about bringing her, because I saw that kid have a hissy fit in Walgreen's a few weeks ago and that screaming would *literally* kill my aunt."

Heat crawled up Grace's chest, and no small amount of anger.

A lifelong introvert who'd do just about anything to avoid a conflict, Grace could feel her whole body recoil in the face of Kitty's personal power. Still, Nikki Lou's needs came first.

"Well, I'm very sorry to tell you that I cannot be there on Thursday."

Kitty's eyes narrowed. "Then give me your presentation and I'll share it with the team."

Grace stared at her. A presentation for a fundraising event to be held in the fall? She hadn't given it one moment's thought.

"I'm sorry, Kitty. My father had a stroke, as you know, and my whole family—"

"I will not accept an excuse," Kitty fired back. "Every single year, one local business spearheads this effort, and once we reach our fundraising goal, the remainder goes directly to the sponsoring business. This is a huge opportunity, and, I'm sorry, but your father's health isn't my concern. This year the sponsoring business is The Next Chapter and as the owner, you have to manage this event. At least tell me what you're planning."

Oh, boy.

Grace sighed, not even sure where to begin with this human bulldozer. She'd given the fundraiser zero consideration. She knew it had to be...a thing. An event somehow related to her bookstore, but creative enough to raise at least the minimum that the organization needed to support programs for local businesses.

Last year, there'd been a 5K race through town that one of the local shoe stores had sponsored. The year before that, the art supply store held a painting contest that had drawn entries from around the country. Over the years, there'd been a contest for ice cream flavor names, and a scavenger hunt, and...a bunch of time-consuming nightmares that just thinking about made Grace want to cry.

A movement outside the window caught her attention just before the door popped open and Nikki Lou came barreling in.

"*Mommmmmmmy!*" Her face was wet with tears, her blond curls mussed, the remnant of something on her T-shirt—was that *blood*?

"Nicolette Louise!" Grace reached down and scooped up her little body, knowing exactly how to calm her wiggles and soothe her during a breakdown.

Walking right behind her, Grace's sister, Rose, wore an exasperated expression.

"I'm so sorry, Grace," Rose said without a greeting. "We were right in the middle of arranging a glorious bouquet of daisies and roses and she got pricked by a thorn. Nothing serious, I promise. It was..."

Grace held up a hand, already knowing what it was. A classic Nikki Lou meltdown.

"She had to come home. It's okay, Rose."

"Hi, Kitty." Rose gave the woman a cursory smile. "Sorry to interrupt, but—"

"It's fine," Grace assured her, so grateful for the interruption that she added a little squeeze to Nikki's squirmy body. "Kitty was just leaving."

"I most certainly was not," she shot back, turning to

Rose, her expression softening, because no one—not even the town's most cantankerous powermonger—was immune to the sweet kindness of Rose D'Angelo. "Rose, talk some sense into your sister. She's trying to weasel out of the LBO board meeting on Thursday, where she's presenting her ideas for the annual fundraiser."

"Oh." Rose's dark eyes widened. "It's your year?" she asked with just enough sympathy and disbelief for Grace to know Rose understood her predicament.

"Evidently," Grace said. "But I have another meeting scheduled on Thursday."

"I told her to give me the presentation right now," Kitty continued. "And she won't even tell me her idea for the fundraiser."

Grace inched behind Nikki Lou's head to secretly mouth, "I got nuthin'!" to her sister.

"Well...of course she won't tell you, Kitty," Rose said cheerily. "That would spoil the surprise of her magnificent fundraising idea."

Behind her glasses, Kitty's eyes flickered. "Magnificent?"

"It's..." Rose added a sly smile. "I think it's one of the best the town has ever done."

Oh, Rose. Bless you.

"Then she must present it on Thursday!" Kitty demanded, looking from one sister to the other excitedly.

"Can you reschedule the meeting?" Grace asked. "I really...have my hands full." As though to underscore the truth of that, the child in her arms shuddered through her last, lingering sob.

"I cannot do that," Kitty said. "And if you want to know what full hands are, be the only person in the family who can take in the lunatic old aunt who spent her life doing God knows what in the Caribbean and now has to pay for her sins by spending her last days in my guest room. Whatever you have planned can be rescheduled. The LBO board meeting is set in stone."

Grace looked at Rose. "I'm meeting with Amanda Alberino."

Rose's eyes registered instant recognition, and understanding. "No, you can't reschedule that, but Kitty, I can present the idea on Thursday. Would you let me stand in for Grace?"

At that moment, Grace never loved her darling sister more...except *what idea?*

Kitty gave a withering look. "It's not the way we usually do things and we already made an exception for Grace. The committee believes strongly in sharing the work among all the local business owners. And if The Next Chapter doesn't sponsor this fundraiser, this store will not be eligible for any of the many LBO benefits, and will be taken off our roster for promotions and tourist communication."

Grace stifled a groan and slowly lowered her now calm daughter to the floor.

"We won't let that happen," Rose replied as she put a hand on the woman's arm and ushered her toward the door. "Where is the meeting on Thursday?"

"My house, of course. I can't leave the old bat alone too long."

Rose smiled. "How sweet of you to care for your aging aunt, Kitty. There's a place in heaven for you."

Grace watched in awe as Rose managed to get rid of Kitty Worthington and still offer her most gracious smile when the door closed.

"Please tell me you have an idea," Grace whispered.

"Not a one, but we'll come up with something."

"Oh, Rose." She reached out and hugged her sister as Nikki Lou scampered away to the kiddie book section to climb into her favorite chair with her blankie. "Thank you."

"Of course. I'm sorry I had to bring her back, but ..." She tossed up her hands. "I lost the battle of wills."

"Welcome to my world," Grace said on a bittersweet sigh. "Thank you for the save and I'm sorry she wrecked your flower-arranging class."

"It's not a problem. The under-five set doesn't have a long attention span and Gabe is finishing the class."

Grace smiled at the thought of Rose's buff firefighter EMT husband teaching a flower-arranging class to little girls in the back of Coming Up Roses. "Of course he is," she said. "Because he's the greatest."

"No argument from me," Rose agreed. "What did Dr. Alberino say?"

The store was still empty, so Grace took her over to a reading nook by the fireplace where they could sit and see Nikki as well as any customers coming in through the front door. There, she filled her in on everything that Amanda had told her.

"This is the best possible outcome," Rose said when Grace finished.

Grace smiled. "Says the most positive person in the world."

"I'm not wearing my rose-colored glasses," she countered. "This really is fantastic. First of all, now you know what you're dealing with. You discovered her condition very young, and she's getting into a wonderful program that will help her, whether she's mainstreamed for school or not, and it's free."

"I do agree with all that, but I'm a tad daunted by the home schooling and special trips and all-new nutrition. I'm underwater as it is."

Rose tipped her head. "You have family to help, hon. Four sisters working on the same street. And there's always Isaiah."

At the mention of his name—and the way Rose lifted her eyebrows—Grace's cheeks warmed.

"Isaiah? He's working at Wingate House," she said. "And as the inn manager? He's busier than ever."

"He'd help you anyway," Rose said. "He'd pretty much do anything for you."

The blush intensified. "Well, he's a great guy and..."

"And so crazy about you."

Grace stared at her. "Rose, stop it. He's just a friend."

She lifted a shoulder. "Call him whatever you want, it doesn't change the fact that the man can't look at anyone else when you're in the room. Plus, he's like a magic elixir for Nikki Lou. He came by this morning to get flowers for the inn and she ran to him like he was Santa Claus bringing her toys."

"Really?" Grace beamed. "She does like Zayah, as she calls him."

"And what about you?"

Grace decided to play dumb. "I call him Isaiah."

Rose dropped back in her chair, eyeing Grace with a smug smile. "We might have different mothers, sister of mine, but you and I are connected at the heart. Don't lie to me."

"I'm not..." She closed her eyes. "Look, Isaiah is a wonderful man. He's strong and steady, he's grounded in a faith that I don't understand but deeply admire, and, yes, Nikki Lou adores him. But that's it. Nothing more."

"Why?"

Grace paused, considering the question and how best to answer it. Honestly, for starters. Rose was right—they were two very deeply connected sisters and lies, or even well-glossed truths, had no place in their relationship.

"He's only a friend, because I will never love again, and Isaiah isn't the kind of man who'd settle for anything less," she said. "My heart and soul belong to Nick Jenkins, even though...that means I'm alone."

"You think Nick would want you to be alone?" Rose challenged. "Grace, you are a thirty-three-year-old widow with a special daughter and your own business."

"So?"

"So, you need a good man in your life. And you just said he is the definition of a good man. He's great with Nikki and strong and kind and, good heavens, he's interested." Rose leaned forward. "I really think you should give him a chance, Grace."

Silent, Grace toyed with the thick gold band hanging on a chain around her neck. The ring she'd once put on her husband's hand. The ring she'd thought lost in a distant desert. The ring that Nick had given to Isaiah Kincaid...for safe-keeping.

Rose's gaze dropped to Grace's fingers. "How could you not love the man who brought you Nick's ring?"

Grace tried to swallow, but the lump in her throat was way too big. She closed her eyes, thinking of the thousands of times she'd agonized over the thought of her late husband's wedding ring lost in Afghanistan after the explosion that took him from her.

She hadn't known Nick had stopped in the mess hall the morning before his fateful patrol, and realized he'd forgotten to take off his ring. He'd given it to a kindly Marine cook, who kept it for Grace and hand-delivered it to her.

"Doesn't that mean anything?" Rose asked gently.

Grace wet her dry, dry lips, knowing what it meant. It meant...Isaiah mattered. He was here for a purpose. Maybe Nick sent him. Maybe the God Isaiah prayed to had sent him. Or maybe Grace was a lonely widow who ached for a companion who wasn't one of her sisters.

She didn't know why he was here, but he made her heart feel lighter, and he made her want something... indefinable. He made her happy, which was something Grace hadn't been in a long, long time.

"Grace." Rose put a hand on her leg. "It would be stubborn and foolish to overlook him."

"I'm not overlooking him," she said softly. "I like him. A lot. But the thought of starting over, of trusting and falling and...and loving again absolutely paralyzes me. I'm sorry, Rose, but it does."

Rose was quiet, studying Grace with a spark of something in her dark eyes. A spirit that reminded Grace of their father, Rex. That twinkle of determination when he wanted to teach his girls about life and the world, or a glimmer of warmth when an idea was brewing.

Then Rose leaned forward. "I'll make you a deal, Gracie."

"Oh, no. Why am I scared of this deal?" Grace asked, a smile pulling.

"Don't be. It's a simple deal." She took Grace's hand. "I will manage the fundraiser from idea to execution. I'll come up with a concept, organize the event, make sure it promotes this bookstore, and make so much stinking money, Kitty's eyes will turn green."

Grace laughed softly. "In exchange for..."

"You give Isaiah Kincaid a real chance. You go out with him, you get to know him, you share your heart with him. You..." She sat back and crossed her arms. "Go on five dates with him."

"Five...dates?"

"Yes, five," Rose insisted. "Three isn't enough to know...anything. I'll do the fundraiser if you go on five dates with Isaiah."

"You...you are not..." Grace just couldn't get the

sentence out, she was so flabbergasted. "You are not serious, Rose."

Her sister lifted one challenging brow as if to say, *"Oh, yes, I am."*

"And by the time the fundraiser is over," Rose added, "if you don't have feelings for him, I'll never say another word."

Grace sighed, torn between a love for her sister so deep she couldn't speak, and raw, unholy terror.

"Rose, we both know you'd do all that fundraiser stuff for me anyway, even if I didn't give him a chance."

Rose just lifted a shoulder. "I'm still making it a fair exchange. Five dates and I'll have Kitty purring."

Grace chuckled. "Okay," she whispered. "You got a deal."

She leaned forward and hugged her sister, holding Rose tight and realizing that the tenuous thread that she thought held her life together was actually tied her to her sisters. That meant it wasn't a thread at all.

It was a lifeline.

Chapter Three

Chloe

Okay, it wasn't like she expected an office with *Chloe Wingate, Junior Weekend Entertainment Correspondent* on the door. Chloe didn't even expect a door when she walked into the West Hollywood offices of *A-List Access*.

But a cube would have been great. Something where she could make a workspace of her own, surrounded by pictures of her family, and some personal items that gave her joy and inspiration.

If life were perfect, the television show where she'd gotten her dream job would be dog-friendly, and Lady Bug could sleep in the corner and make friends with her co-workers as they welcomed her into the journalistic fold.

Sadly, there were no pets underfoot in these offices, but there were plenty of...bitches.

She loathed leaving Lady Bug behind, but had met a fairly responsible neighbor who checked on her dog during the day.

By the end of her first day, Chloe knew that even her low expectations were way too high. She didn't have a cube...or a desk. If she was lucky, she'd get to park somewhere between the breakroom and the actual offices of the higher ups, where she could write *on her own laptop* and use *her own cellphone.* There, she could follow up on leads that were tossed into a competitive pool and gobbled up by the sharks, er, co-workers—not one of whom actually *welcomed* her.

On the contrary, she'd been essentially ignored since she got there. Two other junior correspondents, both very attractive women, had treated Chloe as if she had come bearing the plague. Another reporter, Brandon Monroe, had already hit on her twice, giving her the creeps.

One scriptwriter asked her to stop wearing perfume, because she was allergic to all chemical scents, and the guy who brought the water jugs into the breakroom told her it was raining, which was apparently big news in Los Angeles.

That was the sum total of her co-worker interaction during her first week on the job. Her "work" consisted of following orders that came via email to do research and background checks for the boss she'd barely seen.

But she'd come in this morning with renewed determination to love this career, happy to leave the very small and sparsely furnished one-bedroom apartment she'd rented in the San Fernando Valley.

Surely this coming weekend, she—a *weekend* entertainment correspondent—would get an actual assignment and head off to interview...someone famous.

She didn't really care about the fame of her subject, but this was her first real chance at national television journalism, even if it was for a cheesy syndicated TV show that lived and died on celebrity gossip.

So she waited patiently this morning, camped out in the breakroom, where the producers sometimes popped in with story ideas and breaking news from the paparazzi out on the streets of L.A. When a young woman she recognized as Abigail Ferrari's admin walked in, Chloe sat straight up.

Abigail had "discovered" Chloe after seeing her hosting a series of TikTok videos about the filming of a Netflix Christmas movie on Amelia Island. After several interviews, Abigail hired her.

With an underwhelming salary but promises of more, Chloe had leased a less than awesome apartment in a Northridge complex packed with Cal State students. Not ideal, but it was cheap and less than an hour from work, even in traffic.

And, whoa, that traffic was *brutal*.

Since she'd started, Chloe and Abigail Ferrari had spent exactly five minutes together in a cold conference room when the other woman told her she'd have to be "flexible" and "patient" at first, but after that, things would get easier.

"Chloe?" The admin peered out from under thick, dark bangs that added to her waif-like appearance.

Oh, good. Maybe it was the "get easier" time.

"Yeah, hi. It's Pia, right?" She closed her laptop and stood out of politeness. "How are you?"

She expected a cursory reply and the same question, but merely got a shrug of a bony shoulder. "Abby needs to talk to you."

"Awesome." Finally, a story lead just for her. She could do some research and prep, interview the subject, locate some B-roll, spend a few hours in the editing room, and still have time to record promo before her first report ran on this weekend's show. "Right now?"

"That's what 'needs to talk to you' means." Pia added a slight eyeroll, though it was hard to tell with the bangs and way too much eyeliner.

Whatever you say, cool chick who thinks she's better than everyone.

Chloe tamped down the thought and gathered her phone and notebook with a simple nod. "Lead the way," she said.

Chloe couldn't stand an awkward silence, and this one was deafening as they walked down a wide, empty hall. So, she filled it.

"Been an interesting few days," she said, not really caring if Pia responded. "Still haven't gotten an assignment, though. Is that about to change?"

Pia slowed her step and Chloe couldn't tell if they'd arrived at Abigail's office or she wanted to pause for dramatic effect. Either way, she pinned her eyeliner-y gaze on Chloe, and almost smiled.

"Everything's about to change," she said.

With that, she opened a door and led Chloe into an office that was small, but maybe only seemed that way because it was stacked with moving boxes.

Oh! Was she getting her own office? A thrill danced over her as she peered past a pile of cardboard and saw Abigail Ferrari at the desk, staring at an open file. She didn't look up or speak, so Chloe just stood there, aware that Pia had slipped out without so much as an announcement of their arrival.

Abigail seemed intent on what was in front of her—Chloe's assignment, maybe?—so it felt like staying quiet was the wisest course.

A course that lasted way too long, but finally, the other woman sighed, closed the file, and looked up.

"I want you to stay," she said simply. "But you're going to have to pass a test."

Chloe wished there was a chair she could drop into, lean forward, and do her best "put me in, Coach" speech, but no such luck. Also, something seemed incredibly off about this exchange.

Abby wanted her to stay? The woman had just hired her. Why would she leave?

"Of course," Chloe said instead of peppering her boss with questions. "Whatever you need."

Abigail studied her for a moment, then gave what looked like a very sad smile. "I'm sorry to tell you this, since you flew out and rented a place and all that, but I'm leaving *A-List Access* to work for *TMZ*."

"Oh!" Chloe drew back, not even able to process this news. *Abigail* was leaving? "Well...congratulations."

Abigail shrugged. "I guess. This town is a merry-go-round, the business is a circus, and this building is full of clowns."

"That's...poetic." And depressing as all get out, Chloe mentally added. "Are you not happy about the move?"

She flicked her hand as if her happiness wasn't what mattered. "Cash is king, Chloe. But I've got some loose ends to tie up before I leave and you, my friend, are one of them."

Just what she always wanted to be—someone's loose end. Chloe swallowed, uncertain what to say, if anything.

"My job is being taken over by a man named Rory Sutton. He's British, considered a darling by the powers that be, and a fine producer when he wants to be."

Okay, not the worst news. She'd heard of Rory Sutton, who had a reputation for a big "get"—meaning his stories often led the show and got heavily retweeted. Working for him couldn't be the worst—

"Be prepared to be asked to do...things."

Things? Chloe blinked. Things like...crappy stories? Things like...run the guy's personal errands? Or things like...she didn't want to think about those other kinds of things.

"Not sure I know what you mean," Chloe said, purposely vague. "But I'm certainly not afraid to get my hands dirty on stories no one else wants."

Abby laughed. "You are naïve, but okay. You and Rory will have to hit it off, but he agreed to keep you on for one story this weekend. If you nail it, you stay. Screw it up, and, well, I hope you got a month-to-month lease."

"Are you serious?" Chloe asked as irritation skittered through her. "With all due respect, Abigail, I came out here to work for *you*."

The other woman tipped her head. "And maybe you will, at *TMZ*. I really like you, Chloe, and the camera *adores* you. If you can deliver a decent story, put a fun spin on it, and make viewers think they got an inside look at a real, live celebrity, then you can go far. Unfortunately, I'm not in a position to hire at my new job yet. Sorry."

Abigail picked up the file and tapped it on her desk, sliding it into her bag, silent.

"Is that all?" Chloe asked.

"That's it. Rory's office is down the hall. Just tell him who you are. He can give you the assignment parameters."

Chloe let out a sigh, fighting disappointment, fear, and a little bit of hope. At least *someone* had an assignment for her. She'd knock it so far out of the park that Rory Sutton would give her three more.

"Okay, thanks, Abigail. Best of luck in your new job."

"Yeah, thanks."

With that, Chloe walked out, turning toward the executive production offices, slowing when she reached an open door with Rory Sutton's name on it. There was no admin around, so she tapped on it and inched her head in to see a middle-aged man with unkempt brown hair and a Grateful Dead T-shirt. He stood in front of a window, a phone to his ear.

Not a good time—

"Oh, hello." He lowered the phone and looked hard at her. "New weekend girl?"

She angled her head in concession, certain by the

English accent she had the right man. "I've been called worse."

He chuckled, then spoke into the phone. "Gotta run, luv. Catch you later." He dropped the phone on his desk and walked forward, eyeing her like...yes, like a piece of meat but she'd prefer to think of him as appraising art.

Either way, he stared too hard and too long to be comfortable.

"Seems I've inherited you."

She nodded and extended her hand. "Hello. I'm Chloe Wingate."

He took her hand and held it way past a handshake, long enough for her to be the one to ease her fingers free. "Rory Sutton. How do you feel about ghosts?"

"Ghosts? I'm not scared of them, if that's what you mean." She felt her shoulders square, no doubt an unconscious movement to show she wasn't afraid of the subject matter, or him. "My family owns an inn that is supposedly haunted by my great-grandmother. I've played hide-and-seek with my sisters all over that place, never afraid."

He dragged a dark gaze up and down her, surely breaking half the rules in the HR handbook, if *A-List Access* even had one.

Be prepared to be asked to do...things.

Abigail's words echoed and Chloe swallowed. There were things she wouldn't do—many things. And if this guy thought she was that desperate for a reporting job, then he hadn't met Rex Wingate's youngest daughter. She certainly wasn't afraid of running away from the wrong thing. She'd proven that when she left Hunter Landry at the altar.

"Do you know who Sharon Tate was?" he asked.

Sharon Tate? She frowned, flipping through her scant knowledge of Hollywood history.

"Wasn't she the actress murdered by Charles Manson's gang in the seventies? The crime the book *Helter Skelter* was about?"

"Exactly. I'd like you to interview her."

She choked back a laugh, certain she hadn't heard correctly.

"Well, that's my dream for the assignment," he continued. "Find proof that Sharon haunts the house that has been built on the property where she was murdered. But in order to do that, you have to interview the girlfriend of the rapper who is renting the place, because she claims Sharon is appearing at her bedside every night."

This was her first nationally syndicated news story?

Okay. It stunk. But maybe she could make it funny or poignant or uncover something no one ever expected. "That's great," she said. "What's the girlfriend's name?"

He turned and grabbed a sheet of paper off his desk. "Lacey...something. The rapper is Coo Coo Cooper, or Triple C, Coo-Key, whatever you want to call him. I call him rich enough to rent a twenty-five-thousand-square-foot mansion that has a shark tank in the living room. With real sharks."

Couldn't be any worse than the ones here.

"Has Coo Coo Cooper seen the ghost?" she asked, already formulating the threads of a story.

For a long time, Rory just stared at her, and she wasn't sure he'd heard her.

"Because I'd like another witness to—"

He threw his head back and let out a guffaw so sharp, it would have made Lady Bug cower in fear. When the laugh finally died down, he wiped his eyes and pointed at her, taking a few steps closer.

"You're adorable. Seriously, hot and so funny. I like those qualities in a woman. I like them a lot."

Her skin crawled at the comment, but she held her ground and refused to back down, staring right back at him with what she hoped was a clear *don't you dare* signal in her eyes.

"I better spell it out for you, luv," he said. "Make the girlfriend look good, not insane. She should be sympathetic and..." He waved his hand. "Hot, obviously. But not crazy."

"And if she isn't...sympathetic?"

He narrowed his eyes. "Do you not watch our show? We make stars—and their significant others—look good. Oh, and if you can get me a glimmer of Sharon Tate's ghost—some flashing lights, a shadow in the mirror, some nonsense like that—you can expect lots more stories. If the ghost-seeing chick comes off like a loon, you're finished. Got it?"

"Yes, I do," she said with nod.

He eyed her for a moment, looking a little intrigued and like he had more to say. "You're nice-looking, like Abby said. But you're very small-town. She likes that, but

I don't think it sells Hollywood. Anyway, if your piece airs, we'll discuss where we go from there."

"And if it doesn't?"

He visibly fought a laugh. "What did you say your name was again?"

He'd forgotten it already? "Chloe Wingate."

He raked her with a look that made her want to shudder. "Knock my socks off, Chloe Wingate. And everything else."

She just turned and walked out, a little sick but determined to show him what she was made of.

Chloe pulled into the crowded parking lot of the Meridian Pointe apartments in Northridge after spending the day researching Sharon Tate's gruesome murder and the palace that had been rebuilt on the site in the Hollywood Hills. It left her unnerved and queasy.

The sun wasn't close to setting, even though it was well past seven, but the Cal State Northridge kids were out in the common area, starting the weekend a day early with loud music and enough beer to fill the pool.

She had to pass the group on her way to her apartment, turning down two offers to shotgun a Natty Lite.

Do I look like a college student? She wanted to cry out, "I'm a reporter! I'm an adult! I'm the runaway bride from Amelia Island!"

She was also sad, lonely, and scared.

But not quite as lonely when she heard Lady Bug bark on the other side of the door. When she opened it, the little dog pounced with joy at the sight of Chloe. Her fluffy white tail whipped from side to side as she dropped to the floor, turned over for a belly rub, and dribbled a little in excitement.

"Oh, Bugaboo!" Chloe moaned with guilt. "I'm sorry you're stuck in this ghastly place all day. I really thought I could take you to work."

Tamping down the thought of yet another thing she hated about her new job, she took Lady Bug out to the two-foot section of grass near the apartment and let her romp as much as possible.

A few minutes later, they were back inside the dreary unit.

Yes, she could have spent more money and gotten a higher-end place, but the pay at *A-List Access* wasn't great, and she did just burn through a metric buttload of money to *not* get married.

She was trying to be frugal.

Just as they cuddled on the sofa together, Chloe's phone vibrated with a text, lifting her spirits with the hope that it was one of her sisters with news from home.

"Maybe Mom has an update on Dad," she murmured as she reached for the bag she'd dropped on the floor. "Or maybe..." She inhaled a hopeful breath. "It's Travis McCall."

Lady Bug's tail swished as if she knew the name of the gorgeous firefighter and was thinking about him almost as much as Chloe was.

True, Chloe and Travis hadn't even *kissed* before she left Amelia Island. They'd talked, laughed, watched a movie, and spent a few brief hours together before she took off for L.A. They'd only spent enough time together for him to teach her his personal philosophy of life, which was, "No regrets, coyote."

But today, she was swimming in them.

She pulled out the phone and read the screen, her heart nearly stopping at the name she never, ever expected to see on her phone again.

Hunter Landry.

She hadn't spoken to her ex-fiancé in months. The last time they'd seen each other was the day she left their Jacksonville apartment and moved to Amelia Island, where she'd been living until coming here. She'd heard through a mutual friend that he took the job he desperately wanted out here in L.A., starting his career as a plastic surgeon to the stars with a reputable practice.

She tapped the screen, burning with curiosity to read the text.

Hunter Landry: *Hey, heard you moved to my neck of the woods for a national TV job. Congrats, Chloe. I'm in Sherman Oaks. Where are you living? I'd love to grab a drink and talk.*

She stared at the text, letting it all sink in. First of all, the fact that he even spoke to her was remarkable. Leaving him at the altar in front of one hundred and fifty friends and family was not her finest moment. Not marrying Hunter had been the right thing to do—he was a selfish man who she really didn't know, since most of their relationship had been long-distance.

But waiting until the last possible minute to make that decision had been awful, and she still cringed with shame over her timing.

Second, a drink? Seriously? She couldn't believe he ever wanted to pass her on the street, let alone toast their new lives over cocktails.

And last...Sherman Oaks? That was about fifteen minutes away. The San Fernando Valley was the last place she expected him to live. He had a high-paying job and she imagined he'd have found a place in Beverly Hills or Malibu Canyon.

Dropping the phone on the sofa, she blew out a breath, not the least bit prepared to respond. She needed Raina or Tori or Rose or Grace—*someone* with the last name of Wingate—to help her along. She needed the right words. She needed...a glass of wine.

That was motivating enough to push her off the sofa, and, of course, Lady Bug leaped to follow.

"I bought wine, didn't I?" she asked, trying to remember if she'd picked up a bottle at the supermarket when she'd shopped. "But where did I put it?"

She glanced at the few cabinets in the tiny kitchen, then pulled the door to the one next to the sink, startling when something small and dark scurried across the wood.

Was that...a *roach*?

She smacked the door closed so hard that Lady Bug barked.

This apartment had roaches?

She shuddered and whimpered and took a few horrified steps backwards. At this rent? Well, yes, at this rent. This was a hellhole full of college students who probably let dirty pizza boxes sit out for days.

Letting out a little cry, she went back to the sofa and buried her face in Lady Bug's fur when she jumped up on Chloe's lap.

"What are we going to do, Bug?" Especially because she needed that wine. And a sister, or at least a friend who could tell her she hadn't made a big, fat, ugly mistake.

Her phone buzzed again and she kind of knew who it was before she looked and, of course, she was right.

Hunter Landry rarely took silence or no as an answer.

Hunter Landry: *I know you're probably wondering why I'd reach out, but here's the thing, Chloe. I don't have any friends out here and I figured you don't, either. I say we let bygones be bygones and get that drink. I'm free tonight.*

She closed her eyes but all she could see was the words *I'm free tonight* burned behind her lids. She was free, too. And lonely. And blue. And so, so far from home. And, dang, she wanted a glass of wine, but not badly enough to open that cabinet again.

And here was Hunter, a man she once professed to love, reaching out a hand. What could she say? What *should* she say?

On a sigh of pure resignation, she picked up the phone and responded the only way that was...right.

Sorry, but I can't.

Exhaling sadly, she pushed up and grabbed her purse to head to the store for a bottle of wine. And a can of Raid.

Chapter Four

Rose

"**B**ad news, babe."

Rose looked up from the cutting board, tonight's vegetables forgotten when her husband came into the kitchen. "Don't tell me."

He made a face, but that didn't detract from Gabe's good looks. Somehow, it just made his tanned and handsome features even more attractive. "Okay, I won't, but you already know."

"You have to cover someone's shift tonight," she guessed with a sigh. "How is that possible again?"

He lifted a brow and turned from her, getting water from the fridge. After all these years together, did he think she didn't know when he was...well, not lying. He wasn't capable of lying. But withholding the whole story to protect her from...anything? Yeah, she knew when that was happening when he refused to look her in the eye.

"It's possible, because I'm picking up shifts," he said. "Which can only help the cause."

And Rose knew exactly what cause that was. "No word from the chief yet on that promotion to captain?"

Finishing a gulp of water, his broad shoulders heaved with a sigh. "Nothing official, but he took Hutchinson to lunch yesterday."

"Which means nothing, Gabe. Jeremy Hutchinson might be your competition, but he's not even in your league for leadership, not to mention that your father—"

"Then don't mention it," he interjected sharply, making Rose draw back in surprise.

"Honey." She put the knife down and came around the counter, arms already out in response to the totally out of character tone. "What's *really* wrong?"

He looked like he would deny anything was wrong, but then he shook his head.

"I'm not going to sail into a captain slot just because my father was the chief at this station years ago. Nepotism isn't how it works, even in a town like this. The Fernandina Beach Fire Department is a merit-based organization."

"And who has more merit than you?" she asked.

"Uh, Jeremy Hutchinson, a full-fledged firefighter who has way more hours with a hose than a blood pressure cuff in his hand."

She frowned, searching his face. "Are you saying that the fact that you are the best EMT—and don't even try to argue that—is going to go against you for this promotion?"

"Yes, I am," he said. "Firefighters expect to answer to someone who's been in the trenches with them, full gear, facing...whatever they have to face."

She tried not to flinch, thinking about *whatever they have to face.* She hated when Gabe had to put on that gear and fight a fire. When he was on duty as an EMT, in an ambulance saving heart attack victims or pulling someone from a car accident, she didn't worry nearly as much as when he walked into a burning building.

She swallowed, physically unable to think about the possibility of losing him.

"The fact is, Chief Keating shares that belief," he continued. "So..."

"So you're on firefighter duty tonight."

"The more hours I get firefighting, the better."

Not better for her.

He put a hand on her cheek, his features softening as he no doubt read an expression she couldn't hide.

"Don't worry, babe. It'll be a slow shift, seven to seven. I'll get sleep, and I can work with you at the shop tomorrow." He pulled her closer. "I'm bummed, though, because I know you're going to meet with your sisters after dinner, which usually means you have a little wine." He kissed her, smiling against her lips. "And wine always makes you—"

She inched back, aware of her heart rate increasing, and not because of what he was implying. Silent, she searched his face, a little lost in his blue eyes and that slightly crooked smile that had beckoned her from across a crowded cafeteria when they were fifteen. She'd never looked at another man since that day, and that was just fine with Rose.

"Gabe, do you have to—"

"Stop." He pressed his thumb to her lips. "I'll be fine.

Now, what exactly are you doing with your sisters tonight, besides cracking a bottle of wine and jokes?"

She took a breath and allowed the subject change, knowing she wasn't going to win this one.

"We're getting together at Grace's store to brainstorm an idea for the fundraiser. If you'll be at work, I should probably bring Avery and Alyson with me, since Kenzie was going to babysit Nikki Lou—they'll have their own girls' night. But that would leave the boys here alone," she added, her mother's mind already spinning.

"That'll work," he said, then lifted his brows. "Maybe you can get Madeline or Tori drunk enough to take over your insane offer to run that fundraising thing. You have enough on your plate, Rose."

"It'll be easy," she assured him. "I promise it won't be some massive event. We'll come up with something simple that will raise money quickly and everyone will pitch in."

"I don't want you to be so wrapped up in yet another project that we..." He drew her back into him, even closer this time, nuzzling her neck, giving rise to chills when he kissed her skin. "Miss each other."

"I always miss you," she whispered, holding him a little tighter than usual. "Please be careful tonight."

"I always am." He kissed her on the mouth, a long, warm—

"Get a room, for cryin' out loud." Zach, their oldest at fifteen, loped into the kitchen, holding a bag of chips and eyeing the cutting board. "What's for dinner, Mom? And can I eat early? I'm going over to Tiffany's to watch a movie."

"We'll eat as a family, like we always do," she said. "Then Dad has a seven o'clock shift."

"A movie, huh?" This came from eleven-year-old Ethan, who was so frequently on Zach's tail that the family had dubbed him The Shadow.

"And you're not invited," Zach said.

"Good, 'cause all you're going to do is suck face with your *girrrrlfriend*." He dragged out the last word to emphasize Zach's official status as Tiffany Kaplan's main squeeze.

"Wait, wait, wait," Rose said, holding out her hand.

"Ignore him, Mother," Zach said in his most adult voice. "There will be no face sucking. Well, limited face sucking."

"But there will be Tiffany," Ethan chimed in, adding kissing sounds. "'Oh, Zachary,'" he mocked in a high-pitched voice. "'You're so handsome'...smooch, smooch."

"Shut up, you little—" Zach lunged for him, but Gabe snagged his arm.

"One, don't attack your brother. Two, you're not going to Tiffany's tonight, but she can come here and watch a movie."

"What?"

"I got called in to work, and Mom's meeting up with her sisters and you have to—"

"*Babysit?*" He groaned on the word. "Seriously, Mom?"

"I'll take the girls, but..." She glanced at Ethan, the

imp who'd scampered up to a barstool and was helping himself to carrots she'd just sliced.

"*Moi*," he said with a sly grin. "I'll be here watching you and Tiff watch...each other."

Zach glared at him. "You stay in your room or you're dead."

"Dead?" Ethan lifted his brows. "That's not good babysitting mojo, is it, Mom?"

Her eyes shuttered, fighting the urge to laugh at Ethan—who was hilarious—and feeling sympathetic for Zach. He liked this girl and Rose *had* told him he could go out tonight, but that was before Gabe's schedule changed. She had to come up with *something* for that presentation tomorrow afternoon.

"Mom, please do your sister thing another night," Zach said.

"Or let me stay home alone!" Ethan suggested, stealing a slice of zucchini. "I'm more mature than Romeo anyway."

She considered it for a moment, but Gabe held up a hand.

"Not an option, Ethan," he said. "And, Zach, your mother isn't changing her plans to accommodate you."

"Could you have your sisters here?" Zach pressed.

She shook her head, unwilling to move everyone around. "Ask your friend to come here, Zach."

"Friend?" Ethan scoffed, then added another noisy kiss.

"Permission to kill him?" Zach muttered.

Gabe nodded and started out of the kitchen. "Permission granted." He passed Ethan's chair and playfully bopped him on the head. "Your day will come, little man. And when your sisters are the terrorists mocking you and your new girlfriend, you'll wish you'd been nicer."

Zach gave a satisfied look, then dropped his head back and poured the remnants of the chip bag into his mouth before balling it up for the trash.

"I'm sorry, honey," Rose said softly to him. "I can't reschedule. I have to present to Kitty Worthington's board tomorrow."

He cringed. "Helmet Head strikes again."

Rose fought a smile and didn't bother with the "don't call people names" lecture. Instead, she turned toward her younger son, who had pretty much demolished the veggies she'd cut to sauté for dinner.

"Ethan, did you finish cleaning out Dad's flowerboxes in the greenhouse like you promised you would?"

"Almost. I could use a little help on the last few, because they had oregano in them and that is like pulling out barbed wire."

"Okay, when I get the chicken in, I'll help you, but I do have to make sure Alyson and Avery are ready to go with me tonight. And I should—"

"Relax, Mom." Zach put his hand on her shoulder, looking down with a smile so much like his father's, it made her heart shift in her chest. "I'll help him."

"Thanks, honey."

"Come on, micro-brain. I'll do your chores for you and you can give me half your allowance." Zach nudged him off the barstool and pushed him toward the mud room, the echo of their teasing audible until the door closed.

She picked up her knife to continue cutting, but stood still for a moment, hearing the girls laughing at something in the family room, still tasting her husband's kiss, feeling cocooned and blessed and content in this lovely season of her life.

She never wanted anything to change. She never wanted to be separated from them. The very idea made tears spring to her eyes and put a dark pit in her stomach. That and her husband's determination to get that promotion.

"Oh, Gabe," she whispered to the empty room. "Please don't be a hero."

LATER THAT EVENING, Rose held Avery and Alyson's hands as they walked along the river, heading toward Grace's bookstore, inhaling the brackish scent of the water and appreciating the pink tones of dusk lingering over the horizon.

"All the girl cousins are going to be together!" Avery danced the way only a six-year-old who took tap lessons could—without a care—as they reached Wingate Way. "We can play American Girl dolls."

"Until Nikki Lou starts to cry, pout, scream, or hide." Alyson looked up at Rose with the wisdom of someone far beyond her almost nine years glowing in eyes behind her new purple glasses. "It's just a matter of time, no matter what we play."

Rose gave her hand a squeeze. "And you're always so patient with her, Aly. It makes me proud."

"I know, but..."

"She's kind of a brat," Avery said.

"Hey." Rose slowed and gave her youngest a stern look. "Not nice, Avery. She's not a brat. She's...special."

Avery scrunched up her face, torn between her dislike of being reprimanded and her opinion.

"What makes her special?" Alyson asked. "I mean, she's our cousin, yeah, but why do you always say she's special?"

Rose considered how to answer, and decided not to. Nikki Lou's condition—whatever the doctors called it—wasn't appropriate for her cousins to discuss.

"She's very young," Rose said. "She's only three. Do you realize how young that is?"

"Yes," she said, her expression even more serious than usual. "It's one-third my age after my next birthday and half of Avery's."

Rose grinned. "Look at you knowing your fractions. You are absolutely right, and that 'fraction' of age means you have to let her have her way and let Kenzie call the shots tonight."

They both agreed, but she felt their resentment for always having to bend to the will of their "special" cousin. And that just motivated Rose to march into the bookstore, come up with an amazing idea, and free Grace up to get Nikki Lou into the program that could help her.

When they reached The Next Chapter, she let go of their hands so they could swing through the wrought-iron gate and run down the path to the welcoming sage green doors of the bookstore.

She took a moment to remember how all of the Wingates had gathered to love and hold poor Grace when Nick had been killed. She'd been so scared, so broken, and so pregnant. This beautiful two-story brick building had become available for a new tenant when the couple who'd lived upstairs and run an antique shop on the first floor had retired.

Grace hadn't been quite ready to start over, but with the family rallying around her, she'd moved into the spacious second floor apartment. They'd helped her refurnish the space, turning one bedroom into a sweet pink nursery, keeping an ancient baby grand piano, since no one had a clue how to get it out of there.

Downstairs, the family helped reinvent the retail space as a cozy, inviting bookstore, giving Grace a purpose she desperately needed in those days.

It was on a summer evening much like this when Rose remembered hearing Grace laugh for the first time in so long. They were all together, stacking new books and putting the finishing touches on the space when Rose had referred to this phase of Grace's life as the next chapter.

And instantly, the new bookstore became The Next Chapter. That chapter included owning a small business, becoming part of the community, and being a single mother. And if Rose's instincts were right, it was time for Grace to turn the page and have a little romance.

That was assuming Grace had met her part of the *Isaiah* bargain. Rose was about to find out.

She stepped inside to be instantly greeted by Raina, who came right to her with one hand on her tiny baby bump and a huge smile on her face.

"Hey, Rosebud." Raina reached out for a hug.

"You're looking preggers, Raindrop."

Raina let out a happy laugh, turning sideways to show off her silhouette. "Right? Look at this belly full of two babies."

Rose put a hand on her sister's hard stomach. "Any kicks yet?"

"No. Well, I feel a little fluttering once in a while. But that could be gas."

"You should start to feel them soon." Rose put her arm around her sister and followed Avery and Alyson to make the rounds and greet the rest of them.

Madeline, their oldest sister, was tucked into one of the upholstered armchairs near the fireplace, a book on her lap. She leaned forward to hug Avery, pausing to ask her a question and brush some hairs off her little face.

Not for the first time, Rose's heart cracked at the very idea that not only would Madeline never have a child of her own, but she had yet to wear one of her very own magnificently made wedding gowns. At forty-nine, Madeline had made her way as a single woman and showed no signs of ever changing.

Next to her, Tori was on the floor, sipping wine,

glancing at her phone, and teasing Alyson, who'd come to give her a kiss. Now there was a woman who'd found a little romance, and she wore the glow of it like a fresh summer tan. Dad's stroke had brought Dr. Justin Verona into their lives and into Tori's heart. Just looking at her made Rose smile.

"All right!" Kenzie, Tori's sixteen-year-old daughter, clapped her hands then stretched out her arms. "I need all Wingate women under ten right now."

"I'm not a Wingate," Avery said. "I'm a D'Angelo."

"You're half Wingate," Tori said, tapping Avery's nose. "And that's enough to make you a Wingate woman. Go forth and play."

"Yay!" She scurried off to join the others.

"Now, all Wingate women over ten?" Rose clapped her hands, imitating Kenzie. "Come closer and brainstorm!"

After some small talk and laughter, the five of them curled up in various chairs and on floor pillows in the sitting area by the fireplace that made this unlike any other bookstore in town.

"Okay, who's running this meeting? Let's move it, please," Tori said, picking up her phone one more time.

"Why, you got a date?" Raina asked her.

She bit her lip and gave them all a sly smile. "Not exactly. Justin and Finn are out on the boat and Kenzie and I are going to meet them there later for a rousing game of Scrabble under the stars."

At the reaction and comments about how sweet that was, Tori held up her hands.

"Don't get too excited, you guys." Her smile wavered as she leaned back into Madeline's chair, using her sister's legs as a back rest. "We're cruising into August, and that means my summer of fun will be coming to an end soon. Back to reality and life in Boston, like it or not. And..." She curled her lip. "I don't."

"Oh, Tori." Madeline scooped up a handful of Tori's strawberry-blond hair and started braiding it, taking Rose back to those days when they were very, very little girls. Rose didn't remember much, of course, but she always thought of Madeline as another mommy. She was the big sister who braided hair and made baby doll dresses and was as much a maternal figure as Susannah, who'd come into their lives when Rose and Raina were the same age as Nikki Lou.

"I think you should figure out a way to stay here," Raina said, pointing her water bottle at Tori. "If I've learned anything in the last few weeks, it's that divorce settlements aren't always iron-clad. Maybe Trey will concede and allow you to move here with Kenzie and Finn permanently."

"Fat chance," Tori said dryly. "I'm surprised he hasn't shown up threatening to take them home."

"But he said it was okay for the kids to spend the summer here," Grace chimed in as she put a plate of cookies on a small table and took the empty space on the loveseat next to Rose.

Tori picked up her wine, shaking her head. "It's one thing to fall in love—the best thing ever, I might add. But knowing there's a ticking clock? It changes the game."

Madeline paused in the act of braiding Tori's hair. "I thought you told us Justin was willing to go to Boston."

"Willing, yes. But how can I ask him to leave his neurology practice here on Amelia Island? He's thriving there, loves his partners, and with this weather and sailing? He's happy for the first time in years."

"I think that has more to do with you than the weather and water," Rose said. "You're what he's happy about."

Tori smiled. "And Finn," she added, referring to her twelve-year-old son. "The two of them have just bonded in a way I never expected. I swear they have more in common than Trey and Finn, who share nothing but a name." Tori shrugged. "I don't know what's going to happen, but we have a month left and I'm going to enjoy every minute of it. Including tonight, so step it up, Rosie. Unless this is Grace's meeting. Who's running this fundraiser?"

Grace and Rose exchanged a look.

"Well, it's Grace's thing," Rose said. "I'm just helping her get it off the ground."

"Please." Grace leaned in and looked at Rose lovingly. "You are the literal angel who is helping me out of a bind. You all know what's going on with Nikki Lou. I'm going to put her in a very comprehensive, consuming program that's going to take a lot from both of us. Rose is my savior and she needs all our help, starting with an idea that she can present to Kitty Worthington tomorrow."

A single groan and one meow—courtesy of Tori—filled the room.

"All right," Madeline said, abandoning Tori's hair. "Let's talk about this event. What are the parameters?"

"Something that raises money for the Local Business Organization, as you all know," Grace told them. "It can be anything—an event, a product, a festival, a contest, anything at all. It usually focuses on the sponsoring business, so the owner doing all the work at least reaps some benefit. Raise more than the goal, and the sponsoring business gets to keep it or donate it. So, I'm perfectly happy for this to promote Coming Up Roses as much as The Next Chapter."

"Oh, no," Rose said quickly. "First of all, this is your year and you should get the benefit. I'm up next year. Let's raise money and sell books or at least get new customers in these doors. Who has an idea?"

She looked around the room and saw way too many blank faces.

"Just...anything," Rose begged with a laugh. "Anything that promotes the bookstore and raises money for the LBO. No idea is dumb in a brainstorm."

"I got one," Raina said. "Dress Like Your Favorite Character from a Book Day."

"Okay," Rose said, nodding with encouragement before crinkling her nose. "How does that raise money?"

"Entry fee?" Raina said, then shook her head. "Nah, that's not enough."

"How about a scavenger hunt where the clues are in books or from books?" Tori suggested.

"We had a scavenger hunt a few years ago," Madeline

said. "If I know Kitty Worthington—and, sadly, I do—she'll nix that."

"Meow...*no,*" Tori mewed, making them laugh as she glanced at her phone again.

"I was thinking of a product I could sell," Grace said. "Something so desirable that it would drive people into the store to buy it."

They all liked that, scooting forward with questions and ideas, the energy in the room palpable.

"What's that desirable?" Raina asked.

"This man."

At Tori's comment, they all looked at her, but she was staring at her phone.

"Sorry, but Justin just posted a picture on Instagram with Finn on the boat and, oh!" She dropped her head back and let out a groan. "I *adore* him!"

"You have to stay here!" Raina insisted, coming closer to grab the phone and look. "You cannot leave Dr. Hottypants!"

They all laughed, but Rose held out her hands. "I realize he's desirable, but since we can't sell him, any other ideas?"

"We could sell this picture," Raina said, studying the phone. "I gotta give it to you, Tor. He's a cutie."

Tori took the phone. "Mine," she teased.

"Wait a second," Grace said, quieting them. "What about pictures of handsome men?"

"Like a firefighter calendar?" Rose asked. "Let me tell you, they sell. Gabe was Mr. February once and, whoa. It wasn't cold that winter."

"That's a great idea!" Raina exclaimed. "A calendar that Grace could sell."

"Like Hot Dudes Reading," Tori chimed in, flipping through her phone. "It's a crazy cute Instagram account. Here, look."

She passed the phone around as the ideas started to fly.

"A calendar of men reading!" Madeline said. "Brilliant!"

"All the pictures taken in and around the bookstore," Grace added.

"Twelve hot guys reading...something," Rose said. "Romance? Adventure? Kid books?"

"We have them all," Grace said, standing up as if the idea really excited her. "We could use all local guys, too. The Men of Amelia Island Reading Books."

"We'll need a catchier name," Tori said. "But I love that idea. I'll nominate Hottypants for Mr. August. He looks good in shorts."

Raina rolled her eyes. "You're pathetic."

"Beyond," Tori agreed, laughing.

"Well, Gabe's in," Rose said. "And I'm sure he could scare up a few of the guys at the station."

"How about Dad?" Raina asked. "He's still a handsome man and he'd love that."

They all cheered the idea and threw out more names.

"Don't forget Isaiah," Rose whispered to Grace, the other voices covering hers.

"I could ask him," she said, then lifted her brows. "Would that count as date number one?"

"You haven't had the first one yet?" Rose asked, dismayed. "Yes, this would count if you ask him, but not over text. You have to see him, go somewhere, and ask him real nice."

Grace laughed, shaking her head. "Okay, I could do that."

"That's my girl!"

"We need a name!" Tori's voice rose over all the others.

Rose agreed. "We do. If I have a clever name, this idea, and a timeline for shooting, production, and sales, that's all I need for the LBO board meeting tomorrow. Give me your best ideas."

"Something about books, reading, men," Grace said, snapping her fingers as she thought. "And Amelia Island and..." She threw her hands up. "No. I'm not good at this."

"We'll think of something," Tori said, back on her phone. "Let me Google phrases for books. And men."

"Something about words?" Madeline suggested. "Stories or...literature?"

Tori held up her hand. "Get Lit...with Good Literature."

"How about Storied Heroes of Amelia Island? Or...or Legendary Readers," Madeline suggested, a lone voice of seriousness in a sea of silly.

"I got it," Grace said, surprising them all. "Let's keep it simple and to the point. How about they all read a classic of their choice and we call it...A Year of Classics. We'll make sure all the men look sleek and, well, classic."

"I love it!" Madeline exclaimed.

Raina nodded. "Me, too. It doesn't say 'hot guys,' but that would probably scare old Kitty. She might have a heart attack seeing Hottypants shirtless and reading anyway."

"Mee...wow!" Tori joked.

"I'm taking it to the board tomorrow," Rose announced over the laughter.

"And I'm starting Nikki Lou's program tomorrow," Grace said, putting a hand on Rose's leg. "So I can't thank you enough."

"And I'm going to start taking Justin's pictures tomorrow," Tori said as she pushed up. "No, tonight. Right now, as a matter of fact."

"I have a wonderful wedding photographer we can use," Madeline said. "I've sent her so much business, she owes me a favor."

"We just need to find the twelve men," Grace said.

"I have no one to offer up," Raina replied with a sad smile. "Not even Blake, who is still MIA."

They peppered her with questions about him, but all she could do was shrug. "He's still...lost. And, apparently, he doesn't want to be found. I'm sorry, you guys. I know I promised you I'd find him, but I haven't. My assistant from Miami came up here, as I think you all know, and she's really on the job to find him."

"We haven't lost faith," Rose assured her. "He knows we're his family, even if his father, our actual brother, won't acknowledge that. He'll be back."

"And no one has talked to Dad?" Tori asked. "Not even Suze?"

Madeline shook her head. "She agrees with Raina that Blake should be here in person before we drop the bomb on Dad that he has another grandson. It's been hard enough for him to know he has a son who doesn't want anything to do with him."

"Hard is an understatement," Grace added. "I think that's what caused his stroke."

They were all silent in agreement.

"I'll keep looking," Raina promised them. "And if we find Blake, we'll make him...Mr. September."

Rose reached over and gave Raina's hand a squeeze. "Don't worry, Raindrop. He'll come back."

Raina didn't look so sure. "I hope. Do you have enough for the presentation tomorrow, Rose?"

Rose nodded and looked around, smiling at her beloved sisters. "I have more than enough." And that was the absolute truth. "I'm..." Her voice trailed off as Raina squeezed her hand. Hard. "Are you okay?" she asked.

Raina just stared at her, long enough that the others grew quiet and everyone looked at her.

"What's wrong?" Grace whispered.

"I...I..." Raina put a hand on her stomach. "I just got kicked...from the inside."

The cheer was so loud that the girls came running down from the apartment and happy, happy chaos ensued for the rest of the evening.

Chapter Five

Raina

One of the most comforting changes in Raina's ever-changing life was coming into her office at Wingate Properties and seeing Dani Alvarez already hard at work.

This morning, as Raina came up the stairs, she spotted Dani on a phone call taking notes. She spoke into a headset covered by grown-out ombre chocolate and burnished gold waves that had already escaped her hair tie.

"And these are sent directly to the licensee?" Dani asked as she looked up to catch Raina's eye, adding a thumbs-up and mouthing, "I have good news!"

Raina tilted her head in the direction of her office and whispered, "Come in when you're done."

In the office, Raina wasn't at all surprised that Dani had the shades wide open to let in light. Of course, all of her contracts and important notices were lined up on the desk with military precision, right next to a piping hot cup of decaf from the Riverfront Café with exactly the amount of cream Raina loved.

All that efficiency and she was a dear friend, too.

"God bless you, Danielle Anna Alvarez," she whispered as she came around her desk—*Dad's* desk—and dropped into a chair that was too big, too dark, and too masculine to suit her. Same with the desk, the shelves, the rug, the everything.

If this were her office, there'd be a re-do.

But Dad hadn't retired, he was just recuperating. And Raina didn't really work here, but she sure didn't work at Wallace & Wingate anymore, either.

She was living in limbo, a permanent guest at her parents' beach house, two babies in the womb and no idea of what she'd name them, let alone where they'd settle and how she'd raise them alone. None of that uncertainty sat well on Raina's shoulders.

For the time being, at least until her divorce was final, this was her life.

At the thought, her gaze drifted to the thick manila envelope at the top of the desk with the return address from the Law Offices of Riley, Vitagliano, and Cumberland. Anthony Vitagliano, her attorney, had laid out what she thought was a very fair and equitable distribution of assets, wealth, and...life things. As divorces went, this one could be remarkably clean.

Or not.

So far, Jack had no issues, although things would surely get dicey when it came to the company.

He'd want to keep the business, of course. And she could fight that to the death—there wouldn't be a Wallace & Wingate without Raina Wingate, who'd never even legally changed her name when they got married. She'd contributed every bit as much as he had to the success of their company, and if she wanted to continue as a silent partner, no doubt her attorney could make that compelling argument.

The real question was...custody. That's where things could get complicated and ugly, which just made her so sad, she tried not to think about it too much. So far, his attorney hadn't made an official custody request. Would he want the kids half the time? Every summer? Christmas?

"Ready for my news?" Dani asked from the door, her dark eyes glinting with a secret.

Raina raised the paper cup. "Better news than this excellent decaf? I doubt it. Thank you."

"You're really going to thank me in a minute." Dani came in, holding the notebook with her scribbles visible. "What do you say we bring Blake Youngblood right to our door?"

Raina lifted her brows. "You have news about him?"

"Nothing yet, but not for lack of trying. Are you one hundred percent positive I can't hire an investigator?"

"One hundred and ten," she said. "I can't go hunting him down, Dani. He knows where we are, he knows who we are, and he knows—I *hope*—that we would welcome him into this family. I can't force him to acknowledge the fact that he's my nephew. He has no idea we found the picture of his father in Doreen's arms, identifying that baby as my father's child, but he has to want to—"

"Talk. You have to talk to him."

Raina angled her head in concession. "His cell goes straight to voicemail, his apartment seems to be abandoned, and every time I think I see him, he disappears."

"And I've gone even deeper," Dani said. "I chatted with the people where he banked, shopped, and got his own fabulous coffee. I even found a dry cleaning receipt in the desk and dropped in on those folks."

"And?"

"Nothing. Until..." She arched a brow for dramatic impact. "I contacted the Florida Real Estate Commission."

Raina sucked in a breath. "His license! He was studying to take the test and—"

"He passed," she said. "Just last week."

"Oh." Raina leaned back, letting that sink in. "Then he's not leaving Florida. That's good."

"And..." Dani added with a meaningful look. "They mail those licenses directly to the recipient."

"Okay. Well, when I was at his apartment, his mailbox was overflowing."

"Really?" Dani asked. "Because it was empty when I went. That could mean he's in town, getting his mail but not living there."

"Or that he asked someone to get it for him," Raina said with a pragmatic shrug.

"He might be waiting for that license to arrive so he can disappear to another city and start a life there," Dani said. "And, Raina, we can't just skulk around his mailbox twenty-four-seven and wait for him to show up."

"So, what do we do?" Raina asked, knowing that

Dani rarely presented a problem without offering a well-thought-out solution.

She crossed her arms with a smug smile. "Well, I just made friends with an admin at the FREC who told me they mail licenses on the third of every month, and it's almost August."

Raina nodded. "So if he's waiting for it, he'll stick around for a while and the longer he stays, the better the chance of finding him when he—or someone—gets his mail. That's what you're thinking?"

"That's too...obvious."

Raina laughed. "What would be not obvious?"

"If someone with a little pull in the state real estate industry—someone *who was on the appraisal board of the FREC for two years,* ahem, Raina Wingate—calls and requests that they mail the license here instead of to his apartment."

Raina looked horrified. "Not obvious and also not ethical."

"Really? Then I'm missing something, because I haven't seen his letter of resignation. For all I know, he's on an extended leave, traveling or something. He hasn't quit, Raina. And you could have your assistant call and make this request."

Raina gave a slow shake of her head, feeling this one in her gut.

"Plus, Raina," Dani continued, her gut obviously not having any such doubts. "When he calls them hunting down the license and they say you asked for it to be sent to your office, then he'll know that you want to see him."

"And he could be so mad that I went behind his back to get his license and hold it hostage that he truly never speaks to me again. I'm not willing to take that chance." She stared at Dani, playing each move in her head like a game of chess, but the plays didn't add up. "Nope," she finally said. "I don't want to overstep my bounds."

"You *know* the FREC executive director," Dani reminded her. "You had her to your house for dinner last year."

"And if the ED asks for the request from Blake in writing, which someone with a keen eye will remember is *required in the bylaws* of the state licensing guidelines, I'm screwed and might lose *my* license."

"No risk, no reward," Dani said, pushing back. "Which is something I learned from you. However..." She looked like she'd just thought of yet another solution. "I've seen his signature on plenty of documents around here and I can..." She scribbled in the air.

"Forge it?" Raina choked out. "Dani! Nothing illegal or immoral."

"Fine. I'll go back to mailbox skulking." She flipped her notebook to a fresh page. "New business? Let's start with Charles Madison, who is coming in here on Friday, whether you want him to or not."

She frowned. "Charles...who? New client?"

"Not exactly. He's been Rex's client for years, according to his assistant who called and demanded the meeting. And I do mean *demanded*, because Mr. Madison will *only* work with Rex, period, full stop. She said he spoke with Blake six weeks ago, who informed him—*guaranteed* him was the word used—that Rex would meet with him by the second week of July to take on his listing and promises the house will be sold in no time."

Raina lifted both brows, not sure why Blake would make that promise. "Who is this guy?"

"Charles James Madison," Dani said without a bit of hesitation, once again flipping her pages to some hand-written notes. "Owner of Redbird Management, a company that—"

"Is building Ocean Song, that new boutique hotel south of the Ritz-Carlton," Raina finished. "But my dad didn't have anything to do with that commercial deal."

"No, but he sold Charles Madison a house a few years ago when he started the hotel project, and now he wants to sell. According to some notes Blake wrote in his file, Mr. Madison owns several *dozen*—you heard that right—vacation rental properties in highly desirable locations all over the country. Important client."

"I'll meet with him on Friday." She reached for her keyboard to add that to her calendar but Dani shook her head.

"Not sure you're following. Apparently, Mr. Madison wants Rex to handle the listing, or no one at all."

"He's not getting Rex."

"Then his assistant implied he'd give his listing to another company."

Raina narrowed her eyes, feeling that twist in her stomach when challenged by a problem that need to be solved. Or maybe that was Thing One giving her a kick. Either way, she liked the sensation.

"Does he know I'm taking my father's place?"

"Knows, doesn't care. He is demanding Rex with no substitutes."

Raina considered that, but knew the answer. "My dad's not ready yet," she said. "He's making great progress since the stroke. Walking on his own with a cane, speaking clearly, his brain...pretty sharp. Not the razor's edge it once was, but...no. Not ready to meet with a client."

"Who's not ready to meet with a client?" a familiar voice rang out.

"Suze!" Raina popped up, wondering if she'd heard the exchange. "What a nice surprise! Oh, this is my assistant, who's moved here from Miami, Dani Alvarez. This is my mother, the one, the only, Susannah Wingate."

"So nice to meet you." Susannah reached out a hand but Dani gave her a full hug instead.

"Oh, my goodness, Mrs. Wingate, I've heard so much about you."

"As I have about you, Dani," Susannah replied warmly.

"And, wow, you are gorgeous!" Dani exclaimed. "You could be the eighth daughter."

Susannah laughed off the compliment, but she had to know it was true. At sixty-one, she was still an attractive blonde with a dazzling smile and bright blue eyes.

Only close friends and family knew she also had a

backbone of pure titanium, a determination to protect the Wingate name, and the protective streak of a lioness.

"I'll let you two talk and get back to work." Dani closed her notebook and smiled, moving to step out of the office to give them privacy. "Can I get you coffee or water, Mrs. Wingate?"

"No, thank you, but it's just Suze, sweetheart." Susannah sat in the guest chair with the air of a woman who'd spent many hours there. "I'm sorry to barge in, Raina, but I just came from Wingate House after walking through the empty apartment on the third floor. It's a great space, but I'm here to take you up on your offer to help make it greater."

She *had* offered to help, Raina recalled, but her ideas were forgotten when they discovered the photo of Doreen Parrish holding a newborn with the name "Bradley Wingate" scribbled on the back.

Since realizing Bradley *Wingate* was now Bradley Young, adopted by a farming family in Iowa and the father of her missing assistant, Raina hadn't thought about that apartment too much.

"It's a great space," she agreed. "There's beautiful light up there and with some paint, buffed out floors, and love, that apartment could be a showstopper. And by showstopper, I mean moneymaker. Does Dad agree we should renovate and add it to the inn's room inventory?"

Susannah shook her head. "Honey, I don't think he wants to talk about work. Plus, I'm avoiding anything about Doreen, or the child he had with her fifty-five years ago. I'm petrified the subject of Blake will come up." She looked a little pained by the decision. "I agree with your call on that, but I'm starting to have mixed feelings. Are we sure it isn't wrong not to tell him?"

"Only if we told him without Blake right there. We can't tell him he's disappeared, but once we have Blake, he can be the one to tell Dad the truth, with all of us there to love and support them both."

"I guess you're right, but it's hard to keep this secret from him," Susannah said with a sigh. "Any progress? I was hoping you were talking about Blake when you said someone wasn't ready to meet a client."

"No, we're no closer. And, to be honest, I was talking about Dad."

"Oh." Susannah nodded. "Well, you're right, Rex is not ready. Thank you for being so considerate. And for being here, running everything for him."

"You know I love doing it," Raina assured her. "Real estate is"—she glanced at the fat legal envelope—"the only constant in my life."

Susannah gave a knowing look, then glanced around. "It still feels very much like...a man's office. And a seventy-five-year-old man at that."

"Well, it *is* his office."

"I have an idea," Susannah said. "Come with me to plan some ideas for the new space at the inn and when we shop and design things, maybe we could add a few items to freshen up this office for you. Make it more like Raina Wingate instead of Rex Wingate." She smiled. "Still a Wingate, but lighter paint, maybe a new desk, and please, let's get rid of that leather sofa that screams 'gentlemen's private club.'"

Raina laughed, but appreciated the offer. "Only if Dad agrees."

"He's so happy with what you're doing that he'd agree to anything." She pushed up. "Will you come to the inn with me?"

"Now? Of course," Raina agreed. "If we re-do that space the way I want to, we'll have it booked for top dollar months in advance."

"See? You're so much like your father."

She smiled. "Couldn't pay me a better compliment, Suze."

Dani stuck her head in. "I got that assistant on the phone again, insisting that her boss meet with Rex."

Raina rolled her eyes. "Apparently, I'm not enough like my father for *some* clients. This one is an absolute pain."

"What's his name?" Susannah asked.

"Charles Madison. Owns Redbird Management. Do you know him?"

Susannah lifted both brows. "Oh, yes. He goes by Chase, and your father adores him. He's incredibly charming, fabulously wealthy, and..." She added a sly smile. "Doesn't take no for an answer."

"Great." She looked at Dani. "I'll meet with Prince Charming on Friday and prove to him that I will not take no for an answer, either. It's me or no one. Oh, and Dani, is my calendar free for the next few hours?"

"Wide open," Dani said.

"Good, because my mother and I are going over to the inn for a bit." She came around the desk she would love so much to replace, reaching for Susannah's hand. "Come on, Suze. Let's spend money to make money, as my father would say."

Susannah gave a slow smile. "Be careful, Raina."

"Why?"

"Because...I doubt you've ever met anyone quite like Chase Madison."

The answer surprised Raina, but she flicked it off. "Pfft. He doesn't scare me. By the time I'm done? He'll forget about my father and be madly in love."

"Or you will be," Susannah muttered, chuckling as they walked out of the office.

Chapter Six

Grace

G race huffed out a frustrated sigh when the entry bell rang announcing a customer at six fifty-nine, one minute from her nightly closing time.

Not tonight, she thought as she shelved the last book and stepped down from the small ladder to the floor. Normally, she didn't care if someone came in and lingered this late. Nikki had dinner hours ago and was currently curled up in the kids' reading area, talking quietly to her baby doll.

But tomorrow was a big day and she so wanted her little girl to be in bed by eight, and the bedtime routine could go...a lot of different ways. Easy tonight, she hoped, since she'd already bathed Nikki Lou and had her in pajamas.

"I'll be right there," she called, knowing the customer could be looking around for assistance.

"No hurry, I'll wait."

"Oh!" She let out the soft exclamation at the sound of a baritone voice she'd come to treasure. Before she could get out to the main floor, though, Nikki launched up from her chair.

"Zayah!" she called, using the nickname she'd hung on Isaiah Kincaid the day they'd met.

"There's my girl!"

As Grace came around the bookshelf blocking her view of the front, she saw the big man crouching down to greet Nikki, a flower in his hand. He would never scoop her up or try to hug her—he knew better. Despite his size and big presence, he always managed to bring himself down to her level, and make her comfortable.

He did everything effortlessly like that, Grace marveled. From poaching peaches to singing the hymns he loved so much, Isaiah was comfortable and comforting.

Maybe that was why Nikki responded so well to him. Few people had such an effect on her little girl, and it had made Grace always look forward to seeing him.

She still hadn't met her half of the bargain she'd made with Rose, though. She'd seen Isaiah and...was too scared. That was the truth. For all his ease and comfort and kindness and warmth, something about him scared her.

It was...the potential. She tamped down the thought, staying out of sight to watch the exchange as Isaiah held out the flower.

"For you, Miss Nik."

"Daisy!" She took the stem and gave it a twirl.

"Can you count the petals?" he asked.

"Five! Seven! Nine!" She waved the daisy in the air. "I count!"

"But you *can* count," he said gently. "Show me. Start with number one."

Nikki Lou took a breath and settled, focusing on the daisy. "One, two, three, four..."

"Very good," Grace said softly, getting the attention of both as she came closer. "That was sweet of you, Isaiah."

He stood slowly, his smile widening and his dark eyes glinting with warmth. "I know tomorrow's a big day."

Grace reacted with a flash of her eyes; she hadn't told Nikki Lou anything about tomorrow's appointment, just that she might be meeting some new teachers for a school program.

"Because Thursdays are fun days," he said quickly, instantly interpreting her response correctly.

But the slip was lost on Nikki, who was still counting her way around the petals.

"They sure are," Grace agreed cheerfully. "Thank you for stopping by and *really* thank you for not being a customer. I thought I'd said goodbye to the last one ten minutes ago."

He glanced at his watch, then took a quick step to the door. "Seven on the nose, my friend." He turned the deadbolt and flipped the Open sign. "The Next Chapter is officially closed."

Grace laughed softly as Nikki scampered back to her favorite seat, still counting the petals. Possibly for the third time.

"She likes it," Isaiah said with a smile of satisfaction.

"Likes it? Knowing her, she'll give the flower a name,

demand it sleep next to her bed, and pitch a fit when the petals fall off. That was a thoughtful gesture, Isaiah."

He tipped his head in acknowledgement. "I've been thinking about you and the meeting tomorrow," he said, softly enough that Nikki couldn't hear. "You doing okay, Amazing Grace?"

"I am," she told him, smiling at the nickname that always rolled off his tongue. It gave her the strength to power through her inexplicable fear and meet her half of Rose's bargain, looking up at him. "Nikki's eaten already," she said, "but would you like to stay for dinner? Just a salad, nothing fancy."

"I'd love that."

See? So easy. Did that count as date number one? Maybe. In any case, she was happy he'd said yes, but suddenly wondered if the invitation seemed weird.

"We can talk about what I can expect tomorrow, not that either of us know, but..." Her voice died out along with the thought.

"What's going to happen is what's going to happen," he said as they walked toward the stairs that led to her apartment. "Hey, come on, Nik," he called, waving her over. "Did you give that flower a name yet? Daisy doesn't count."

She smiled up at him, stroking a white petal. "You name it, Zayah," she said, holding the daisy up to him.

"All righty, I will."

Grace started up the stairs, turning when she realized they were still at the bottom. There, Isaiah stood very still, staring at the flower.

"Solomon," he finally said.

"Solomon?" Grace and Nikki Lou asked in perfect unison.

"Eww," Nikki said. "Daisy is better."

"I admit that's not what I'd have expected," Grace agreed.

Isaiah laughed and gestured for Nikki to go up the stairs before him. "I'll explain in a minute, if your mother has no objections to a quick Bible lesson."

Grace met his gaze and nodded. "We can do that instead of her bedtime story," she said.

"Do you have a Bible?" he asked.

"Not our own." She pointed toward a shelf in the Religion and Spirituality section. "But I've got six right there. Feel free to grab the version of your choice."

A few minutes later, after Grace had helped Nikki Lou brush her teeth, Isaiah joined them in her room, taking a seat in the rocking chair while Grace and Nikki rested on the bed. The daisy was in a small juice glass of water on the nightstand.

So far, so good on the bedtime routine, but with Isaiah here, that didn't surprise her.

"Okay," Grace said, tucking Nikki closer in her arms and stroking her soft hair. "Why would you name that poor daisy Solomon?"

Nikki Lou popped her thumb out of her mouth. "Solly. I like it."

Isaiah laughed heartily and opened the Bible he'd brought up. "I don't know if King Solomon would approve of that nickname, but who knows?" He rustled a few pages. "Here we go. Matthew."

"I thought Solomon!" Nikki Lou said, sitting up as if something wasn't right in her brain.

"It is *about* Solomon," Isaiah said gently. "But the man who wrote the story is named Matthew. He has his very own book that's part of this book, the Bible."

Instantly calmed, Nikki dropped back on Grace's chest, thumb returned to mouth, her free hand clinging to her worn pink blankie.

"In this chapter," Isaiah said, "Jesus is talking. Do you know who Jesus is, Nikki Lou?"

She looked at him, thinking. "The man in church?"

He smiled. "That'll do."

"Sorry," Grace whispered. "I haven't—"

He held up a hand. "No worries. In fact, that's the whole point of this story. Jesus is telling people not to worry about anything, not about money or time or food or clothes. On the subject of clothes, he said, 'Consider, er, look hard at the flowers of the field.'"

"This one?" Nikki asked, pointing to her daisy.

"Yes, indeed," he said. "Take a good look at that flower."

She turned and stared at it, narrowing her eyes and pursing her lips in concentration, making them both laugh softly.

"Then Jesus says, 'See how it grows?'" he continued. "'The flowers do not labor or spin. Yet I tell you that not even Solomon—'"

"Solomon!" Nikki exclaimed.

"Yes, you're getting it," Isaiah said, showing remarkable patience despite the interruptions. "'Not even Solomon in all his splendor was dressed like one of these. If this is how God clothes the flowers in the field, which are here today and gone tomorrow, will He not clothe you more?'" He grinned. "I took a few liberties with that," he added softly. "But you get the idea."

"No, I don't," Grace admitted. "I mean, I do, but can you explain it to us?"

He leaned forward, his elbows on the Bible, his dark eyes looking from one to the other. "He's saying that our Father in heaven takes care of everything for us, and we just need to trust Him."

"My father is in heaven," Nikki whispered, making Grace suck in a soft breath.

"Oh, honey, he means—"

"Yes, he is," Isaiah said quickly. "And he doesn't want you to worry about anything, Nikki Lou. Not about what you'll wear, or if you meet new people who might seem unfamiliar to you, or even if you wake up and Solomon is a droopy daisy."

Grace's heart shifted in her chest. *If you meet new people who might seem unfamiliar to you.* How kind of him to prepare her for the day ahead like that.

"I like Solomon," Nikki announced, leaning over to gently tap the flower. "Night-night, Solomon."

Grace rose from the bed, her whole being feeling lighter and brighter for their Bible lesson. Maybe she got the point—*don't worry*—but the real reason she felt better was because of the compassionate and considerate man who'd told them the story.

"Night-night, Nikki Lou." Grace leaned over and kissed her forehead, pulling up the comforter. "Sweet dreams, my angel."

"Good night, Nik, and good night, Solomon," Isaiah added, closing the Bible and standing in the doorway while Grace turned off the light and gave Nikki one more kiss.

As she closed the door, she heard Nikki Lou whisper, "I love you, Solomon."

Unexpected tears sprang to Grace's eyes. "Oh. Thank you, Isaiah. You're so..." She looked up at him and couldn't think of any word that could adequately describe him. "Just thank you," she finished, feeling a little lame.

He merely smiled. "Let me make you some dinner, Grace."

"I have a salad."

"I can do better." He winked at her and led her to the kitchen.

BY THE TIME Grace finished the best omelet she'd ever eaten and sipped some herbal tea she didn't even know she had stashed in a drawer, she was beyond relaxed. She credited it all to Isaiah, who'd taken over her kitchen like the pro he was and somehow managed to erase all the stress she was feeling about the next day. About everything.

"You have a superpower, you know," Grace mused as she tucked herself back into the chair at the kitchen table and surrendered the fight to clean the kitchen. No one was going to get between that man and his dish towel.

"A superpower?" He turned from the sink, a sly smile lifting his lips. "Like a comic book hero? I can fly? See through steel? Make diner-quality omelets from scant vegetables and yesterday's leftovers?"

She laughed. "You certainly can, but your super-power is...peace." She breathed the word as it came to her.

"You think?" He looked intrigued.

"I know. And so does Nikki Lou. You spread peace wherever you go. That's why she's still and comfortable with you. You are...a peace spreader."

His smile grew, but he didn't say anything as he smoothed the towel against the side of the sink and walked into the living area, looking around.

"Interesting lamp choice," he joked, running his hand over the worn leather shade of one of Grace's most prized possessions. "I'm guessing Nikki Lou picked this out?"

Smiling at the lamp, which was, indeed, interesting, she came into the room. For a moment, she just gazed at the thin and aging leather shade at the top of what had to be the world's oddest table lamp. The base was cut to look like the trunk of a tree with two metal bees perched on the branches, plus a dangling plastic beehive that functioned as a nightlight.

"Actually, it's a family heirloom."

His brows shot up. "The Wingate family? Sure haven't seen anything like this at the inn."

"The Jenkins family," she said. "It was in my husband's nursery and he kept it, and carted that thing around to every base and new assignment and apartment we had. He was determined that it would be his child's lamp and nightlight, too."

"Why don't you keep it in Nikki's room?"

"I did until the other night, but the light comes on and off at weird times and sometimes it flickers, which upsets her."

"Sounds like it's a broken filament." He reached for it, ready to look at it, but Grace put her hand on his arm.

"No, don't fix it."

He gave her a surprised look.

"I like when it flickers," she admitted. "I feel like... you know." She rolled her eyes, knowing it was insane.

"You think it's Nick," he suggested softly.

She nodded. "I know, I know. Silly, but it's comforting."

"I get it," he said, abandoning the lamp and turning to the other interesting item in the room—the baby grand. "This is quite an unexpected addition to your house. Yours?"

"It was here when we moved in." She put her mug of tea on an end table and joined him at the piano, opening the keyboard cover to reveal yellowed keys under the faded mahogany wood. "It's likely out of tune but it's become part of our home somehow."

"Baldwin," he said, reading the word embossed over

the center of the keyboard. "I think that's a decent brand."

"It's not worth a lot," she said. "I had it appraised and it would cost more to get it out and over the balcony—which is how it must have gotten in here at some point—than I would make selling it. Plus, sometimes Nikki Lou tinkers on it. Can you play?"

He smiled and looked down at the keyboard. "When I was thirteen or so, the pianist at my church died. No one could play the hymns and my mother was in the choir." He grinned. "A big Black Baptist gospel choir that didn't need any instruments, not with those voices. But she begged me to learn the songs every week, which I did. Never read music, but I could pluck out a tune. My entire repertoire consists of gospel music and hymns."

Grace gestured toward the bench. "Please. I'd love to hear something."

He hesitated, then pulled out the seat. "I won't be loud," he said. "I don't want to wake Nikki Lou."

"She's a sound sleeper." Grace went to the sofa, picking up her tea and settling in to listen.

"I'll play my favorite song," he said with a smile.

Looking down, he played one note, with one finger. He held the second, then the third, one key at a time.

Of course, she recognized the melody to *Amazing Grace*.

"Your favorite?" she teased.

"Absolutely." He used his other hand to hit a soft chord, then started over.

"*Amazing Grace, how sweet the sound...*" He sang

softly, in his distinct baritone. *"That saved a wretch like me."*

Chills she didn't expect blossomed over her arms. "Wow."

He added the slightest bit more force on the keys, playing with, well, amazing grace.

"Do you know the words, Grace?"

She shook her head. "I don't think so."

"It's the most recorded song in history," he told her as he continued to play. "Written by a man who captained slave ships but was saved by the Lord."

Fascinated, she just sighed as he sang the next verse to a song she really did know, no doubt from going to church with her family. She never went now. She certainly didn't pray or listen to hymns. Not after...

She lifted her gaze to the lamp, willing it to come on at that very moment, aching for Nick to somehow communicate that it was all right to have this man in her home, in her life.

But the light didn't flicker, so she looked up and studied the framed picture of Staff Sergeant Nicholas Jenkins, her heart heavy with confusion and guilt and the familiar ache of missing him.

Isaiah followed her gaze and let the piano fade out.

"I better be going, Grace," Isaiah said quickly, lifting his hands from the keyboard and closing the cover. "I didn't mean to take up so much of your evening, especially when you have such a big day tomorrow."

"Oh, no. I've enjoyed this so much. Thank you."

With a quick smile and a nod, he slid off the bench

and pushed it back under the piano. "Anytime you need a little church, I'm happy to play."

"And read the Bible," she reminded him.

"That's...my role." He took an awkward step away from the piano and she instantly stood, a question rising from her heart. Was this right? Was it wrong? She didn't know.

All she knew was that he gave her peace and she needed it.

"Would you..." She swallowed, and blamed Rose before diving in. "Would you go with me tomorrow?"

His dark eyes widened in surprise. "With Nikki Lou? To her first day of the program?"

"I totally understand if you can't," she said quickly, the reality of what she'd just asked hitting her. "It could be hours and so boring to just sit through testing, so please, if you're busy, and I know you are, just forget I asked. I only—"

"Yes, of course."

She blinked at the answer. "Really? You will? You don't mind? You can—"

"Grace." He angled his head. "Why do you think I came over here?"

"To be invited to spend half your day at a psychologist's office?" she asked in disbelief, because that was a stretch, even for a good man like Isaiah.

"I knew you hadn't asked Rose, because she's doing the fundraising meeting, and I saw your mother and Raina today at the inn, and overheard them talking about various plans tomorrow. I started to suspect that you might be taking her all by yourself, because you didn't want to trouble anyone."

She sighed and smiled. "Yep. But now I...don't want to go alone."

"You shouldn't," he said. "My schedule is clear. I'll take you and Nikki Lou tomorrow. We'll bring Solomon, too."

She gave a soft laugh at that and resisted the urge to throw her arms around him and hug him tight. Barely.

After they set plans and she walked him down to the front door to say goodnight, she stood for a long time in the quiet of the bookstore, feeling things she didn't understand at all. Gratitude. Joy. Hope. And, yes, peace.

And she texted Rose to tell her that she'd had Isaiah at her house for dinner and had scheduled "date" number two. Her sister responded with five red hearts that made Grace smile as she turned off the lights and went back upstairs, humming the melody stuck in her head.

How sweet the sound indeed.

Chapter Seven

Rose

"Will it be clean and wholesome? No naked men! There won't be undressed men, will there? Or...will there? The Amelia Island Local Business Organization is a family-friendly operation, so will there be... man chest?"

Rose fought a smile of amusement, because there was something in Kitty Worthington's barrage of questions that sounded like she *wanted* bare-chested men in the calendar, no matter how much she insisted the opposite was true.

"Heavens, no, Kitty," Rose promised her. "Maybe a wee little bit of...skin...showing, but nothing that would make you blush."

"Everything makes Kitty blush," joked Sarah Beth, a fairly new store owner who'd come from Sanibel Island to marry her high school sweetheart. She might be new to the town, but she'd made lots of friends and ran a popular boutique, and Rose knew she could count on her vote.

"Not me," another woman said, crossing her arms under an ample bosom. "I love this. Count me in for ten copies, Rose. I'll give them as Christmas presents to my old—and I do mean *old*—sorority sisters. That crew loves the hot guys."

That got a good laugh from the small group of a half-dozen board members, comprised of local business owners. Kitty had brought them out to her screened porch with brusque instructions to keep it down, since her aunt was asleep upstairs.

Rose pitied the poor woman, forced to live with Kitty Worthington, of all the unsympathetic caretakers. But Rose forgot about the houseguest as she finished her presentation, doing her best to convince the board members that twelve attractive men reading well-known books on a calendar would be fast, easy, not terribly expensive, and would sell well.

They seemed to agree. Well, all but one.

"I still think it objectifies men," Kitty said. "We'd be furious if the idea of this calendar featured scantily-clad women."

"No one will be scantily—"

Kitty flicked her hand to stop Rose from speaking.

"It's the principle, dear," she sniffed, adjusting her glasses. "I think that you and your sister should get back to the drawing board and present a new idea."

Frustration spiraled through Rose, but she kept her smile in place. "I don't think that's necessary," she said with false cheer. "Unless the rest of your board agrees with you."

The others shook their heads, several of them chiming in with how much they loved it.

"I think it will sell like hot cakes!" exclaimed Elaine, who owned a frame shop. "It's fun, playful, and showcases our, uh, local talent. I love it."

More of them nodded in agreement, giving Rose the confidence she needed to power on.

"I promise you there will be nothing unseemly at all about the calendar," Rose said. "But it will let the world know we have no shortage of good-looking men in our small town, and that they are well-read and intelligent."

The only man in the group, Peter Salentine, owner of a very popular souvenir shop on Centre Street, ran a hand over thinning hair. "I don't know if I qualify as handsome, well-read, or intelligent, but I certainly would not feel objectified, Kitty. Maybe I'd find the love of my life."

The women laughed and teased him, with Elaine giving him an elbow jab of encouragement. "You should be Mr. February, Peter."

"Because I'm short like that month?" he asked on a laugh.

"Because you're romantic."

That got a big reaction from the group, confirming Rose's sense that this was going her way and Kitty was the only stumbling block. Did the chairwoman's vote count more than the others'? Rose didn't know.

"What books will they hold in these pictures?" Kitty demanded. "Smutty romance novels?"

Sarah Beth snapped her fingers playfully. "Don't knock the romance novels! After my husband and I fell back in love after forty-five years apart, I feel like I'm living one."

"Well, we've called it A Year of Classics," Rose reminded them. "And every man will be classically handsome in his own way, and reading classic literature."

Kitty still looked doubtful. "Who decides what's a classic?"

"We're letting each man pick his book, and for my husband?" Rose shrugged her shoulders. "That could be anything from *The Farmer's Almanac* to *When I Grow Up, I Want to be a Firefighter*. He liked to read that to our kids."

"Oh, Gabe's going to be in it?" Diane, the owner of a precious antique store where Rose shopped all the time, pretended to fan herself. "I'll take a few dozen copies."

Rose laughed at that and started packing up the papers from her presentation, feeling confident she could win this vote and start scheduling the photo shoots and production.

"Can we vote and move on to the next agenda item?" Peter asked, sounding impatient. "My afternoon cashier needs to leave early."

"Yes, please, it's inventory day for me," Diane added.

But Kitty remained unconvinced, so Rose leaned in to close the deal. "You understand how precious time is for local business owners, Kitty. You and your husband have run your jewelry store for, what? Twenty-five years? Let's just move on this and make it easy on everyone."

"Easy for you," she said. "When the morality police come after us, I'll be the one on the firing line."

"We don't have morality police on Amelia Island," Rose said, patience waning. "You and your group should discuss it privately and I'll step out for the vote."

"Fine," she said. "But if you bump into a confused old woman named Annabelle, don't believe a word she says."

Rose gave a smile and slipped back into the house, walking through the kitchen toward the front room to wait there. As she passed the stairs, she heard a reed-thin voice calling from upstairs.

"Are you there, Kitty?"

Rose's heart dropped at the sad sound, and she barely gave it a moment's thought before she started up the stairs.

"Kitty's in a meeting," she called as she reached the top and looked down the hall. "But I can help you."

"I need some water."

Kitty didn't give her aunt water? With more irritation pumping through her, Rose followed the sound of the woman's voice, stopping at the door to a dimly lit bedroom.

"Annabelle?" she asked as she stepped inside and looked at a four-poster bed.

"That's me. Annabelle Greene. Who are you?" A slender woman who barely made a bump under the comforter lay in the bed, with thinning gray hair mussed over the pillow.

"Hello, I'm Rose. Do you need a glass of water?"

"It's there. On the dresser. I left it and I just can't get up."

"Of course." Rose grabbed a water tumbler and

walked to the side of the bed, sliding open some plantation shutters as she passed to let in some light. "Too bright?" she asked when Annabelle covered her eyes.

"No, no. I like it. Sunlight always makes me feel better."

The other woman blinked and managed to push herself up on a few pillows, letting Rose see that she was likely in her seventies and looked like she'd lived hard through every one of those years. Not ancient and decrepit like Kitty made her sound, though she had a network of creases all over her face and around faded green eyes.

"Oh my goodness!" Annabelle gasped and slapped her hand to her chest. "Am I dead?"

Startled by the question, Rose drew back. "Absolutely not," she said, holding out the water. "You're just thirsty. Here you go."

"But...but..." She ignored the water and peered hard at Rose, the little bit of color she had draining from her face. "Yes, I'm dead. It's you! It's *you*! I told you God would make us roommates in heaven, Charlotte Lillian Long!"

Rose nearly dropped the tumbler, her legs suddenly weak. "You...knew...my...mother?"

"Your mother? Char! Your mother is...wait. Aren't you Charlotte?"

Chill bumps rose over her arms. "I'm Rose, and Charlotte was my mother. Did you know her?"

"Know her? She was my best friend for two summers

when I came to Fernandina Beach to visit my grand-parents."

"When was that?" Rose asked.

"The summers of *love*," she said on a chuckle. "Well, for some of us. It was 1965 and 1966. See, I can remember that but not what color my panties are." She took the tumbler and sucked down some water, then set it on the nightstand to stare at Rose some more. "Probably red or black, 'cause I'm wild like that."

Rose chuckled and perched on the edge of her bed, utterly fascinated. "I can't believe you knew my mother," she said.

"Oh, yes, and you are the spitting image of her. It's like looking at Char only...you're older. She was just sixteen, but so pretty. So, so pretty."

"Why, thank you, Annabelle." Without thinking, she took the woman's hand, suddenly wondering about Char-lotte. If she'd lived this long, would her mother have a few age spots? Would her neck sag and would she have gray hair and lines in her face?

She couldn't imagine her mother as anything but the young and vibrant woman she'd seen in pictures and old videos Dad had. And, yes, Rose certainly favored her in coloring and features, far more than Madeline, Tori, or even Raina.

Rose sat still and mesmerized, not even knowing where to begin. She rarely met anyone who'd known her mother, and if they did, they didn't talk about her.

"She's gone now," Rose whispered, realizing she might be bringing sad news to this woman.

"Oh, I think someone told me that," Annabelle said. "A long time ago."

"She died in childbirth when my twin sister, Raina, and I were born."

"We were best friends, did I tell you?"

"Yes, ma'am, you did. What did you two do together?" she asked, hungry for more.

"We had fun, that's what. We flirted with the Navy sailors all over town, and went to the shrimp boat races. She'd never miss that. And the Fourth of July street fair when we got..." She placed her hand on her chest, feeling around, then sighing. "It's long gone, I suppose."

"What's that?"

"Just...a trinket. Something from your mother." She took another sip of water and Rose waited, giving the woman's old brain a chance to remember things Rose was aching to hear.

In truth, Charlotte was a bit mythical to Rose, and she longed to know more about her mother's history, the color and details of her life, her dreams and desires. Could Annabelle tell her...or were those memories long gone?

Maybe the latter, since the older woman fell back on her pillow with a sigh of pure exhaustion. But Rose felt like she had to ask a question before Annabelle fell asleep.

"How did you meet each other?" she asked.

"We worked together," she said, looking off into the distance with a smile. "At the five-and-dime down on the river."

"Wait a second." Rose sat straighter. "The five-and-dime was on Wingate Way, right?"

"Big brick house with an apartment upstairs," Charlotte said. "I think it's still there."

"Oh, yes. That's the bookstore now," Rose told her. "My sister's bookstore, The Next Chapter."

"Ah, well, back then, it was just penny candy and comics, fabric and sewing notions. Bits of things, like hats and household goods. We had such good times together in those days. Char was so bright and fun." She rubbed her breastbone again. "I wonder where I put that thing..."

A stabbing pain nearly took Rose's breath away, and for the first time in her life, she felt cheated in the mother department. Of course, she loved Susannah wholly and unconditionally; she'd been—still was—a spectacular mother to all of them.

But...*Charlotte*.

"It's probably still there at the five-and-dime," Annabelle said, touching her neck again.

"The trinket? Oh, I doubt that," Rose told her. "That store has been remodeled a few times over the years."

"Did they take down the brick wall?"

Rose frowned. "There's some exposed brick along the back, but it has bookshelves built over it now."

"Well, back in my day, those bricks were loose and we hid things behind them. Fun things." She gave a shaky smile. "Secret things."

Rose smiled at the idea of teenage girls hiding trinkets, but Annabelle suddenly looked lost, her gaze blank as she groaned, sliding deeper into the covers.

"Are you okay?" Rose asked. "Can I get you anything?"

"I'm dying," she said, the simplicity of the statement a little shocking.

"Oh, I'm so..."

"It's fine," she said. "I know where I'm going and it's better there. Anyway, Kitty doesn't want me around much longer."

"Oh, I'm sure she does! You're her aunt."

The older woman studied Rose for a long time. "You even sound like Char," she said softly. "Always something kind to say."

That gave Rose an actual thrill. "I'm optimistic by nature," she said. "My sisters tease me for always being positive, and my husband calls me 'Rose-Colored Glasses' but he says it with love."

"You come by it naturally," Annabelle said, sighing again. "She was a pretty one, that Charlotte Long. The sailors loved her, but she just wasn't interested. She liked some boy named Rex."

A new set of chills rose. "She married that boy. He's my father."

"Always wore yellow," Annabelle added, maybe not even hearing what Rose had said. "I called her 'Sunshine' and it was true. Always had a sweet smile and..." She frowned, thinking. "We were best friends, did you know?"

Ah, yes. Annabelle could be spinning tales in a mind that wasn't nearly as sharp as it once was.

"Yes, you said that," Rose reminded her gently.

"She was so bright. So alive and...nice..." Her chest rose and fell with sleep.

"I wish you could tell me more," Rose whispered as she tucked the comforter around the woman's tiny shoulders. "Dear Annabelle, who was my mother's friend. I wish you could tell me more."

"Rose?" Kitty barked from the bottom of the stairs. "We've voted. You've won. You can make your vulgar calendar."

She stood and closed the shutters again, looking at the woman.

"Yes, I have won," she whispered. "You told me something I never knew and now? Now, I just want to know more."

TORI CALLED for a get-together that night so they could find out about the meeting with Kitty and how things went for Grace with the specialist that day. Once again, they decided to meet at the bookstore, since Grace didn't want to leave Nikki Lou with a sitter, but being there made Rose obsess even more about what she'd learned that day.

This old house had always had some sort of retail on the first floor, with the second floor used as a place to live. Looking around, Rose tried to picture her mother here in the 1960s, selling candy and sewing notions.

Grace was still upstairs putting a very exhausted Nikki Lou to bed when Raina and Tori arrived.

"Who wants chocolate?" Tori called when she breezed in, her whole demeanor so much lighter and happier than when she'd arrived on Amelia Island from Boston. Yes, they had all been upset about Dad's stroke, but a certain doctor had sure put a bounce in her step and a light in her eyes. "I got a box from our girl in Belgium today!"

"Sadie sent chocolate?" Madeline, who'd arrived at eight on the dot, looked up from her cozy corner in the seating area, a long white piece of fabric in one hand and an embroidery needle in the other. "Gosh, I miss that girl."

"I called her and got five precious minutes," Tori said. "She just got back from Paris, is home in Brussels for two days, then jets off to...Munich? Milan? Somewhere that starts with an M."

Madeline laughed. "Madrid. Suze talked to her, too, and gave me an update."

"Oh, Sadie," Raina said on a sigh. "I know she's having so much fun and loving her continental life, but I just wish she'd—"

"Our mother worked in this very store!" Rose exclaimed, the words coming out like they had a life of their own, silencing everyone.

Madeline frowned. "Suze never worked here."

"Not Suze," Rose corrected. "Our...biological mother, Charlotte Lillian Long."

Raina drew back, frowning. "That's right. Her middle name was Lillian. I like that. Maybe if one of the twins is a girl—"

"You can find out the sexes, Raina," Tori said, flipping open a box of dark chocolate. "I don't know why you wouldn't."

"I like being surprised."

"And this news doesn't surprise you?" Rose insisted, shocked that her sisters didn't pounce on this information like she had. "Charlotte worked here when it was a little general store, a five-and-dime they called it."

"Riverview Five & Ten was the name of it," Madeline supplied, folding up her white fabric as though she instinctively knew it couldn't be in the same room as that chocolate. "I used to go there with her. Who told you this?"

Rose explained the circumstances of meeting Kitty's aunt, Annabelle, including how she remembered such specific details, like a trinket from a fair, but was forgetful and sick.

"So, not the most reliable witness from the past," Tori said.

"No, but..." Rose sighed. "Some of the details were just so clear, they had to be right. Did you know she worked here?" she asked Madeline.

"I'm not sure," she admitted, her dark eyes shuttering. "Some things I don't know if I really remember, or if I heard a story about them from Grandma Lolly."

"Aww, Grandma Lolly!" Tori exclaimed. "She died when we were so young."

"She was broken and lost her will to live after her Charlotte died," Madeline told them. "Oh, and Raina? She was Lillian, but everyone called her Lolly."

"I love that," Raina said. "Great family name."

"I wish I knew more!" Rose moaned. "How can I not know everything about her?"

Madeline smiled. "I barely remember her and I was six when she died, so you can't be hard on yourself, Rose. Dad has let her memory fade and we all know why."

"Respect and love for Suze," Tori said. "Which is one of the reasons we adore him."

"I should ask him about her," Rose said with a sigh. "But I always feel like it's...I don't know. Like you said, it's disrespectful to Susannah."

"It's not," Madeline said. "Susannah's position as our mother—as the matriarch of this family and the woman we all look up to and love wholeheartedly—is not in question."

Rose nodded, almost taking that as her oldest sister's approval to seek more information, but then Grace came in and it was easy to see she was tired and stressed.

"Hey, Gracie. Have some of Sadie's chocolate and tell us about Nikki Lou's program," Madeline said, smoothly changing the subject. "Will it be good?"

"So good." Grace sighed, leaning over the open box and plucking out a piece of candy before sliding onto the loveseat next to Madeline. "These people are so smart and caring and Nikki Lou did great. Isaiah said he'd never seen her so happy."

"Isaiah?" Rose exclaimed with the others. That was the date? Taking Nikki Lou to her program?

"Yes, Isaiah," she said, taking a bite of her chocolate

then letting out a moan. "How does Sadie live with this much chocolate around her?"

"Happily," Tori said, helping herself to another. "And don't change the subject, which was Isaiah."

"He came with me," she said, dabbing at her lips as she finished the bite.

"You took Isaiah and not any of us?" Raina asked, looking a little hurt.

"You had three showings today, Rain, and shopping with Mom for the inn," Grace said. "Madeline had back-to-back fittings. The café was slammed for Tori, and you" —she pointed to Rose, her delicate fingers holding the last bite of her chocolate—"were already handling my workload."

"And you are meeting your end of the bargain, I see." Rose grinned. "I will count that as date number one."

"Wait—what?" Raina sputtered.

"A date?" Madeline's voice rose.

"Hold up there, cowgirl." Tori was the loudest of them all. "You're *dating* Isaiah, Grace?"

"No! I'm..." She looked at Rose and laughed. "I'm paying for Rose's time on my project by following her silly rules."

"Not silly," Rose shot back, crossing her arms with a challenging look. "You all see how he looks at her. I just think it's something worth pursuing. Am I right?"

They all agreed, but Grace just smiled. "We're friends and that's all," she insisted. "Now, please tell me all about how it went with Kitty."

"Perfect," Rose assured her. "Once I convinced her

that the calendar wasn't going to be Amelia Island's version of *Playgirl*—is that still a thing? Anyway, we got the approval, and the photo shoots will start next week. Oh, and I..." She glanced around, hoping the others didn't mind her bringing it up. "I met Kitty's aunt and she knew our mother, Charlotte. Did you know she worked here, Grace? In this very store when she was a teenager and it was a little general store."

"Oh!" Grace's eyes widened. "That is such an amazing piece of history. How did we not know that? Why wouldn't Dad tell me that?"

Because he never talks about Charlotte, Rose thought, while the others chatted and the subject changed. Which made her wonder and worry if it was Rex they were protecting by not talking about her, and not Susannah.

But before she could give that more thought, Tori reached for another piece of candy. "Speaking of missing sisters," she said. "Chloe has her first legit interview with a celebrity tomorrow."

They pounced on the news, asking for details, and conversation naturally shifted. That was fine; Rose understood. She joined the conversation and put thoughts of Charlotte out of her head...at least for now.

Chapter Eight

Chloe

H oly cow. That wasn't a house. That was the most stunning Mediterranean palace Chloe had ever seen.

"Nice, huh?" Brian, the CO—camera operator—who'd been assigned to accompany Chloe on this story, looked up from his phone for the first time since they'd gotten into her car to drive deep into the Hollywood Hills.

Even that had been another disappointment. The TV show just sent them off with no crew, no truck or van, no nothing. Just Chloe and some kid right out of school who could hold the camera. Everything else was up to her.

"Have you been here before?" she asked.

"The guy who owns it throws sick parties," he said. "I've covered a few. But he moved to Miami, and Coo's been renting it. No wild parties that I know of."

"Just ghosts." She hit the gas on her sluggish little crossover, rounding a hairpin curve to get an even better look at the jaw-dropping mansion. "Of Sharon Tate."

"Is that why we're going here? I heard Coo might be switching labels or recording something new in secret." He sat up, pushing hair from his face. "Sorry, but I do not do ghosts. Especially..." He curled a lip and looked around like someone might jump out from the side of the road and attack them. "This is where the Manson murders were? Gross. I'm not going in."

"What?" She choked the question. "We've got an interview with Lacey Britton, Coo Coo Cooper's girlfriend, in ten minutes."

"No, dude, *you've* got an interview with her. Set up the camera on a tripod. But this dude?" He pointed to his chest with two thumbs. "Does *not* go near the otherworld. There are portals and...no, not going in. No way."

Portals? She pulled up to the gate and pressed the call button, wanting to get into the only portal she cared about—the front door. *Could* Brian refuse to work? Wouldn't that cost him—

"Can I help you?" a male voice called out from the box.

"This is Chloe Wingate with *A-List Access* and"— she threw a look at her pathetic passenger—"my camera crew. We're here to interview Ms. Britton."

After a few seconds of silence, the iron gates parted and they were able to drive through and round yet another curve, coming around a bank of grass and trees to get the full impact of the home known as Casa Grande, a monster of a mansion perched on so much land it looked like a national park, all overlooking Los Angeles.

"Don't you even want to see it in the daylight?"

Chloe asked Brian, hoping for a different response this time.

"Sorry, I'm out."

"Out?" She turned to him. "I can't do my first story without a camera operator."

"If Sharon's ghost gets you, it'll be your last." He held up the phone, showing a page from Amazon. "*Helter Skelter*, man. Have you read it?"

"You can't be serious." She shook her head, fury shooting through her. Was there anything about this operation that was professional? "We have a job to do."

"I'm dead serious, if I can make that pun."

Biting back a curse, she pushed open the door and climbed out.

"Just go talk to her and set up your shots," he called through her open door. "I'll show you how to mount the camera."

She answered by slamming the door and marching to the front of the house, half expecting the guy from *The Wizard of Oz* to open the door and tell Dorothy to go home.

But the heavy wood door opened fully before she even found the bell, and a thirty-something man in clean jeans and a white linen button-down greeted her with a nod.

"Hi, Ms. Wingate. I'm Garrett, the Coopers' personal butler. You can come with me." He peeked past her into the driveway. "Your crew?"

Her crew of one scaredy-cat? She just smiled as she pushed her sunglasses up to her head. "I thought I'd talk to Ms. Britton first and set up our shots and locations rather than having the camera operator trampling through the house."

His smile grew a little when he got a look into her eyes, or maybe he just liked how considerate she was. She didn't have time to think about it, though, because her reporter's Spidey sense just got tweaked.

"Did you say 'the Coopers' live here?" she asked. "Have they gotten married?"

Because *that* might be an actual story for *A-List Access*. Nothing earthshattering, but wasn't that more interesting than ghosts?

He threw her a sly smile. "You'll have to talk to Lacey about that."

Which would be a yes. Mentally filing that, she followed Garrett through an entryway the size of her apartment, with gold accents on the walls, heavy pendant lights, blue crystals for doorknobs, and a sea of white marble floor as far as the eye could see.

She suddenly longed to show Raina this house and get her opinion—and appraisal—or hear Tori joke about the utter lack of practicality of these floors. Kenzie would do a hilarious TikTok of the aquarium—holy heck, that *was* a shark—and Grace would run off with Nikki Lou and play endless hide-and-seek and...

Stop, Chloe. You're alone in this haunted, over-the-top mansion, so do your job and stop being homesick for the family that isn't here.

"Can you shoot outside?" he asked.

Without a camera operator, she wasn't sure she could shoot at all. "Sure...I guess."

"Perfect, then you can step right out there." He gestured toward a wide bank of French doors, all open and leading to an infinity pool and two-story waterfall made of natural stone. "Lacey is sunbathing."

"Thank you." Outside, she pulled the sunglasses from the top of her head to protect her eyes from the onslaught of...sunshine and beauty. Sparkling blue water, cream stacked stone, green grass, red umbrellas, and...a not exactly *dressed* woman lying on a double-bed chaise...thing.

"Uh, hello," Chloe called. "You must be Ms. Britton."

Very slowly, the woman rose. She wore giant sunglasses, so Chloe couldn't really see much of her face, but she sure could see the woman had miles of gorgeous hair. And she was definitely not going to get a tan line.

"*A-List Access?*" she asked.

"Yes, ma'am. I'm—"

"Did you just 'ma'am' me?" the nearly naked woman coughed with disgust as she grabbed something to pull over her head and cover herself. More or less.

"I did, but I'm from the South and that's..." Jeez. Apologizing already?

She could practically hear her favorite journalism professor in her ear. *Do not let your interviewee put you on the defensive.*

"How about I just call you Lacey?" she asked, shaking off any nerves.

"How about we just pick the best lighting and I'll go get my makeup done?"

"Why don't we talk for a few minutes first." Chloe came closer, then perched on the edge of a chair, despite not getting any invitation to get comfortable. "I'd like to prepare my questions and I thought we might chat before cameras start rolling."

Lacey pulled the big sunglasses down to reveal giant eyes that looked like the makeup artist had already done a lot of work. "*Chat?*"

"Yeah, I mean..." Was *chat* uncool? "Talk about...your experiences."

"My what?"

"I understand you've had some sightings of Sharon Tate's ghost."

She stared a second longer, then fell back on the bed, cursing under her breath. "Of course they sent an idiot."

"Excuse me?"

She pushed up to her elbows, whipping off the sunglasses completely. "You do not really think for one moment that I'd be living—and sleeping—in this house if I thought there was a ghost of someone who'd been murdered running around here?"

"I was told that's why I'm here. You have a better story to give me?" Chloe asked.

"I got plenty of stories, Blondie, but none of them are for public consumption yet."

"Like your secret marriage to one of the most famous rappers in the world?"

Her jaw slipped open, then slammed shut as she

leaned forward, narrowing her gaze. "Print that and you will never work in this town again."

Chloe almost laughed at the cliché and swallowed the urge to remind this rocket scientist that she was a television journalist, not print.

She did neither, but took secret pride in the fact that her reporter's instincts were still strong. She had sniffed out the marriage. And it was a decent story. Not exactly Pulitzer Prize-winning, but at least it wasn't the ghost of poor Sharon Tate.

"Someone's going to find out that you're married someday," Chloe said. "So, first, congrats. And second, let me have the scoop and I'll make it awesome for you."

"No can do. We promised it to *People*. Or *US Weekly*. Or some rag. You get the ghost stuff. Just don't make me sound dumb, and don't take one drop of video from my left side or you'll never—"

"Have you or have you not had an encounter with Sharon Tate's ghost?" Chloe pressed.

"Tate? Is that her name? Like Tater Tot?"

Chloe winced, thinking of all the research she'd done to prepare for an interview with what her nephew Zach would call a micro-brain. Not to mention the abject disrespect for a woman who died far too young, way too violently.

"She was considered a great beauty," Chloe said. "Without a doubt one of the most gorgeous women in Hollywood at the time. Have you seen her picture? Or just her ghost?"

"Now we're talking," Lacey said, sliding her feet to

the ground. "Let's tell people I see her because...only equally gorgeous women can see her. Will that work for your angle or whatever?"

"My angle is usually the truth. Have you seen her?"

She leaned forward, all pretense gone. "Honey, you're not here because I saw a ghost, okay? You know that and I know that. You're here because my husband has a lot of favors owed to him and I want a story that's going to make me look beautiful, smart, and talented enough to get me the part I just auditioned for. Got it?"

She was starting to.

Lacey stood, showing off legs that went on forever, a model's body, and, oh, her hair. Well, *someone's* hair. "I'm going to get made up. Find a spot and get your camera. We'll figure it out."

"Hang on a second," Chloe said, not quite ready to sell out *that* easily. "I'll do that story if you like, but can't you give me something...real, too? If not your nuptials, then maybe the fact that Coo is recording? A new label? Any truth to those rumors?"

Lacey closed her eyes and dropped her head back. "What are nup...things."

"Nuptials? It means...a wedding."

"I told you, no! No to the wedding story, and if you breathe a word, one single word, that Coo is recording for a new label?" Her eyes tapered to slits, not looking nearly as beautiful as before. "You'll be as dead as the Tater Tot."

"So he *is* recording for a new label?" she asked, choosing to ignore the threat.

"Garrett!" she hollered. "Someone get this woman out of here."

The understated butler appeared in an instant. "Is there a problem, Lacey?"

"I don't have time for this. I need a good story to run about me or I'll never get a part!" she whined, flouncing off and leaving Chloe with her jaw hanging open and a sick feeling in the pit of her stomach.

She was definitely not getting on air this weekend... unless she could find herself a source and some B-roll. Maybe this story wasn't quite as dead as poor Sharon, not yet.

"Right this way." Garrett gestured for her to follow him back the way they'd come.

"Of course." She took a few steps and paused, soaking up the details to add color to her story. "Is Coo recording here?"

The man shot her a look, clearly uncertain how to respond.

"It's fine, Lacey already told me. More of the same, or is he breaking into something new?"

He just eyed her, the slightest secret smile pulling as he studied her face. She'd seen that look before, the interest, the acknowledgment that Chloe was easy on his eyes. She'd sworn she wasn't going to use that God-given attribute in her career, that she was smart, too, and a darn good journalist.

But right now, she just wanted to get a story on air this weekend, so she held his gaze and smiled.

"He is, isn't he?" she asked.

"Downstairs in a sound-proof studio." He inched closer. "It's his best work."

"No surprise, he's so good." She wasn't a fan of his music, but Chloe had done plenty of research before this interview. Maybe she could use some of it after all. "Is it like *Hit Me Up* or is he going back to his roots from the *Generation Coo* album?"

"It's his roots," Garrett said. "With a sour twist that is going to blow people away."

They reached the door. "Oh, man," she gushed. "I cannot wait to hear it. How long until release?"

"Secret drop date, but my guess is they're close. Maybe this fall?" He smiled. "You didn't hear that from me or Lacey...Cooper."

"Oh, she changed her name after they got married?"

He gave her an impressed look. "You're good."

"Thanks." If only someone other than the butler would acknowledge that.

"I guess you won't be back?" he asked with a knowing smirk.

"Don't be so sure. I think she liked me, don't you?"

He laughed. "Don't take it personally. She's not a fan of competition, so most attractive women get shown the door."

She smiled at the compliment, thanked him for the help—more than he realized—and stepped out into the sunshine, her story forming in her head. Hopefully, the useless cameraman wouldn't slide through a portal to the netherworld if he just got some B-roll shots of the outside.

Then she'd work her magic and make a story out of it.

IF YOU NAIL IT, you stay. Screw it up, and, well, I hope you got a month-to-month lease.

Her former boss's warning rang in Chloe's ears while she stood in the chilly, windowless editing room waiting for the verdict from her new boss, Rory. Pia said twenty-five minutes ago that he'd "be right there," but Chloe knew the oh-so-important news producer could be doing something more critical than previewing her story for the Saturday broadcast.

But she wasn't worried. She'd totally nailed this story. It was fun, broken up with bits of Coo's most famous songs, and included a few shots of the jaw-dropping house, so she was able to get the Sharon Tate connection in, as instructed. She'd peppered the edit with stills of Coo and the new Mrs. Coo, and led with the news that the now-married rapper was changing labels and reportedly dropping a new record in the fall.

Chloe's presentation was serious but warm, with just enough humor to show she recognized that this might not be a breaking headline, but fans would care a lot.

The digital editor seemed to like it, but he was a Coo Coo Cooper fan and the news of a fresh record appealed. The marriage? Not so much, but Chloe knew the *A-List Access* demographic skewed heavily female, and they would gobble up the secret marriage.

"Ping me when he shows." The editor, one of a string of Gen Z employees who seemed to populate this place, stood and pulled out a vape. "I need some nicotine."

"But can I start the tape if he—"

"Ping me!" he called as he slipped out into the hall, leaving her a little uncertain as to what he meant. Call him on his cell? Ask someone in the department? Or—

"Show me Sharon Tate, newbie!" Rory's British-accented voice preceded him into the editing studio.

His long hair still hadn't gotten cozy with a comb or maybe a shampoo bottle, and his Led Zeppelin T-shirt had seen better days. Why had she imagined these people as polished professionals?

"I don't have Sharon Tate," she said with a smile. "I have something much, much better."

His eyes flashed with dissatisfaction. "No ghost? That's a bloody shame, because—"

"Rory, I have a *scoop*. Trust me. You're going to want to watch this and prepare plenty of teasers for the syndicates to run tonight and tomorrow morning, because this is *news*."

He stared at her. "I didn't send you out to get *news*."

She almost laughed, assuming that was, well, a joke. "You sent me to get a story that no one else would have. One that would make Lacey Britton—spoiler alert, she has a new last name—look good. And I have the added bonus of breaking a huge story about Coo Coo Cooper's career. Take that, *Entertainment Tonight*."

She glanced over his shoulder for the editor, but he was a no show, so she turned to the bank of equipment, determined to start the video herself rather than wait for him. She leaned over and touched the Start button.

"Here. You can see—"

Rory grabbed her hand. "Where is the ghost, Wingate?"

At the ground-out words and his way too harsh touch, she straightened and slid her hand out from under his.

"There is no ghost, Rory. Lacey had never seen a ghost and even if she had, I would have had a hard time getting an image of it because, one, it's a ghost, and two, the camera operator was too scared of it to go in the house."

"But I—"

"So I found a better story. Three of them, to be fair. Not only did I uncover that the Coopers have secretly married, but Coo is recording a new album *and* he's changed labels. I didn't get the name of the label, but I do know that his new sound is back to his roots." She added a smile and tried not to be smug. "Would you like to see the report that will have the competition scrambling and likely using our footage with attribution?"

"No." He crossed his arms and looked at her. Hard and long, like it was the first time he'd really seen her. "I realize you're very fresh, very educated, and probably very idealistic. Maybe a touch naïve, hoping that the people who make decisions in this industry will look past your pretty face and see your substance."

She swallowed, absolutely hating that it was all true, because she knew the rest of his speech wasn't going to make her all aglow with pride in her accomplishment.

"Here's the *news* you're looking for, angel," he continued. "Coo's record company—the new one—is owned by the same company that syndicates this show and signs

your paycheck. Anyone at the top of the food chain—
which you are not—knows that and is keeping it a big, fat
secret. The marriage is about to end, which is why we
were trying to help out Coo by throwing a bone at his
babe so she didn't go psycho when he tells her to leave.
Oh, and by the way, the record he's dropping is utter
garbage, so the last thing they want is pre-release
publicity."

She managed a shaky breath. "Oh."

"Get over yourself, luv," he said in a low voice. "Can
you do that?"

"I don't..."

"Because if you can't, there's about six hundred—no,
six *thousand*—pretty girls who can look into the camera
and deliver the story *I told them I wanted*." He leaned in
to make his point. "And they are lined up outside waiting
to kick you to the curb and make me happy."

With that, he walked out, leaving Chloe to swallow
the lump in her throat, nearly choking on the bitter taste
of disillusionment.

Chapter Nine

Raina

Pregnancy hadn't slowed Raina...much. Even though Dr. Milwood said she could continue exercising, Raina had downgraded her runs to fast walks, now taken at sunrise on the beach almost every morning.

Sometimes she felt like the change in her workout mirrored the change in her life since leaving Miami, ending her marriage, and finding out she was pregnant with twins.

Before all that, Raina exercised daily, worked fifty-hour weeks, conducted showings and open houses—in high heels—every weekend, wined and dined clients regularly, and generally zoomed through life at breakneck speed.

Now, she was...slower.

This morning, she strolled the sand, leisurely enough to spot pretty shells or watch the clouds change from pink to cream as the sun peeked over the horizon. She inhaled the salt-tinged air and refused to think about deep, timed running breaths. She listened to the gulls squawk their morning greetings, and enjoyed the soft whoosh of the surf on sand.

Best of all, she could look to the left as she walked north and take in the variety of architectural styles of the homes along the shore of Amelia Island. Some were tiny and forty years old, others were rambling with add-ons, still more were brand new, and every one unique.

She always took time to gaze at one of her favorites, only about a mile from Rex and Susannah's house, but a world of difference in design.

The Sanctuary, as the small hand-carved sign at the beach access steps read, appealed to her more than any other place along this stretch of sand. So much, that she sometimes fantasized about trying to buy it and live there when her babies were born.

Every time she passed, her heart tightened with an inexplicable longing. She ached to cozy up inside that weathered cedar shake beach house, and gaze out the mullioned windows that brought a quaint and coastal New England charm to the place.

Today, the rising sun glinted off the French doors along the deck, blinding her a little as she stared and let her fantasies run wild. She could see herself out there, maybe with two covered baby swings and...and...her thoughts faded as she saw a man walking under the deck, partially hidden by the dunes.

Was that the owner? The house rarely showed signs of life, although once in a while, when she walked by after sundown, she thought she saw a light on inside. She assumed it was a snowbird's winter home, so perhaps they'd rented it for a week in the summer.

But maybe it *was* the owner. Maybe he'd come down to check on things and he happened to notice that the market was picking up steam, and maybe he'd let her make an offer. It wouldn't be the first time Raina walked up to a stranger and convinced them to sell their house. She'd done that for a number of clients willing to pay top dollar for something they'd dreamed of owning.

Maybe she was the client, and this was her dream.

Raina took a few steps closer, watching the man doing something under the deck. Was he searching for a leak or a foundational problem? She should know that before—

"What?" Raina gasped as he straightened and stepped out from under the deck into the light.

Blake! It was Blake! She knew it instantly and the familiar blue hoodie, hanging open with the white circular logo visible, confirmed her guess.

She started to run, then froze. Could she just pounce on him? What was he even doing there? Was he living there? She stared at his figure as he walked toward the side of the house, having no doubt whatsoever that the man was Blake Youngblood, her biological nephew.

With chill bumps on her arms, she started toward the house, slowly, tracking his movement up the north side of the house. She recognized his walk, his dark blond hair, even the jut of his chin with what she once thought was arrogance and now knew was self-preservation.

Then he disappeared, and she couldn't tell if he'd

gone inside or to the front. She was certain he hadn't seen her.

As she walked closer to the dunes around the beach steps, she realized she was shaking. This mattered to her, and she didn't want to blow it. Yes, she had the element of surprise on her side—unless he was staring out the window and spotted her.

If he did, would he come out? Would he run and hide somewhere farther away? What was he doing here?

Very, very slowly, she walked up the wooden stairs that led to the outdoor deck, unable to stop herself. Her heart slammed against her chest, her whole body vibrating with anticipation.

What would she say? Just the obvious, she supposed, the words forming as she climbed the stairs.

Please, come and be part of our family...

Suddenly, one of the French doors whipped opened so hard and fast, it forced her to grab the handrail, she was so startled.

"Can I help you?" A man stepped out into the light, tall, dark, and certainly not Blake Youngblood. He looked to be in his late forties, with enough dark hair for it to flutter in the morning breeze around arresting features.

He wore a pair of old cargo shorts and a faded T-shirt, but the clothes could have been garbage bags and they'd probably look good on that physique.

"I'm, um, looking for Blake."

"Who?"

Was he going to deny that she'd just seen him go inside?

"Blake? The man I just saw"—she pointed to the side of the house—"there?"

Thick brows knit as he followed the direction of her finger, then he shook his head. "You're mistaken. No one was there."

Oh, really?

Ohhhh. Really. Suddenly things made sense. Blake had never mentioned a partner, only that he was gay, so maybe this was his—

"There's no one else here, so what can I do for you?" he asked, taking one step closer so she could see that his chiseled jaw was set with determination—probably to get her to leave.

And she should. She'd overstepped her bounds by a mile. Blake had made it clear he didn't want anything to do with her or any Wingates, and now she'd found where he was hiding, maybe with someone he wanted to keep secret. She had no business here.

But she had to let Blake know he was safe with her, with all of them. And she had something else she'd wanted to say for a long time.

"Look, I know he's here." She climbed to the top step but didn't go any further. "I just want to see him."

"No one else is here, ma'am."

She barely heard the words. "I wanted to thank him," she said softly. "He might not have told you, but he saved me and..." She put her hands on her belly. "My babies. I'm having twins."

"Good for you." He sounded like he meant it, which gave her a little incentive to take one step closer.

"I might have lost them if not for him and I've so desperately wanted children, but I thought...anyway, I wanted him to know—"

"There's no one else in this house," he said, his tone leaving no room for argument. "I'm sorry, but you're mistaken."

She released a sigh and nodded, understanding that Blake wanted privacy more than he wanted family. Who could blame him? He'd come out to his family in Iowa and they'd disowned him. No wonder he distrusted everyone.

Plus, if he wanted to talk to her, he'd probably step outside, because she *knew* he was hiding in that house, most likely peering out one of the many windows and wishing she'd just go away.

She held up a hand. "Thanks, anyway," she finally said, not waiting for his response as she turned and walked back down the stairs, and headed home to the beach house.

The near-miss with Blake haunted her all morning. She couldn't shake the frustration and disappointment even after she got to Wingate Properties a few hours later.

She told Dani the whole story, but that only made her assistant want to go back to Plan A and call the FREC headquarters and make up some story about Blake's license.

"Not happening," Raina said, finally settling at her desk. "What's this file?"

"Everything I could find on your next meeting.

Remember? Charles James Madison, the man who wants Rex and gets you? Raina, you're going to want to list this house."

She rolled her eyes. "I am so not in the mood to beg for business."

"You'll get in the mood when you look at his portfolio," Dani said, sailing out the door as the phone on her desk rang.

"Maybe that's him," Raina said hopefully. "Canceling at the last minute. Yay for me."

Just as she reached for the file, one of the babies gave her a solid kick, making Raina giggle at the sensation she doubted she would ever get used to.

"Well, hello down there, Thing One." She pressed the little bump, marveling at how hard it was getting. She stood because sometimes that made Thing Two wake up and join in. These babies could kick her senseless and Raina would love every minute of it.

She turned to the window, using the heel of her hand to coax them into moving again as she stared down at the cobblestones of Wingate Way. Across the street, she could see Madeline in the front window of her store, changing the wedding gown on one of her mannequins.

"There's Auntie Maddie," she whispered to her babies. "You'll love her. And she'll love you, especially if you show up on your due date. And next to her studio is the ice cream shop that I think you two are just a little too familiar with lately."

In fact, she visited so frequently that Silas, the man

who owned the business, started scooping Rocky Road whenever Raina walked in.

"And there's Aunt Rose's flower shop." She pointed to the pink stucco flower shop on the other side of Madeline's. "Less calories, but just as glorious. Maybe we'll go there this afternoon instead." She wanted to tell Rose about what had happened this morning. In fact, she didn't want to wait one minute. She wanted to go—

"Raina?"

"Please tell me he cancelled," she called. "Because I want to see my sister more than I want to kiss the royal behind of some entitled millionaire who goes by the incredibly made-up millennial name of—"

"Charles Madison."

At the sound of the man's voice, she whipped around on a gasp. Oh, she didn't just—

"It's *you*." They both said the words at exactly the very same moment, and what felt like an electrical current arced through the room as they realized they'd already met...this morning.

She bit back a moan, but he just gave a wry smile.

"But I do go by Chase, thanks to my mother, because my grandmother wanted me to be Carlo. As for entitled? I prefer to think of myself as discerning. And speaking of things that are made up," he continued, ignoring her shock, "you were looking for some man under the deck this morning? Please."

"Oh, well, I..."

"You could have said you were doing some intelligence

on the property I'm about to list." He let a beat of time go by while Raina tried—and failed—to conjure up something to say to the man who looked bigger, darker, and even more imposing than he had in shorts and a T-shirt. "Because Rex Wingate would never have lied about why he was at my house. So, this is hello, Raina Wingate. And goodbye."

With that, he turned and gave a silent nod to Dani, who still hadn't closed her wide-open mouth, and marched toward the stairs while Raina's brain screamed things that didn't add up until they did.

That was his house? He's listing it? And he is my only connection to Blake!

"Don't leave!" she yelled, barreling around her desk. "Please, Charles...Chase...sir! Don't leave!"

She zipped past Dani, who raised her brows. "And you weren't going to beg."

She ignored the comment and followed the man who seemed to be sailing down the marble steps.

"Please don't make me run!" she called. "I'm four months pregnant."

"With twins, I know." He didn't turn, but stopped at the bottom of the steps. "Congratulations," he said over his shoulder, then strode toward the door.

Muttering a curse, she followed without running, but bolted to the door once she was off the steps, throwing it open and looking left and right and all around for any sight of him.

There! Right outside Madeline's shop.

She waited for the only car to pass, then rushed

across the street, finally reaching him just as he passed the ice cream parlor.

"Please," she said, putting her hand on his arm, breathless when he stopped. "Please let me talk to you."

He turned and looked down at her, easily over six feet, his dark, dark eyes intense. Maybe a little angry, too, which she understood.

"I don't think we're going to do business together, Ms. Wingate."

"Just tell me about Blake," she said. "Blake Young-blood. I saw him today."

"Ah, your mystery savior." He shook his head. "Sorry, but I don't know who you're talking about. The only Blake I know worked for Rex, and I've never met the guy. I talked to him once when he told me Rex would be ready, willing, and able to meet with me and get my listing in six weeks. That was six weeks ago. Here I am. Where's Rex?"

"Where's Blake?" she countered.

"I don't know." He sounded disgusted—and genuine. "And, frankly, I don't care. I need to find the best Realtor in town and if Rex isn't available—"

"You're looking at her."

He scoffed. "Not sure I like your style."

She let out a slow breath, confusion mounting enough that she had to have answers. "Can I buy you an ice cream?" she asked, tipping her head toward the entrance.

"No, thank you."

"Well, I want one and I also want ten minutes of your

time." She leaned in. "Five. Please. If nothing else, I want to make an offer on your house."

His eyes flashed and the slightest hint of a smile lifted the corners of his lips. "Fine." He turned and opened the door to let her in. "Five minutes."

It was all she typically needed to close a new client deal, but she already realized that nothing about Chase Madison was typical.

BY THE TIME they had coffee and a scoop of Rocky Road that, for once, Raina didn't really want—and Chase kindly paid for, since she'd come with no phone or purse —Raina believed that he had no idea who Blake Young-blood was.

So she told him the whole story, which took a lot more than five minutes, but at least he didn't run away. In fact, he listened intently, barely sipping his coffee or taking his unwavering gaze off her.

"So, this man—Blake Youngblood—is your nephew and you're searching for him and thought you saw him at my property this morning," he recapped when she finished.

"Oh, I saw him. I just don't know why he'd be there if you aren't his...if you don't know..."

"I'm *not* his friend or acquaintance or anything else," he said with a sly look, making his point clear. "I did speak to him, but not in person."

She stared at him, part of her brain trying to go

through the list of reasons why Blake might be at his beach house, the other part trying not to get distracted by those impossibly deep eyes.

"Oh, I bet I know," she said, grateful that the correct half of her brain was still working. "Have you listed that house for luxury vacation rentals? That's your business, correct?"

"It is, but I don't rent this one. I sometimes let family stay there, and I stay there when I'm in town."

She considered that. "And he said specifically six weeks to you?"

"Yes, that's when he said Rex would be ready to meet, which worked for me."

"Maybe—and I'm just guessing here—maybe he wants the listing and was waiting until he had his real estate license, which he just got. Then he planned to take the listing if you learned Rex wasn't available."

"That makes sense, but speaking of Rex, I'm sorry for not asking sooner. How's he doing?"

"He's doing well, thank you. Greatly recovered but not quite..." She sighed. "I'm not sure he's coming back full-time. I think he's enjoying being home with Susannah more than he thought he would. I've been standing in for him since he had the stroke."

He searched her face, seconds ticking by as the moment lasted too long. "You're the one who loves real estate." It wasn't a question.

"Of his seven daughters?" she guessed, imagining her father and this man having personal conversations over long dinners. She could see that Dad would like him. "Yes, that would be me."

"I thought you lived in Miami and had a business there with your husband."

She smiled, a little surprised. "You *are* a good listener. I do—I did. I'm..." She cleared her throat, fearing she'd already aired enough dirty family laundry with this man. "But I'm not living there now," she finally said.

"But surely you want to get home before..." He dropped his gaze. "Four months, you said?"

Yes, an incredible listener. "I'm due in late January. And, I'm, uh..." She didn't want to tell this man who looked like he had no weaknesses that her own life was... in shambles. That she lived with her parents, got cheated on by her husband, and...yeah, no. "I'm sticking around here for as long as I'm needed to run Wingate Properties," she said, feigning confidence.

"And as long as it takes to find your missing nephew, I'm guessing."

She nodded, happy to get off the subject of where she lived and with whom. "Yes. And seeing him today is making me certain he's hoping to get your listing." She sighed in frustration. "It seems like every time I get close, I lose him."

"Well, if he does contact me, I'll lure him in and call you."

She felt a smile pull. "Thank you, Chase. That's very kind."

He tipped his head in acknowledgement. "So what about my listing?"

"The one that you're giving to me?" She lifted her brows.

"I thought you wanted to buy the place."

"With my whole heart and soul," she said. "But...it might be a pipe dream. I'm not sure I'm in a position to buy right now."

He nodded, scanning her face again as he waited for her to elaborate. She wasn't about to.

"But someone will buy it," she said instead. "And if you're ready, I'd be happy to prepare a listing and hold an open house and have that beautiful property sold in no time. Top dollar, likely over asking."

A smile spread over his face, which was a little like the sun sliding from behind a cloud to pour light over the world.

"Spoken like the daughter of Rex Wingate."

"Thank you very much." She leaned in. "Can I have the listing?"

"Depends."

She grunted. "What hoops do you want me to jump through?"

"A woman who's four months pregnant? No hoops for you. Just the truth."

"I've been extremely honest, Chase. I've told you more about Blake Youngblood than even my father knows. I haven't lied about a thing."

"Lie of omission," he countered. "What aren't you telling me?"

She just looked at him, feeling a little blood drain

from her face. Dang. He was such a good listener, he heard things she didn't even say.

"Come on," he urged. "Full story or no deal."

She laughed softly. "It's personal."

"Which..." He leaned in a centimeter and pinned her with his espresso eyes. "Makes it even more important to me."

"Why?"

"Because I only do business with people I know, trust, and approve of their choices in life."

"That's kind of...judgey," she said.

He shrugged. "I'm Sicilian and we're a judgey people."

"Madison is Sicilian?" she asked, the question heavy with doubt.

"My mother's maiden name was Cardinale, and she was born and raised in Palermo."

She searched his face, definitely seeing the dark coloring and strong classic Roman features. "That's where you get Redbird?" she guessed, remembering the name of his company.

He smiled and nodded. "Exactly. Now, what aren't you telling me, Raina Wingate?"

She let out a soft moan, knowing that if she did business with him in any capacity, the truth would eventually come out.

"I'm not living in Miami because I'm getting a divorce from my husband of sixteen years who cheated on me, but I didn't know that when we, uh..." She flicked her hand in the general direction of her stomach. "Oh, and I'm currently living on the third floor of my parents' beach house, which is pretty mortifying for a forty-three-year-old woman." She gave a tight smile. "That's what I'm hiding. My personal...mess."

He stared at her for a long time, then finished his last drop of coffee. Silent, he pushed back from the table, the legs of his chair scraping over the tile. Then he stood to his full six-feet-plus and looked down at her.

Here it comes, she thought. *Thanks but no thanks, crazy, complicated lady.*

"You've got the listing, Raina."

She sucked in a breath, her jaw loose. "Really? You're not afraid of my mess?"

"It's not your mess I'm afraid of." He angled his head. "I've got to go. You can start the paperwork and come over for an appraisal at your earliest convenience. Thank you for being honest."

With that, he left the ice cream parlor, and Raina sat there with a big smile and a melted bowl of Rocky Road.

Wait a second, she thought, sitting up a little.

What *was* he afraid of?

Chapter Ten

Grace

"You know this is going to make her want a puppy, right?" Isaiah whispered the comment to Grace as Nikki Lou danced around the apartment in a dress covered in tiny dachshunds. "I mean, we're taking her to the Puppy Parade, so you gotta be prepared."

"I am," Grace assured him. "But this event meets all the at-home program criteria—stimulating, fun, outdoors, and extremely active."

"And we have to practice our part," Isaiah added. "You remember our part?"

She smiled, touched by the use of *our*. After spending so much time with Nikki Lou at her program, Isaiah was no longer an "outsider" observing or even understanding the process. He was a hands-on participant and, as such, had cleared his day for their first big "homework" assignment to take Nikki Lou into a highly stimulating environment.

"Our part is to help her handle stimulation and take note of what...puts her off-center," Grace said. "Which is a lovely euphemism for an NLM."

He frowned. "I don't remember that acronym."

"Because I made it up. It's a Nikki Lou Meltdown, and it's never fun."

"Some things aren't fun," Isaiah said calmly, smiling at Nikki when she crawled around the piano legs pretending to be chasing an invisible dog. "But everything she does is kind of...special."

Grace smiled contentedly as she checked her bag for the necessities she never left without, instantly pulling out the small container of Twizzlers.

"Nope. I'll take an orange, but no sugar," she murmured, tossing the candy in the trash. "And the other part of what we're supposed to do?" she asked Isaiah. "Make sure she's...connected or involved? I can't remember the word."

"Engaged," he supplied.

"Oh, yes. Engaged." The word touched Grace's heart as she gazed at her daughter and suddenly imagined her... engaged. In the diamond-ring, big-girl sense, not the connected-mind of a child on the spectrum sense. Would that ever happen?

"What is it?" Isaiah asked, studying her as intently as she was studying Nikki Lou.

She swallowed, remembering how Nick always said she was an open book with expressions that gave away her every thought. And with a man as intuitive as Isaiah, she had to expect he'd read those expressions accurately.

"I was just thinking about her future. Will it be... normal?" She barely breathed the last word.

He put a strong hand on her shoulder. "Nothing is

abnormal in God's world. It's up to us to find the beauty and hope in every situation."

She looked up at him and wrinkled her nose. "Come on, Isaiah. Be real with me. I don't need a Bible platitude."

He wasn't even fazed by the comment, but grinned at her. "I don't do platitudes, Amazing Grace. I think the answer to your question is to redefine 'normal' and let Nikki Lou be Nikki Lou. Also, you better want a dog."

"I know," she admitted. "And Dr. Alberino did say a pet would help her, remember?"

He frowned. "I didn't spend a lot of time with that doctor. I was in the blocks and coloring room. But I did hear her say to trust your gut. If Nikki Lou seems to thrive with a dog, well, then..."

"She misses Chloe's little Lady Bug desperately."

He nudged her closer. "Let's see how today plays out. There are adoptions at this event."

"Are you sure?"

"I looked it up."

She let out a grateful sigh. "You are something, Isaiah Kincaid. How can I thank you for all you've done to help me with this process?"

He just gave his deep chuckle and pointed at Nikki Lou. "Come on. Let's get her...engaged."

She tamped down the first thought about that word and concentrated on its second meaning—connected to reality and the people around her. And, maybe, some dogs.

"Let's go before all the good places along the parade

route are gone," Grace said. "Nikki Lou! It's Puppy Parade time!"

"Yay!" Another twirl, another giggle, and off the three of them went to the annual Fernandina Beach event that brought lots of tourists, lots of traffic, and lots of dogs to the small town.

Even Wingate Way was crowded as they stepped out, with people and puppies of all sizes.

To protect Nikki Lou and because it felt totally natural, Grace and Isaiah each took one of her hands and walked toward Coming Up Roses, where Avery and Alyson were playing with some flowers in front of their mother's shop.

"Aunt Grace!" Alyson called, arms out, her smile wide as she adjusted her purple plastic glasses that were so much a part of her, Grace forgot she wore them.

In that instant, Grace thought about how Rose and Gabe had handled the news that their very little girl needed glasses when she'd been not much older than Nikki Lou. They'd been...calm, at ease, and raved about the doctor.

Was that because there were two of them to share the burden of whatever got thrown at them as parents?

She greeted Alyson with a tight squeeze of love, and gathered Avery in, too. She was only six, and so protective of Nikki Lou, and because of that, held a dear place in Grace's heart.

The cousins greeted and hugged and danced around with anticipation while a few more dogs went by, increasing the general excitement level.

"Oh, there you all are!" Rose stepped out the front door of the store, pausing to fix one of the many buckets of bouquets that spilled over the front porch display. "I just finished the day's orders. My manager, Lizzie, is on duty. Let's watch the Puppy Parade!"

The six of them set off, waving at Madeline as they passed her dress shop and studio, and turning the corner toward the street that had been blocked off for the parade.

The summer sun was blistering, but this particular avenue was lined with lush oaks that had grown for decades to shade the entire street and sidewalk.

"Gabe set our chairs up already," Rose told them. "The whole fire department was out here early, so he got us a fantastic place."

"Yay for Daddy!" Avery exclaimed, prancing ahead like she was starting the parade right now.

Alyson looked up at Grace. "She has to lead everything," she said with no judgment, just a factual smile. "My dad says it's because she's the baby and no one pays any attention to her."

They all laughed, but Rose grabbed Grace's arm and tugged her closer.

"Look who's there," Rose whispered, pointing into Honeycomb, a quaint honey store owned by a local couple. "We need to persuade Pam to let Bill be in the calendar."

"He doesn't want to do it?" Grace asked, thinking about Bill Dunbath, the husky and handsome beekeeper with a big beard and infectious laugh.

"Oh, he does," Rose replied. "But Pam thinks it's cheesy, making me suspect Kitty's been whispering in her ear. Help me convince her it's for a good cause."

Grace glanced at the girls, all of them itching to get to their spots and see all the dogs.

"You go," Isaiah said, tipping his head toward the store. "I got these three."

"Are you sure?" Grace asked.

He gave a hearty laugh. "I could manage the two dozen grunts who kept my mess hall running in Afghanistan. I think I'm good with three little girls at a dog parade."

Rose beamed at him. "Yes, you are, and thank you."

Before Grace could reply, her sister tugged her away toward the patio outside of Honeycomb. "She'll need to hear it from you, since this is technically your fundraiser."

Grace shot her a look, somehow doubting that was Rose's only motivation for separating from the group. "You've convinced everyone else on your own, Rose," she said. "No one can say no to you."

They waited as a group of tourists, kids, and three dogs passed between them and the store.

"I had to get you alone for a second," Rose said. "And Pam's a tough sell."

"Alone...why?"

Rose gave her an *are you serious?* look. "Isaiah! Is this date number three or four or...?"

"This isn't a date, Rose. He came with me to the program session last week, and we got so much information and homework with Nikki Lou, he wanted to help. Am I meeting my end of your silly bargain?"

"Silly? You don't look like you hate the idea and he's so...oh, I don't know. Awesome comes to mind and then I see him with Nikki Lou and I change my vote to amazing. And wonderful. And, whoa, he's got it bad for you, so let's call him...perfect."

Grace laughed at the gush, which was over-the-top even for her uber-optimistic sister. "He is a great guy, but...slow down, okay?"

"Okay, okay. But do you like him?"

"There's nothing not to like about Isaiah Kincaid," Grace said, sliding past the question and the next group with ease. "Come on, let's talk to Pam."

"Wait." Rose held her back. "Isn't it more fun to do life with someone, and not alone?"

Grace looked at her, not sure what to say, since Rose's words so closely mirrored her own thoughts.

The answer would be...*Yes, it sure seems that way.* But now wasn't the time or place.

"Is that a rhetorical question, Rose? Of course it's easier and better to have a partner. But I'm not ready to fall into something with someone. Could there be a worse time with all that's going on with Nikki Lou?"

"Could there be a better time?" Rose countered. "You need him. And, good heavens, Grace, when he looks at you, it's like he's seen his future."

Grace's heart rolled around in her chest. "Really? I mean...no. Stop, Rose. I'm just not ready."

"Okay, I get that, but if you were ready, would it be Isaiah?"

"Rose, please, I..." She exhaled noisily, knowing she owed her sister the dignity of an honest reply. Plus, if she didn't, Rose would never back off. "I admit, he's one of the nicest, sweetest, kindest, all-around best guys I've ever known."

"Yes!" Rose fist-pumped, making Grace laugh.

"*One* of them," she repeated. "Nick is still..."

Rose's expression grew serious. "Nick isn't here anymore, Grace. And for all you know, he's up in heaven making sure you're taken care of."

"I'm taking care of myself," she said, her throat growing tight.

"I know you are, and doing a phenomenal job. But, honey, life is—"

"I know." She stopped the diatribe with a light hand to Rose's lips. "I'm just not there yet, okay?"

"Okay. But he is. I can tell."

"Hey, Rose! Grace!" They turned to see Pam Dunbath waving them into her store. "Come and try my newest orange blossom honey! It'll cure what ails you."

"I need some of that," Grace said cheerily, steering Rose inside, grateful for the reprieve. "My daughter's doctor says her sweets should come from local honey."

"I got what you need, then," Pam said, but she gave Rose a playful look. "And I heard *you* need my husband."

"Not exactly," Rose said with a chuckle. "Just to take one picture of him."

"I know he loves books," Grace said as she inspected

a jar of honey. "I keep the beekeeping section stocked just for him."

"I know you do, Grace, but..." Pam leaned in to whisper, "Kitty says he might have to take his shirt off."

"I knew it," Rose muttered.

"Sorry, but that six-pack is just for me and me alone," Pam joked.

They laughed, but something inside Grace twisted as Rose assured her that Bill could stay fully dressed.

What was that feeling shooting through Grace? Jealousy? Not of Bill Dunbath's six-pack, but she was definitely envious of something.

Of their *partnership*. The intimacy between a husband and wife. She longed for it, couldn't stop thinking about it, and was truly envious of others who had it. And that felt like all kinds of wrong.

"Oh, all right!" Pam said, flicking her wrist to bring Rose's sales pitch to an end. Honestly, Rose did not need Grace for this job.

"Really?" Rose asked. "That's a yes?"

"Of course. You can take pictures of him reading. But I get to be there! Oh, and he'll want April, because that's my birthday month."

"So sweet," Rose cooed. "You got it! I'll call you with some open dates for the photo shoot."

"And I'll take this honey," Grace said, holding up the jar.

When they finished and walked back to the chairs that Gabe—who daily earned his nickname of "Angel

Gabriel"—had placed for them, Rose elbowed Grace and gestured toward the rest of their group.

Isaiah was seated in one of the canvas-backed chairs, keeping a close watch on the girls. Avery and Alyson stood protectively on either side of Nikki Lou, who was sitting on the ground with her arms around the neck of a little dog that looked exactly like the ones on her dress.

"Oh, boy," Grace murmured. "That didn't take long."

"Mommy! Weiner dog named Slinky!"

As Grace got closer, she saw the dog's handler, a woman with the name of a pet rescue on her T-shirt, the bright colors matching the "Adopt Me Today!" kerchief tied around the little dog's neck.

Isaiah stood and smiled down at her. "I hate to break the news to you, Amazing Grace. But when Slinky slinked up and looked at Nikki Lou, it was game over."

She gazed up at him, feeling very much the same way. Was this...game over?

She sighed and took his hand. "Then I guess we know what we should do, huh?"

There was nothing but joy in his eyes when he squeezed her hand, no words necessary.

Isaiah ended Nikki Lou's day with a Bible story. Like before, he managed not to make it "religious" but to craft his story about people in a way that any mother, a believer or not, appreciated.

But this time, a brown dog with a long nose and a

longer body was curled up on the bed next to Nikki Lou. Slinky, who was about four years old, give or take, and blessedly housebroken, already knew who was his real owner and where he would sleep.

Nikki Lou had vibrated with excitement all day, but they hadn't had one meltdown. Yes, everything had gone her way, but both Grace and Isaiah were able to put a few specific things they'd learned into action. They used verbal and physical calming techniques like massaging her hands and quietly taking her away from a situation when they saw she teetered on the edge.

They added the words of affirmation when she needed them, and, of course, healthy foods, which had been the biggest challenge. But when they passed the ice cream, Nikki Lou accepted yogurt and drizzled the local honey on top, which Grace considered a win.

So it was no surprise that evening that Grace got to experience something rare and wonderful—relaxation. Curled on the bed with her daughter and their new dog, she closed her eyes and listened to the deep voice that soothed...everything.

Tonight's story was about Ruth and Naomi, most of which went way over Nikki's head and even a little bit over Grace's as she listened to a sweet tale of a mother-daughter relationship.

"But Ruth didn't leave Naomi," he said. "She stayed with her, even though Naomi said it was okay to leave. Ruth said, 'Where you go, I will. Where you stay, I will stay. Your people will be my people. Your God will be my God.'"

He lowered the Bible and looked at them. "Do you understand what happened in that story, Nik?" he asked.

She pulled her thumb out of her mouth. "She stays..." Then she patted the dog's head. "Like my buddy. Good dog, Slinky. Stay."

Slinky replied with a slap of his tail against the comforter, already at home. When they'd filled out the paperwork and finalized the adoption earlier, Isaiah had said God knew what he was doing when he sent this dog. Grace was starting to believe it.

"She stays because family is a very important part of God's kingdom." Isaiah closed the Bible, no doubt sensing that anything more than that would be too much for her tonight.

He glanced at Grace with a question in his eyes, but stood before asking it.

"I'll let you two say goodnight now," he said. "I better get back to the inn. But it was a wonderful day, ladies, and I'll never forget it." He reached down and gave Slinky's head a rub. "Welcome home, little soldier."

With a quick salute, he headed to the door and Grace sat up, not quite ready for him to leave so quickly.

"Wait a sec," she called as he stepped into the hall, then realized that sounded a little desperate. See? She wasn't cut out for this...dating stuff. Was that what this was? "I'll, um, lock the door behind you."

"Sure," he said, but she heard his footsteps heading out.

"Night-night, sweet baby girl," she said quickly, dropping a kiss on her hair.

"Mommy." Nikki Lou reached up and wrapped tiny hands around her neck, pulling Grace closer.

Grace felt the urge to draw back and run to Isaiah, but she squelched it, knowing this moment with Nikki Lou was every bit as important as the one she wanted with him.

"Yes, honey?"

"Today was the best day of my life. I love Slinky."

Talk about gratitude and affirmation! The doctor said when Nikki Lou started to give those back, then she was making progress. Great, great progress.

"I love Slinky, too," Grace replied, hugging her. "And I love you."

With another goodnight kiss, she headed out into the hall and through the front door of her apartment, wondering if Isaiah understood that her request that he wait was about more than locking the door.

Would he be gone when she got to the bottom of the steps and into the bookstore? Or would he—

Her heart did a really weird jump that felt all wrong and all right at the very same time when she saw him waiting by the front door.

For the first time since she'd met this man, his posture wasn't straight and strong like a Marine. He didn't look... confident. He shifted from one foot to the other, his hands in the pockets of his cargo shorts, his shoulders almost hunched as if he was bracing for something.

"Thank you for waiting," she said, surprisingly breathless, since she'd only come down a flight of stairs. "She's so happy, Isaiah. Today was a smashing success."

He turned to face her as she came closer, revealing another emotion in his dark eyes that she certainly had never seen before. Was that...fear?

"What's wrong?" she asked. "Are you worried about the new dog? Think it wasn't a good idea? No, no," she added when he didn't answer. "You don't worry about anything. And you're not afraid. Haven't you told me 'don't be afraid' is in the Bible 365 times?"

She knew she was rambling, but her heart was pounding against her ribs and he was so quiet. What was the matter?

"Isaiah?"

"I better go," he said simply, reaching for the door.

"Not until I say thank you from the bottom of my heart."

His hand stilled as it reached the knob. "It was nothing, Grace."

"No, you're wrong." She took a few steps closer, able to clearly see his face even though the only light was from a streetlamp outside.

But it was enough to confirm all her suspicions that he was...afraid. Of her?

"It was *not* nothing," she corrected. "It was everything. You made today so easy. You make everything with Nikki Lou so much more fun. She just told me how happy she is, and that's progress. All of this...well, it's so much better to not have to do this alone."

The words spilled out like she'd opened a faucet and nothing—not even the glimmer of real surprise in his eyes—could stop her.

"I almost can't imagine how I'd do any of this without you," she continued. "And not just with Nikki Lou, but...life. My life. It's..." She bit her lip, apparently the only way she—the quietest of seven sisters—could shut up.

But before she took her next breath, he leaned down and brushed her lips with a featherlight kiss.

Well, that was another way to quiet her.

It was fast, brief, barely a touch, but every cell in Grace's body woke up, shook off, and suddenly begged for attention.

"You're..." For once, Isaiah seemed at a complete loss for words.

"Welcome," she finished for him. "When someone says thank you, you just say—"

"Grace." He put his hands on her shoulders, a light touch but enough to draw her closer.

One step and she closed the space between them so that their bodies came into direct contact for what might be the first time ever.

She looked up at him with the shocking realization that he was trembling, too.

For a long time, they just stood like that, silent, still, and barely breathing.

"Surely," she finally said softly, "you have a Bible quote for this moment."

"A thousand," he replied. "But my mind is blank and my heart is...hopeful."

She felt a smile lift her lips. "I have a lot of hope, too."

"Do you? I'm not imagining things?"

She sighed into him. "You're not imagining anything, Zayah."

He smiled at Nikki Lou's beloved nickname, gliding his hand from her shoulder to her cheek, cupping her jaw in a palm that was somehow rough and tender at the same time.

"I'm not sure what I'm feeling," he said softly. "But it's real and it's powerful and...and...today was the best day of my life."

"Exactly what Nikki Lou just said."

"I guess we're all making progress," he whispered.

With one tender hug, he placed a kiss on her forehead. "Goodnight, Amazing Grace."

Long after he left and she locked the door, Grace stood in the quiet of her bookstore, more amazed than *amazing*.

For the first time since a Marine officer showed up at her door with his hat in his hand and grief on his face, Grace's heart felt light.

Yes, this might have been one of the best days of all their lives.

Chapter Eleven

Rose

Saturday nights in the greenhouse were special, romantic, quiet times for Rose and Gabe. With the moon high over the glass ceiling, the younger kids in bed, and Zach with some school friends at Tiffany's house, this one had real potential for romance and sharing.

Add in the fact that she and Gabe had both brought wine out for their alone time instead of their usual non-alcoholic drinks, and Rose hummed with anticipation for her low-key but high-quality date night with her husband.

Until they sat in dead silence for ten minutes, with Gabe staring off into space. He'd had a long week, many shifts, and had to be tired. Maybe Rose had to carry the conversation.

"So, we have officially reached the limit of three fire-fighters for our calendar," she said. "You, Travis, and—"

"If you say Jeremy Hutchinson, I'm bailing out."

Whoa, he was in a bad mood. "First of all, no, he isn't on the list. It's Alex Karakostos."

"Good."

"It great, because he's exceedingly easy on the eyes."

He barely grunted, still staring ahead, which was weird after a comment that would usually get him to crack a joke.

"And his classic book of choice is Plato's *Republic*, which I think is hilarious, since you told me his nickname is 'Greek.'"

"Yeah." Gabe took a sip of his wine, made a face, and put the plastic cup down with a little more force than was necessary.

"Something wrong, honey?" she asked.

He just closed his eyes and sighed. "I'm gonna get passed over for that promotion." He spoke so softly she almost didn't hear it. "Even my dad thinks so. EMTs simply don't make captain with the same frequency as someone who spends the majority of their time in the heat."

She shifted on the loveseat they shared, inhaling the earthy scent of tomatoes and basil that filled the greenhouse, trying to think of the perfect thing to say.

"You're the best EMT in that station, maybe the county," she told him. "And EMTs *do* make captain."

"Not with Hotshot Hutchinson in my way." He grunted and shook his head. "Forget about it, babe. What were you talking about again?" He turned to her, but there was no spark in his eyes. "Something about...the calendar thing?"

She just smiled and took his hand. "Gabe, you of all people know that you do your best, you accept what happens."

"Please. You don't understand."

A punch of rare irritation hit her. "Then why don't you try and explain it to me? I'm here for you."

He puffed out a breath, silent for so long she started to give up hope that he would say another thing. But finally, he turned to her, a world of pain in his eyes.

"You don't understand, because your father raised a family of people who never quit."

She leaned back a centimeter, not expecting that. "Rex hates quitters, it's true, but your dad is no slouch in the motivation department."

"I can't decide what's worse. Being a quitter, or not making captain."

"You're thinking about...quitting?" she asked, unable to keep the shock out of her voice. Gabe D'Angelo had been a firefighter for...well, not forever, but since Zach was born. "Leaving firefighting?" It was unthinkable.

"I quit once, you know. And it still bugs me."

"You quit...oh, medical school." Dang, she hated this topic. Absolutely hated it. The decision to quit Brooks College of Health, the medical school associated with the University of North Florida, had been one of the hardest they had ever made as a couple.

Gabe had been deep into his third year when Rose got pregnant with Zach. Could they have done it? Could they have scraped by and had a baby while he finished and went through a residency then worked until he was forty to pay off the loans? Sure.

Gabe had been gutted to have to give up his child-hood dream of being a doctor. But his father had been a firefighter and, at the time, was the chief in Fernandina Beach. He longed for Gabe to bring his skills there, and it just made so much sense. It still did—to Rose.

He went in as an EMT and eventually passed the tests to become a firefighter, but he'd been pigeonholed as a medic from the beginning. A leader, a lifesaver, and a well-liked member of his team, but a medic.

"The road not taken," she whispered. "I wish I knew the rest of the expression." Because she would say or do anything to erase that look on his face.

"That road makes you miserable to think about," he finished.

"Why?"

"I feel like being an EMT is...is...a poor man's version of a doctor."

"Now you sound like Chloe's arrogant ex-fiancé," she said. "You're wrong. You wanted to be an internist, Gabe, and if you were, you'd be doling out antibiotics and up to your eyeballs in paperwork. Now you save a life on every shift."

He stared ahead, silent.

"EMTs save lives," she insisted. "Just ask my dad how important they were when he had his stroke. And you personally carried my sister into the ER and saved two babies!" She sat up, determined to make her point. "And I love when you are on EMT duty—"

"Because you know I won't be in any *danger*," he finished, slathering disgust on the last word. Disgust for... her? "I know, I know," he added quickly. "That's why I chose this route and now it's costing me a promotion."

"It's *my* fault you're not making captain?" she asked, not even believing he'd said that.

"No, no, I didn't mean that, Rose." On another noisy exhale, he put his arm around her. "It's fine. I'm just frustrated and feeling...mediocre."

"Mediocre? The world's greatest husband, father, son-in-law, and the man who holds my entire heart in his hands? That's mediocre?"

"I guess everyone's definition is different," he said. "I'm...struggling. Maybe it's my turn for a midlife crisis."

She snorted. "If you pull a Jack Wallace and fall in love with a co-worker, cheat on me, and file for divorce, you *will* be in danger."

"Please." He squeezed her. "I love you, Rosie."

She snuggled into him, somewhat appeased, but still worried. "You'll get the promotion," she said. "You've been at this station longer than Jeremy, and your dad..."

"Is not the chief. The fact that he was could work against me." He shook his head, then leaned forward to get his wine and take a deep sip. "Let's forget it tonight." He pulled her closer and kissed her hair. "I love you."

She gave a contented sigh. "I love you, too, Gabe. There's nothing mediocre about you. Nothing."

"Certainly not my wife," he said, adding another kiss. "Now, tell me all about this calendar. Greek's reading Plato? Tell me again, because I wasn't paying enough attention before."

She loved him for his honesty and happily changed the subject. The truth was, a captain could be in as much danger, if not more, on that job. Was it the end of the world if he didn't get the promotion? No. But if something happened to him, it would be the end of hers.

ROSE WENT to visit Annabelle the next day after church, while Gabe took the kids to the beach house for a family Sunday with Rex, Suze, and the cousins. With a promise to meet up later, she parked her car and walked along the side street to Kitty's house with a surprising amount of nerves pulling across her chest.

How would Annabelle Greene feel today? How clear was her head? Would her memories be accurate? And would she share more about Charlotte? Tidbits about her personality, the way she talked, the music she liked, her favorite dessert, her pet peeves, and big dreams? Why didn't Rose know all this?

Because she'd been one hour old when her mother died, and Charlotte had been an only child who left no sisters or brothers to share her story.

But Rose had Annabelle now.

The front door opened while she was still coming up the walk, surprising her when Kitty appeared in silhouette.

"Rose?"

"Kitty, I'm sorry I didn't call, but—"

"How did you know?" she asked, hanging back in the house without stepping into the sunshine.

"How did I..."

"I guess news travels fast in this town, especially to

the local florist." Now she came out, the light revealing that she didn't have on a drop of makeup behind her glasses, her normally poofy hair was flat and unbrushed, and she looked like she hadn't stepped outside in days.

No. Rose's heart dropped so hard she could have sworn she felt it hit the ground.

"How sweet of you, Rose," she said as she reached for the flowers. "I guess this place will smell like a funeral home soon. No pun intended. She's at the real funeral home."

"Oh." She whimpered the one syllable. "Oh, Kitty...I didn't know."

"You didn't? I thought..." She lifted the flowers.

"No. I came to see her and..." Disappointment strangled her, but Rose had to remember this wasn't about her. "I'm sorry, Kitty. When did it happen?"

"Yesterday," she said, bringing the bouquet to her nose and inhaling. "She would have liked these."

Rose sighed. "Was she in any pain?"

"Not a bit. Just went to sleep and never woke up, which I guess is the way to go. But it was a bit of a surprise, since she'd been doing so well since your visit. You two must have really hit it off, because it was all she talked about after you left. She knew your mother. Your real one."

She tried not to react to that.

"She told me that," Rose said. "And I was..." Another long exhale helped to process the bone-deep frustration that she hadn't come sooner. "I was hoping to see her again. I'm so, so sorry."

"Come in for a moment, Rose," Kitty said. "She left something that she asked me to give you."

"Me? She did?" All the disappointment evaporated and Rose's heart climbed back up again. "What is it?"

"A necklace. Nothing we'd sell at *our* jewelry store, to be certain, so don't expect to retire early on diamonds," Kitty remarked as she led Rose inside. "But she made me go through her boxes after you left, like I have time for that kind of thing."

The necklace must be the trinket she mentioned. For some reason, that eased Rose's pain. "That was sweet of her," Rose said.

"Just wait here." She pointed to the dining room, which needed windows and flowers and, whoa, better wallpaper. "I'll put these in water and get that thing."

That *thing*?

Kitty's words and dismissive tone echoed as Rose pulled out a chair and sat at an ancient maple table, her thoughts all over the place as she came to terms with the fact that she'd found a Charlotte connection and lost her just as quickly.

She heard footsteps overhead, then down the stairs, then in the kitchen. The whole time, Rose sat completely still except for her fingers, which grazed the edge of the table runner the way Avery used to stroke the satin edge of her blanket to calm herself.

"Of course, I never knew what was real and what wasn't with her scrambled brain," Kitty said as she breezed in from the kitchen, a white envelope in her hand. "So, everything Aunt Annabelle said had to be taken with a boulder of salt, if you get my drift."

"She really didn't seem that...foggy to me," Rose said. "I mean, she repeated herself a few times, but who doesn't?"

"Me, for one," Kitty said, crossing her arms and leaving the envelope on the table in front of her, so Rose could see her name written on it in shaky script. Rose felt like Chloe's little fur baby when they made her sit but held a treat overhead.

Just give it to me already!

But she smiled at Kitty instead. "Then you're very lucky, Kitty."

"If I were lucky, Annabelle would have left me a million bucks and a house on the water with a handsome handyman living next door. Like the nice aunties in those books, you know?"

She held the smile in place. "You were very kind to give her a comfortable home in the end."

"Well, no one else would." She inhaled sharply. "Anyway, you must have brought some kind of sunshine to her, Rose, but then, you're sweet like that."

"Thank you." She tried—and failed—not to let her gaze drop to the envelope. "Did she say anything in particular about our visit?"

"She just gabbed on and on about...Charlotte? Was that your real mother's name?"

The phrase irked again. "Yes, Charlotte Lillian Long Wingate. As you know, Kitty, she died in childbirth when

Raina and I were born. Your aunt was her friend when they were teenagers and both—"

"Worked at the store, yes, yes, yes. Please. I heard every story forty times. I don't know about your...Charlotte. But Annabelle was a wild woman. Did you know she was some kind of hostess at Club Med in the Bahamas? Club Med! I've heard anything goes at those hedonistic places. Then she was a waitress on cruise ships and God knows where. She drank a lot, probably smoked some of the funny stuff, and must have slept with one too many men, since no one wanted to marry her."

"Kitty, please," Rose said, anger rising. "The woman just passed and you...*we* shouldn't judge her. She was my mother's friend, so I'd rather not speak ill of her."

Kitty eyed her for a second, looking like she had a lot more to say but somehow found the dignity not to say it. Then her expression softened and she closed her eyes.

"Aunt Annabelle said you were the spitting image of your mother, Rose," she added softly.

"She told me that, too."

"She also said that your mother said she'd name her first baby Annabelle." Kitty gave a derogatory snort. "Guess she forgot that promise, or Madeline would be Annabelle."

Rose just looked at her, mulling over this new piece of information, torn between chiding Kitty again and wondering if her mother had been serious. And did Madeline know this?

"Or Rex didn't like the name," Kitty added. "Your father doesn't hold back his opinions."

"No, he doesn't," she said, giving up the fight and pointing to the envelope. "May I?"

"Yes, yes. Of course. She said that she and your mother went to some festival or carnival or something. I don't know. Anyway, they bought these cheap necklaces that they used a machine to engrave. Annabelle got a C for Charlotte, and Charlotte must have gotten the other half, presumably with an A. With some words. I don't know. She was rambling while I had to sift through a pile of garbage to find this. She said she wanted to give it to you, so...here. Like I said, it's cheap."

She finally pushed the envelope across the table.

Trying not to tremble, Rose opened the flap and pulled out a tarnished metal semi-circle hanging on a chain. Oh, no, not a circle, she realized as she lifted it. It was half a heart with a C engraved on one side and the word *Apart* on the other.

"Oh," Rose whispered. "My little girls got these at the town craft fair last year. They each wear the other's name, since they have the same initials, but...but..."

"Rose! Don't cry! It was *my* aunt who died."

Rose didn't even realize tears had sprung, but the simple, cheap necklace blurred in her hand. It couldn't have cost two dollars. Heck, in 1965, it might have been fifty cents. Her father had given each of Charlotte's daughters far more valuable pieces from their mother's small collection of jewelry.

But somehow this inexpensive tin bauble mattered. It might as well have been made of solid gold and covered in rare stones.

"Thank you, Kitty," she said softly. "I hope..." She looked up, a little surprised to see Kitty's eyes glinting with tears, too. "I hope they've found each other in heaven."

She saw Kitty work to swallow, then stand. "Well, if you believe in that sort of thing. Anyway, thank you for the flowers, Rose. And for being so kind to her when you met."

"Of course." Rose slid the necklace back into the envelope and tucked it in her bag, touched to see that Kitty had a heart after all. "Again, you have my condolences, Kitty."

She nodded. "You better be prepared to meet with my board soon and give us an update on that project you're working on. Because all I see is your sister gallivanting around town on Isaiah Kincaid's arm."

Maybe not *that* much of a heart.

"I'll be ready, Kitty. The photo shoots shouldn't take long, then we'll present a mockup calendar to the board for final approval. It'll be selling in no time."

"And no skin."

Rose laughed softly as she walked to the front door. "No skin."

But her smile faded when she sat in her car and pulled out the necklace one more time.

C for Charlotte.

She brought it to her lips and gave it the lightest kiss before putting it around her neck to fasten it, thinking about the word engraved on it.

"Apart," she whispered with a sigh, pressing her hand

over the half-heart. "We are apart, dear mother of mine. But now I have one more piece of you, and I'll always wear it near my heart."

After a moment, she started the car and headed to the beach, wondering what ever happened to the other half of that necklace. It was lost, like so many memories and moments of Charlotte Wingate's life.

Chapter Twelve

Raina

These days, for Raina, the only thing better than an incredible pastry and a cup of decaf at the Riverfront Café was an incredible pastry, decaf, and the current proprietress of the Riverfront Café at the table with her.

Having breakfast with Tori was the perfect way to start what Raina hoped would be a perfect day and a perfect week. She had new listings, Dani was a dream, and the babies were growing, healthy, and kicking up a storm.

As she listed her litany of life successes, Tori nodded, but looked a little less enamored of the world at that moment.

"I'm hogging the conversation," Raina said quickly. "Everything okay with you? This place is hopping, the kids are happy, and you..." She fluttered her fingers around Tori's pretty face. "...you got that Hottypants glow about you, so..."

"Yes, everything is great," Tori agreed with a sigh that contradicted those words.

"What's wrong?" They were too close to beat around the old bush.

"Nothing, except...it's flying by too fast. It's August now. In three weeks, we are officially in BTS, the second-worst season of motherhood."

Raina shook her head. "BTS?"

"Back to school. When they hit you with lists of things to buy and dates and classes and books and all the joy fades away and summer becomes fall and that means...sports and homework and teachers and..." She groaned. "I hate the end of August."

Raina never even considered that. Would she hate BTS times two? "And that's the second-worst season? Do I even want to know what's the worst season of motherhood?"

"May. End of the year. Six million events and awards and projects due. By the last day of school, mothers everywhere are begging for mercy."

Raina laughed. "You're killing me."

"I don't want to leave Amelia Island," Tori said simply.

"You don't want to leave Dr. Justin Verona," Raina volleyed back.

"No, I do not." She smiled. "He said he'll come to Boston once in September, again in October, and we're all coming down here for Thanksgiving and maybe Christmas, if Trey the Bonehead lets me."

"So you'll only see Justin four times before the new year?" Raina asked.

"Shut your mouth."

"Why? It's the truth. I mean, if you count each visit as once. Think about this, Tori. You don't want to leave. The kids don't want to leave. Justin doesn't want you to leave. And don't start me on how much *I* don't want you to leave!" She heard the whine in her voice and didn't care. "Things One and Two need Auntie Tori."

A smile lifted Tori's lips. "I cannot bear the thought of missing you being a mom. It's...everything."

"I'll need help and you know it. Twice as much as your average mother, and remember, I'm working and will be forty-four by then." She shivered. "What have I done?"

Tori laughed. "Help is in abundance around here and you could run a real estate business in your sleep, especially with Dani here. Also, forty-four is the new twenty-nine—haven't you heard?"

Raina snorted, then leaned in. "I need *you*. I need someone who is brutally honest and funny and experienced and...and...you." Raina reached over the table. "Is it really impossible to even consider relocating down here?"

"I haven't...well, that's a lie. I *have* thought about it. Non-stop, to be real. Talked to Kenzie and Finn. I even floated the idea to my two sous chefs who are running my catering business, and they're salivating to buy out my equipment and client list. I could sell the Wellesley house—"

"In a heartbeat, and I know a great Boston-based agent."

Tori took a sip of her own coffee, the light in her hazel

eyes dimming for the first time since they'd sat down together.

"So?" Raina prodded.

"So I cannot, Raina. Period. End of story, end of discussion. The court says I can't take the kids out of the state of Massachusetts without some serious legal wrangling. Which would be expensive and miserable and I'd probably lose."

Raina slumped, defeated in the face of that argument. "Wow, divorce is ugly."

"You have no...well, maybe you do. Any word from Jack?"

"No, nor his lawyer, but the whole thing is like a black cloud over my otherwise sunny life."

"A black cloud that never, ever goes away." Tori made a face, then the light was back in her eyes. "But except for that? Wow, this is a blue-sky summer. Have I told you lately that I'm in love?"

"Not since two minutes ago," Raina cracked. "Do any of Justin's trips to Boston include interviews with neurology groups up there?"

"He said he would relocate, but no." She shook her head. "We haven't been seeing each other long enough to make that kind of change."

"You moving here would be that kind of change," Raina countered.

"My moving here would be a dream," Tori said. "A dream that my ex-husband does not want me to have." She leaned across the table and whispered, "Be very, very careful what you accept in that settlement, Raina.

I've been divorced for five years and until Finn is eighteen, I'm still, for all intents and purposes, in Trey's prison."

On the table, Raina's phone flashed with a text from Dani that she would have ignored except it said *URGENT!!!* in the first line. "Whoa, hang on a sec. Maybe it's about Blake."

She tapped the screen and read the rest of the text.

Dani: *Jack is here waiting for you.*

"Oh..." Raina felt lightheaded just reading the words.

"She found Blake?" Tori asked.

Raina slid the phone across the table so Tori could read the text. "Speaking of prison and divorce settlements," Raina said. "What in the name of all that's holy is he doing on Amelia Island?"

"*Oof.*" Tori closed her eyes. "Whatever you do, Regina Deborah Wingate, you may not go back with him. I don't care if he grovels on both knees, offers the moon, and swears on his mother's grave that he'll be faithful, you can't—"

"Tori, stop. I'm not. He fell in love with another woman."

"And if he fell out of love with her? Sorry, I usually am very careful with what I say to you, because I don't want to sound bitter, but I get scared."

"There's nothing to be afraid of," Raina said as she reluctantly put her napkin on top of the rest of her pastry even though she wanted it more than her next breath.

But every bite would just sit like a rock in her already nervous stomach. "Nothing to be afraid of," she repeated.

"Who are you reminding? Me or you?" Tori asked with that sly smile.

"Both." She stood and slipped her purse off the back of the chair. "Wish me luck."

"Just please don't fold like a house of cards the minute he begs."

"Give me a little credit, sis." Raina blew her a kiss and hustled out of the café, a sheen of sweat on her neck before she got ten steps down Wingate Way.

And that wasn't only because it was ninety degrees and humid. She didn't want to see Jack. She didn't want to look at his face and remember...sixteen years of what she thought was happiness.

This is happiness, she realized with a start. *This*.

She paused mid-step and looked around, seeing the sunlight glistening off the river, the charming red brick buildings, the familiar gates and arched windows and tall oak trees that lined the avenue that had always been *home* to her.

Then she touched her baby bump and shivered in that heat and humidity. Also this. And her sisters, her business, her life. This was happiness. And that old life was...

Standing right in front of her.

"Hi, Rain."

She stared up at the man who'd been her world for so long, it felt a little disloyal to have been reveling in a world that he wasn't part of. But he wasn't, and she couldn't forget that.

Nor could she melt under his warm and familiar

gaze, with nothing but Tori's parting shot echoing in her head.

Don't fold like a house of cards...

"Hey, Jack. What are you doing here?"

He angled his head as though he'd expected that would be her first question. "I wanted to talk and see you and see how...you've changed." His gaze dropped to the body-hugging dress she wore, easily able to see exactly how she'd changed. "Wow. Babies. Two of them."

She nodded and put a protective hand on her stomach. "Yep."

"You feel okay? Everything's good? After that, um, near-miss you had?"

"I'm fine. They're fine. Everything is..." She screwed up her face as the sheen became actual perspiration that dribbled down her neck. "Can we go back into A/C?"

"Yeah, yeah. I heard Dani say you were at the café, so..." He turned toward the Wingate Properties building. "We can go inside. Where?"

"My..." Something twisted inside her, and it wasn't a baby. She didn't want him in her office, or even in the building. But she was melting, so sitting on a bench outside wasn't a good idea. She gave a nod and walked toward Wingate Properties, then asked, "Are you staying long?"

She was already dreading the possibility of him coming back to the beach house or, God forbid, staying with her.

"Nah, we just came up last night and will go back tomorrow."

We. She felt her whole being clench as they reached the door. How easily he'd became a "we" with Lisa Godfrey. It was shocking. And a big clue that he wasn't here to grovel, beg, or otherwise fulfill Tori's prophecies.

"And here it is," he said as he pulled the heavy door and held it for her. "The white elephant of Wingate Way."

She shot him a look, too hot to argue.

"But now that you're calling the shots, Rain, maybe you'll do what I always said. Repurpose this puppy into condos and retail and head straight to the bank with bags of cash."

She stepped inside, the cold air like a balm on her irritated heart. "The bank was built by my great-grandfather, Jack. A Wingate has worked here for more than a hundred years. Do you really think I'm going to turn it into *condos?*"

"Oh, please, Raina. I know you. But I also know this town, and you'd probably have to sleep with the mayor to get that approved."

Seriously? He'd dragged her from a pastry and a heart-to-heart with her sister for *this?*

She *really* didn't want him upstairs, so she led him to a small sofa in the reception area. Ellen, the receptionist who normally manned the desk out here, must have been in the kitchen or copy room, leaving the area empty enough for whatever he needed to say.

"So, what can I do for you?" She used her most businesslike voice and perched on the sofa's edge like he was an annoying sales rep and she was simply being polite.

He gave her a look and glanced left and right, then looked hard at her. "Here? Really?"

"I could ask the same thing, Jack. What are you really doing here, out of the blue, at my office?"

"So it *is* your office. You've officially taken over from Rex?" He nodded a few times. "Good. That's good, Rain."

"Why?"

His eyes flashed a little, then he closed them, looking like he was gathering his thoughts, but she knew him too well. He was pausing for dramatic effect. He did that right before he accepted an offer, so the buyer thought Jack was making a huge concession.

"I have an idea, Raina, and I wanted to just...bypass the lawyers."

Tori's *other* warning suddenly crystalized in her head...

Be very, very careful what you accept in that settlement, Raina.

So she stayed quiet, looking at him and waiting for the lawyer-bypassing idea to tumble out like it was so much in her favor when really it was all for him.

Oh, *man*. How had they gotten this far so fast?

"We are thinking about selling to RE/MAX."

She gasped, not sure which word in that sentence was more appalling. *RE/MAX* or *selling* or *we*.

"Selling? Wallace & Wingate?"

"There's no Wingate working there anymore," he said simply.

"Well, there certainly wouldn't be if you sell," she

fired back. "Is that why you'd consider doing this? To wipe every last molecule of me from the place?"

He regarded her for a moment and looked like he was about to say something, but then cast his gaze to the ground.

So, that would be yes, that was exactly why they would sell.

"Raina, please," he said. "We all know what happened."

"You cheated on me," she ground out. "And you fell in love with your mistress, who is now apparently calling the shots about the business *we* took a decade and a half to build from the ground up with sweat and tears and...love."

He stayed silent, the tiniest bit of color in his cheeks the only reveal of a temper about to blow.

"I'm sorry I hurt you," he finally said in his most controlled voice, the words sounding practiced. Had he rehearsed this speech in front of Lisa? "You didn't deserve that, but you cannot fight...feelings."

"Oh, *I* can. *You* can't. And neither can Lisa." She crossed her arms when one of the babies moved a centimeter out of spite, unwilling to share even that much of the experience with him. "So, what are you proposing?"

"A buyout. Straightforward and simple. I'll split the profit with you from the sale, pay you for half the house and divide our investments. Easy-peasy. And fast."

She searched his face, kind of liking the idea, but not

willing to give in so easily. There had to be a catch. There was always a catch with Jack.

"Buyout before or after the sale is finalized?" she asked, knowing he could easily cheat her out of thousands if she agreed to a number and he ended up getting more for their business.

"After," he said, appeasing her.

"And everything else, just...fifty-fifty?"

"Fifty-fifty and fast."

Fast must be very important to him...or Lisa.

Another kick in her gut reminded her of the one thing they hadn't discussed. The only thing that mattered. The most important thing—or things—of all.

She sat up a little straighter, one hand on her belly. "We have two children, Jack."

His gaze dropped. "Yes, of course. The twins." He shifted on the sofa and visibly swallowed, and during that split second of time, her body braced the way it would if she were flying down the highway and saw a truck coming at her head on.

"I'd like to, um, relinquish my rights."

And...*crash*.

"Excuse me?" she asked in a whisper of disbelief.

"Well, Rain, let's be honest. I'm in another town, in another relationship, and we're...we're..."

"You don't want to have *anything* to do with them?" she asked, shock and pain sending sparks to every nerve in her body. Hadn't he made his big "they're my kids, too" speech the day he showed up to hear the heartbeat? What happened to that?

Lisa Godfrey happened. *She* didn't want him connected to those babies or Raina, and she had some unfathomable sway over him.

He cleared his throat, clearly nervous. "We're trying to have one of our own now, Lisa and me, or we will once the divorce is finalized and we get—"

"You're serious." She simply couldn't believe it. She couldn't process it. "You don't *want* to be their father?"

"Rain, it's not like they're people I've met," he shot back. "I don't have a connection to those kids and you have this monster of a family up here and—"

She stood on shaking legs. Her whole body, in fact, was trembling with rage and agony and resentment and oh so much...*rejection*. He didn't want her *or* their babies! The business they built? Yeah, she understood that. The marriage they'd created? She'd accepted that was over.

But he *didn't want his own children?*

The idea hurt so much, it left her breathless. What was wrong with him?

"Just...please..." It was hard to form a word but she forced herself, vaguely aware that Ellen had returned to her desk and was within earshot. "Leave now," she finally managed to say.

He looked up, a question in his eyes. "Do you want time to think about it?"

"I want..." She tried to swallow, but it hurt, so she just covered her stomach with two hands as if she could possibly protect these tiny creatures from all the pain ahead. All the questions and confusion and hurt and *why didn't Daddy want us?* "I want you to leave."

He finally stood. "Should I go back to the lawyers?"

She smiled sweetly, mostly for the benefit of the receptionist. "You should go to hell, where I'm pretty sure there's a special corner waiting for a man who doesn't want anything to do with his own children."

With that, she rushed straight to the stairs, congratulating herself on every step that she made without collapsing in a heap of tears.

Upstairs, she sailed past Dani, practically dove into her office, slammed the door, flipped the lock, and fell onto the sofa as the first sob ripped her throat.

"Raina? Honey? Please let me in."

Raina blinked as a suffocating fog started to lift, almost surprised to see she was on the sofa in Dad's office, her face wet and smashed against the leather, her whole body wrecked from weeping. Her eyeballs literally hurt.

"Dani?" She groaned as she moved and realized with a thud that it hadn't been a nightmare. He really wanted—

"I need to come in and talk to you." Dani's voice was a hushed whisper, like she was pressing her mouth to the door jamb. "It's super important."

"No." She pushed up, swiping hair from her face.

"Chase Madison is here."

She almost gagged on a dry laugh as she wiped her face and looked at the smear of mascara on her fingers.

"No," she repeated.

"He has news...about Blake."

Muttering a curse, she sat up. *Now? Really?*

"What kind of news?" she asked as the fog lifted a little more.

"Unlock the door, Raina. Please. I'll help you."

But no one, not even her well-meaning friend and assistant or any of her sisters or her parents or her missing nephew or some stupid, stupid client out there could help her.

Jack's betrayal had shattered her on so many levels. What had she done to deserve this? What had their babies?

"Please," Dani asked, jiggling the doorknob.

Raina stood and took a few steps to the door to flip the lock. Slowly, it opened, as if Dani were uncertain what she'd find on the other side.

Dani slipped in through the narrow opening and closed the door behind her, flinching when she got a good look at Raina.

"Oh, sweetheart." She reached her arms out, but Raina shook her head, not sure she could be touched right then.

"It's fine," she lied. "I'm fine. I...I'm...it's fine."

"What did Jack want? What happened?"

"To sell the business and relinquish rights to the babies." Even as she said the words, they stuck in her throat like she'd swallowed a handful of gravel.

Dani's eyes flashed. "Whoa. Wow."

Raina grunted and shut her eyes. "I just feel kicked in

the teeth and the belly." She rubbed her stomach. "These are my babies, and his. It just hurts so much."

"At least you don't have to deal with shared custody."

She nodded. "I know that. I also know that this is probably a—well, not a good thing, but convenient. That doesn't make it less emotional for me. I hurt and I think that someday these kids will hurt, too, when they realize their own father didn't want them."

Dani reached out her hand. "They will be so loved, so buried in Wingate comfort and assured of their mother's love that it won't matter."

Raina nodded, knowing she was right but it wasn't enough. Not yet. "What does Chase Madison want? He found Blake?"

"He said he wants to talk to you. He has a plan to facilitate a meeting with you and Blake. He seems genuine, and nice. And really doesn't want to leave without seeing you."

She rolled her eyes, biting back a comment. Why did powerful men always get what they wanted, when they wanted it? And when they didn't? They just...relinquished.

Wincing at the word, she smoothed her hair and didn't even want to imagine what she looked like after her breakdown.

"I need to go to the bathroom. Put him in the downstairs conference room. Give him coffee and tell him I need five more minutes."

It took ten, even though all Raina did was wash her face with ice-cold water. That did very little to reduce the red rims around her eyes and the blotches on her cheeks. But she didn't care what she looked like. If this hadn't been about Blake, she'd have sent the man packing without a second thought for the dream listing she'd lose.

She'd get through this meeting for Blake. Her soon-to-be-ex-husband might not value family connections, but she did.

She stepped into the conference room, grateful this one didn't have glass walls so anyone could see in, like at her office in Miami. It did have windows, though, which flooded the room with sunshine, and no doubt highlighted her dreadful appearance.

At least, that's what she assumed from Chase's not-so-imperceptible reaction when she walked in.

"Raina," he said as he stood, his voice surprisingly husky. "Are you okay?"

"No," she replied, taking a seat at the head of the table. "Dani said this was urgent and concerned Blake Youngblood."

Sitting kitty-corner from her, he narrowed his eyes, scrutinizing her. "We didn't have to—"

"Please. I don't want to discuss anything except my nephew."

He exhaled softly and nodded. "He contacted me."

"Oh?" She sat up. "What did he say?"

"Confirmed your suspicions," he said. "He is now an independently licensed real estate agent and wanted to discuss the possibility of me giving him the listing."

She gave a soft grunt. "A tad uncool to poach your former employer's clients, but—"

"He acknowledged that, several times. He said he would only talk if I had made the decision *not* to work with Wingate Properties. If I hired you or even discussed the property with you, he didn't want to steal the business. And, yes, that was him checking out the property the other day before he knew I was there."

She nodded, knowing that Blake's move was entirely acceptable if the seller had decided not to work with Wingate. Except...he had. At least verbally.

"I almost told him no, you already had the listing, but I know you want to talk to him, so I thought you might see this as an opportunity to make that happen."

She did, and she appreciated him understanding that. "How?" she asked.

"I thought we could work it out so that you and Blake both met at the house at the same time. He'd come for an interview on the listing, and you'd show up or already be there. That way, you could have the opportunity to talk to him. Is *that* uncool?"

It was sneaky, but Blake was giving her no option.

She looked up to meet brown eyes, which didn't look as dark as she remembered. In this light, she could see they were flecked with gold, and fringed with an unfair amount of lashes. If she had those lashes, she wouldn't have cried off every molecule of mascara.

"I don't relish the idea of an ambush," she said. "But all I need is a few minutes with him. How he accepts what I have to say is up to him."

"Then I'll make that happen."

She searched Chase's expression, seeing him differently than she had in the ice cream parlor when all she'd wanted was a good listing. Now, she saw him as a man with a surprising amount of compassion in his eyes and more silver at his temples than she'd noticed before.

"Why?" she asked softly, saying out loud the one-word question that had plagued her since Jack dropped his bomb. But that was why was Jack so awful, this was why was Chase being so...nice?

"Because you were forthcoming with me, about everything. I appreciate that."

"I'm not...being forthcoming now." She brushed under her eye where she'd obviously shed more than a few tears. "Am I?"

"Want to tell me about it?"

"Not really." She leaned back and sighed while he waited without saying a word. "My life is a dumpster fire, as I believe I told you," she finally admitted. "And my about to be ex-husband and father of my children just... relinquished all custody."

"He *what?*" He jerked forward like he couldn't believe the words.

She gave a tight smile at the response, mostly because it vindicated her own. "I hope that doesn't color your opinion of me," she added.

"Are you..." He shook his head, speechless for a moment. "I'm sorry."

"Thank you." And she meant that, appreciating again that he even cared about this embarrassing aspect of her life.

"Raina," he said, leaning forward. "I like that you care

about your nephew. I am impressed that you stepped in to help your father. And I respect that you met with me even though you really didn't want to. What color is that opinion?"

She glanced at his temples again. "Silver. As in you sure found the silver lining in my otherwise dark cloud."

He nodded a few times, searching her face. "It does end eventually. Divorce, I mean."

"You've been through it?"

"Twice."

She grimaced. "Then you're a better man than I am."

"I know two women who would disagree," he said, his voice surprisingly sad. Without elaborating, he stood. "I'll get you in the same room as your nephew. After that, it's up to you."

"Thank you, Chase." She looked up at him, wondering what he did to fail in two marriages. He certainly seemed good-hearted enough and very attractive. But then, Jack probably seemed like both of those things to Lisa Godfrey. "And, um..." She stood. "What about the listing?"

"Well, now I'm talking to this other guy..." He gave a slow smile. "May the better agent win."

Her jaw loosened and he just chuckled and showed himself out.

Chapter Thirteen

Chloe

T he entire time Chloe talked to Rose on FaceTime, Lady Bug's tail fluttered from side to side.

"Somebody misses you," Chloe said, redirecting the phone so Rose could see her on screen. "And she also hates it here."

"Oh, Chloe." Rose looked like she wanted to climb through the phone and offer tea and sympathy and all the right words. "It'll take time, but I am certain you'll slay this new job and city."

"Save your optimism, Rose. I've yet to get on air, my social life is a complete bomb, and don't forget the disgusting little critters that are renting out my kitchen cabinet."

Rose made a face. "You can't live like that. All of that stuff is just wrong, hon."

Chloe moaned. "I just have to come up with the right story to get air time. And force myself to get out and meet people. Oh, and buy stock in bug killer. Enough about me. Tell me everything about home."

Home. Even as she said it, Chloe's heart shifted a

little. She'd lived in Washington, D.C., suburban Virginia, Jacksonville, and now L.A., but the cobblestone streets of Fernandina Beach and the familiar live oak- and palm-lined streets of Amelia Island would always be home.

And right now, she was next-level homesick.

"What do you want to hear about?" Rose asked.

Chloe switched the phone to her left hand to get comfortable. "Travis McCall," she whispered without hesitation. "Unless he's already met someone else. Then I'd prefer to hear about anything else."

A smile pulled at Rose's pretty face, her brown eyes glinting. "He asked about you at his photo shoot yesterday," she said.

"He did? Oh, my gosh, he's in the calendar you're doing! You better have stolen a few pictures of him for me. Was he in uniform?"

"Hang on." Rose looked down and the screen went blank, then her face reappeared. "I just texted you."

A second later, Chloe got a notification that Rose had sent an image.

And what an image it was. Probie Travis McCall in a Fernandina Beach Fire Department T-shirt that clung to his impossibly broad shoulders and biceps, leaning against the brick and wrought-iron gates outside of The Next Chapter, holding...

"Is that Shakespeare he's reading?" Chloe asked, using her fingers to zoom in and read the book spine.

"For his classic, Travis chose a compilation of the romantic comedies of William Shakespeare."

"No!" Chloe threw her head back and laughed. "We had a discussion about Shakespeare's rom-coms the first night we..." Her voice faded out as the bout of homesickness blended with an unexpected longing for the night Travis had showed up at Rose's house and they'd watched *Pretty Woman* together. "He likes rom-coms," she finished softly. "He watched them with his mom before she died."

"He misses you, too," Rose said softly.

"He told you that?"

"No, to be honest, he didn't. He played it very cool with me. But in a moment of weakness, he told Gabe. Well, more specifically, he asked if you were doing okay, and what it was like to be the only male in-law in a family full of Wingate women."

"Oh." Chloe put her hand over her mouth, tucking away that anecdote to be carefully considered later. "He's...sweet. And gorgeous. And three thousand miles away."

"Not if you come home."

"Stop." Chloe ran her hand over Lady Bug's silky coat and knew she had to change the subject or burst into tears. "How is that calendar project going, anyway?"

"Really well," Rose said with a soft laugh. "The guys are totally into it. It's going to be such a cute calendar with a small-town vibe and Grace's store showcased."

"Send me one the minute you can."

"Sure! You can get all your Hollywood connections to buy them."

Chloe rolled her eyes. "If I had any. Has Gabe done his photo shoot yet?"

"Oh, yes. He lounged in Grace's front display window, full gear, a helmet in one hand and *The Adventures of Huckleberry Finn* in the other."

"No! So cute!"

Rose smiled—and maybe it was the FaceTime connection—but Chloe could have sworn she didn't look that happy. "It was his favorite book as a kid and now Ethan's inhaling it, with the two of them quoting their favorite lines at dinner." She gave a soft laugh. "When he's here for dinner and not picking up firefighting shifts."

"Ah, I miss those D'Angelo family dinners." When she'd lived with Gabe and Rose, they had dinner with their four amazing kids in the dining room every night that Gabe wasn't on duty. Zach was always talking smack or secretly texting his girlfriend, and Ethan teased everyone. Alyson and Avery were like little baby doll bookends, just so sweet, both of them slipping scraps to Lady Bug under the table.

"Well, those dinners are rare these days."

Chloe frowned, so not used to anything but light and optimism from Rose. "Is everything okay?" she asked.

For a moment, she thought Rose looked a little...lost. Then she nodded and smiled. "Of course! We just miss you so much, Chloe."

"And I miss you guys."

"I know, honey. And as much as I want to beg you to

come home, you have to power through and see if this was the right move for you. You can't quit yet."

"I won't," she promised. "I had a long talk with Dad last night—he sounds really good, by the way—and he gave me the ultimate 'Wingates aren't quitters' talk, which, for the record, was *not* what he said moments before I called off the wedding."

"True, but Wingates *rarely* quit." She sighed as if the subject somehow pained her. "But I think he's right. You are not quitting yet. Can you make a girlfriend out there? Have you met anyone at work you could have drinks with?"

"If I didn't mind getting arsenic in my vodka-tonic," she said dryly. "The women at work kind of hate me. And each other. Everyone's so competitive out here, it's downright ugly. It's very hard for me to trust anyone, to be honest."

"And, I hate to ask this, but...have you heard from Hunter? I know you said he texted you once."

"Yeah, but I haven't seen him. We talked briefly on the phone and we text once in a while. I have to say, he's been very nice, considering I literally left him at the altar." She shifted on the sofa. "I hate to admit I'm almost ready to say yes to his offer of drinks."

Rose lifted a shoulder, considering that. "Maybe you should. I don't think he's trying to get back with you, Chloe."

"No. No, he's not. He's seeing someone. Not serious yet, but it made me feel better. He made it clear this would be friends having drinks."

"Then maybe you should go," Rose said. "For one thing, if you smoothed over all the hurt, I think you'd stop suffering from the guilt you feel for leaving him at the altar."

That was probably true, Chloe thought.

"And for another, he could be a friend who might introduce you to others. Maybe someone who works at his office? Or one of his neighbors? Other women who might not be as competitive, because they're not up against you for air time on a TV show."

"That makes sense, Rose." Chloe took a deep breath. "You think I should see him?"

"As long as he knows it's not romantic and it's cool with whoever he's seeing, then what's the harm? You're lonely."

"You can say that again," Chloe said glumly. "So lonely I'm staring at this picture of Travis McCall and starting to think I should just text him and have a long-distance something with this cute probie."

Rose gave a look that said she didn't agree.

"He really liked me and I...went off to find fame and fortune in L.A."

"You didn't go off looking for fame or fortune," Rose said sweetly. "You're following your professional dreams and I, for one, am so stinking proud of you, little sister."

"Thanks."

"But Travis is looking for someone...serious," Rose said.

Chloe fought a little groan. "And he'll find someone in a heartbeat."

"He hasn't yet, but he's told Gabe that he wants... well, he wants what we have."

"Who doesn't?" Chloe cracked. "Fairy-tale marriages aren't that common, you know."

"I know," Rose said. "He's got such a sweet spot for you, he might give in to a long-distance romance. But, is that fair to either of you? He wants the whole deal—marriage, kids, and a happy ever after."

Rose was right and Chloe knew it. "So you really think I should text Hunter and have a drink with him?" she asked.

"I do, as long as you're both clear why."

Chloe blew out a confused breath. "Maybe I will. Give everyone a kiss for me, okay? All the kids." She lifted up Lady Bug and made her little paw wave. "Lady Bug misses your girls! Oh, Grace tells me Nikki Lou is doing so well in her new program."

"Yes, she is," Rose cooed. "Nikki Lou's going alone tomorrow. Well, not alone. Isaiah is taking her in and keeping the new dog all morning, because we're doing Dad's photo shoot at the store. Then Isaiah's shoot is in the afternoon. Everyone is going to come and watch Dad, of course."

"Not everyone," Chloe said glumly. "I'm not."

"Come on, Chloe," Rose said in her most cheer-leadery voice—and she had plenty of those. "Give it a real go out there. This is your dream!"

"Yeah, yeah, yeah." Chloe smiled. "Or my nightmare."

"On that happy note..."

Chloe laughed. "It'll get better, you're right. Love you, Rosie."

She blew Rose a kiss and signed off, sitting in the silent apartment for a good five minutes before she picked up her phone again, staring at Travis's picture.

"Marriage, family, and happily ever after," she whispered to the image. "I sure wish—"

Her phone vibrated with a text from Hunter.

Hunter: *Hey, what's up?*

"Okay, Hunter," she mumbled while tapping the screen. "Let's set some boundaries and follow Rose's advice. I need a friend."

With a lump in her throat, she typed: *Hi! What are you doing?*

She knew that would start the ball rolling. Okay, maybe he wasn't the friend she hoped to make out here, but...

Five minutes and three exchanges later, she pushed up to get dressed and go meet him for a drink.

"Don't look at me that way," she said to Lady Bug. "Desperate times call for desperate measures. And, baby girl, I am desperately lonely."

Lady Bug wagged her tail, but Chloe could have sworn there was some harsh judgment in her brown eyes.

SITTING across from Hunter in a painfully hip rooftop bar overlooking Sunset Boulevard, Chloe couldn't help wondering...*why*.

Not why she was there—she knew that. But why would Hunter ever want to look at her again, let alone make small talk and show interest in her work?

He'd never been that invested in what she did for a living, to be honest. His medical degree, residency at the Mayo Clinic in plastic surgery, and his bright future as a doctor was always the first, last, and favorite topic on the table.

But even beyond his politeness, why would he want to bring his ex-fiancée to this snazzy bar and...reconnect? Why didn't he hate her for humiliating him in front of his entire family, all his friends, and graduating class of residents?

"So, have you met any celebrities yet?" he asked, twirling the straw in his Roku Gin and bergamot orange cocktail while she nursed a glass of pedestrian red wine. She never remembered him drinking much at all, but then, he hadn't worn black T-shirts and jeans with boots, either. He was the original "wear scrubs whenever possible" kind of doctor—scrubs impressed people.

But she forgave the rock-star outfit and figured he was just trying to fit in, or maybe these clothes had been too hot for Florida.

"Celebrities? Well, I passed someone who looked like Leonardo DiCaprio in the hall," she said. "But it might not have been him."

"Come on, Chloe. You're working in a celebrity hotbox."

She wasn't sure what a hotbox was, so she let it go. "Well, I was in Coo Coo Cooper's house, which is where

Sharon Tate was murdered, of all gruesome things, and I met his girlfriend. Does that count?"

He nodded, looking intrigued. "How's she?"

She curled a lip. "Not that nice."

"She looks good, though."

"Yeah." She eyed him. "Not really someone I'd think was your type."

"No, no, that's not..." He laughed. "So, do you have any cool interviews lined up? Even B-list stars must be fun to meet."

"Honestly, Hunter, I'm having a bit of a rough go of it at this job," she admitted. "The person who hired me has moved on and the guy who inherited me is not sold on my talents as of yet."

"Who's that?"

"Some guy named Rory—"

"Sutton," he finished, as if he'd been spending his days reading *The Hollywood Reporter*. "He used to date that Ecuadorean model, Daysi...something. That'd be a great person for you to meet."

So great he couldn't remember the woman's last name. "My job is less about meeting famous people than looking for news."

"But aren't the celebrities the only news that matters at that place?" he asked.

"More or less," she agreed, a little tired of rehashing the issues at *A-List Access*. "How's the plastic surgery practice? Do you like the group you joined?"

He tipped his head in an expression that anyone else would read as noncommittal, but she knew Hunter

Landry much too well. He didn't like his job, she'd guess, but he just didn't want to say it. Maybe he'd made a bad choice, but he hated to be wrong about anything.

"It's not fun to be the new guy. Bottom of the ladder has never been my favorite place, as you know."

She smiled, a little touched by this new Hunter. Could her public breakup with him have erased some of his arrogance and left behind the man she once loved?

"You'll climb fast," she reassured him. "You are such a quick study and you're a fantastic surgeon. Have you done any noteworthy work? Introduced your colleagues to that new grafting technique you were so excited about for burn patients?"

He snorted. "We don't get burn patients," he said. "We get people who want an upturned nose with a depression in the nasal bridge. Or, my favorite, the Kardashian butt lift." He rolled his eyes. "That's honestly the number one request I hear."

"Eesh." She took a sip of wine, considering the slight bitterness in his tone. "You had to know that was going to be the L.A. clientele, right? Anyway, who does a nose job better than you?"

"Six hundred surgeons on the Westside," he joked, surprising her again with that lack of ego. "But it's fine. Pay's great. My apartment's the bomb, and..."

"And you're seeing someone, right?"

He gave a casual shrug. "Sort of. I'm, uh, taking it easy after my last breakup." He grinned, looking very much like the charismatic medical student she'd met when she was a cub reporter working on a healthcare story at Johns Hopkins.

"Oh, Hunter." She crossed her arms and braced her elbows on the table, her heart softening. "You're too kind to forgive me for what happened."

"Based on what you said in that church, Chloe, I'm the one who needs to be forgiven."

Seriously? He was acknowledging his flaws? Humble Hunter was a wonderful change.

"We both had problems," she said, aching to get all the apologies out. "I shouldn't have waited until the last possible moment."

"And I shouldn't have been a jerk about your dad on a walker."

The words stunned her. "Shocking to think we could get past that and be friends, Hunter, but I'm so very happy to do so." She offered a handshake over the table. "Truce, my friend?"

He took it, shook it, and nodded. "Absolutely."

They toasted after they shook and then he wanted to know everything about the Sharon Tate house, which she shared, including the part about getting the boot from a nearly-naked Lacey Britton.

"Are they real?" he asked, lightly gesturing toward his chest.

"Nothing is real about her," she replied. "She probably has her own parking spot in the back lot of your practice."

He laughed at that and finished his drink. "Well, you

keep your eye out for celebs, Chloe. They're your bread and butter, even if you want harder news."

"Well, I've been assigned a party—which, in my job, is the closest thing I'm going to get to an actual desk assignment—at Woody Renault's house in Laurel Canyon. I should certainly see some famous faces there."

"You need a date?" he asked with an uncertain smile. "I mean, I know it's work, but I'd go with you."

She drew back, really not sure how to answer.

"Why would you want to be my date, Hunter? I get apologizing and I'm glad we did, and I am grateful to know someone in this overcrowded town, but..." She laughed softly, shaking her head. "I am surprised to hear you use my name and 'date' in the same sentence."

"Chloe, come on. We can't be enemies forever."

They weren't enemies, they were exes, she thought as they gathered their things to leave.

"But you'd want to go on an assignment...as my date to a party? You have to admit that's a little strange."

He flicked his wrist. "Hey, we'll go as friends, extending our truce. What's worse than walking into some big star-studded affair and not having anyone to talk to? I just wanted to offer my company if you feel like that would make it easier."

She searched his face for a moment, still so confused by this new version of Hunter Landry.

"I don't think I'll have a problem, but it's really nice of you to offer. A little weird, but nice."

He laughed, acknowledging that. "Hey, I'm as curious

as the next person about how someone like Woody Renault lives. And maybe if you don't blow in with the 'I'm here to do some journalism' hat on...you'll get your story."

"Thanks," she said, not quite sure how to take that. From Old Hunter, it would be irritating. But he was trying so hard, she gave him some slack. "I'll do my best, even though I *will* be there to do actual journalism."

"I know, but I can tell you as someone who has to deal with these people a lot, they prefer it if you don't hit too hard. Just sayin', Chloe."

She thought about that and considered that maybe he wasn't wrong. "Thanks for the advice," she said as they walked out. "I'll think about it and let you know before Friday night."

They parted outside when her Uber showed, saying goodbye with an extremely platonic hug. As the car pulled away, she turned and watched him walk down the street, a cocktail of emotions brewing.

A little sadness, plenty of relief, and a teeny bit of affection for the man who clearly wasn't holding a grudge when he had every right to.

Maybe Hunter Landry had changed, and maybe her decision had caused that change. She wasn't sure, but she was glad she'd seen him tonight.

Still, on the way home, she tapped her phone and looked at Travis McCall's picture the way a hungry woman might read a menu for a gourmet restaurant...that was three thousand miles away.

Chapter Fourteen

Grace

The minute Dad walked into the bookstore, leaning on his cane and looking summery and comfortable in his red, white, and blue shorts and shirt, Grace forgot that she'd sent Isaiah off with a tearful Nikki Lou and a very excited Slinky just a few minutes earlier.

She tamped down the guilt about not taking her daughter to her special classes that day, because this photo shoot was too happy an occasion to miss, despite Nikki's breakdown when she found out Grace wasn't driving her.

"Mr. July is here," Dad announced as he gave Grace a kiss on the cheek. "Make me look handsome, smart, and sexy."

"Like you could be anything else," she teased, giving him a hug and looking over his shoulder to watch her mother greet Madeline, who'd come over early, of course, along with Tori and her kids.

"And there's a peanut gallery!" Dad joked, holding Grace with one hand and deftly lifting his cane with his right hand—the one that worked perfectly—and using it to point to the group.

"You look great, Daddio," Tori exclaimed, coming closer to give him a hug.

"Good enough to be a cover boy?" Dad struck a pose, making them laugh.

"Better you than me," Finn said as he hugged his grandfather.

"And I'm putting the highlights on TikTok," Kenzie called from behind them, her phone up as she recorded every minute of the Wingate life. "You know my followers love you, Grandpa Rex!"

Rose and the photographer were already setting up along the back wall, where a flag hung and a display of American history books was spread out. Dad had chosen to hold David McCullough's *1776* and sit in a wingback chair for his photos.

Before he headed back there, he stopped to greet Raina and Madeline with hugs, making them all fuss over how great he looked and how far he'd come since his stroke four months ago.

Next to him, Susannah beamed. As she should, considering all she'd done to get him from there to here.

"I trimmed his hair myself," she whispered to Grace. "He didn't want to go get it done. Is it okay?"

"It's perfect," she assured her mother, adding a hug. "You're perfect."

Rose suddenly appeared next to them, sliding her arms around both of them. "You can say that again," she whispered, and kissed Mom on the cheek. "You're my queen, you know that? He looks amazing."

She inched back, smiling at Rose. "Don't look too close at the back, because I didn't have sons and I don't know how to use those clippers."

"We're only shooting the front," Rose assured her. "You want to go help him get settled? The photographer's name is Mel, and she's great to work with."

"I'm going right now." But she didn't move, looking from one to the other, her blue eyes bright with what almost seemed like unshed tears.

"Are you okay?" Grace and Rose asked in unison, making her laugh. And that made a tear spill.

"I'm just so happy," she said softly. "He dressed himself completely this morning. He stood after breakfast and put his dishes in the sink. He held me all night long and slept like a baby."

"Oh, Mom," Grace sighed. "It's the little things, isn't it?"

"Five months ago, I would have laughed if you said I'd celebrate Rex dressing himself or putting a dish in the sink," she said. "Today, I feel like it's a major victory for the team and I'm the coach."

"Indeed you are," Rose said, reaching for her again. "He's so lucky to have you." Her voice cracked a little and they all hugged again.

"Oh, I hear him calling me. I better go." With that, her mother slipped away to go check out the staging.

"Hang on a sec," Rose said, snagging Grace's arm before she could follow. "I need an Isaiah update."

"No update," Grace said. "He took Nikki Lou to her program—"

"What date are we on now?"

Grace shrugged. "Three or four, I suppose. He came over a little later last night, after the inn went quiet for the evening and we..."

"Yes?"

"Talked," she said.

"And that's all?"

Grace swallowed. "There might have been a good-night kiss. Very brief, very...not kissy."

Rose gave a soft laugh. "I don't know what that means, but...do you like him? And don't you dare say, 'There's nothing not to like.'"

"There's nothing to report, Rose. If and when something happens, I'll let you know. Right now, we're friends."

"Who kiss," Rose added.

"Our lips barely brushed."

"Also known as a kiss," Rose teased.

"Mostly we talk and share things and simply...be. Is that good?"

"Good?" Rose's brows shot up. "You just described what makes a great marriage."

Grace recoiled. "*Marriage*? We went from five loosely defined dates to..." She couldn't even say the word.

"You're the one who said he wouldn't be casual, Grace. You're either on your way there, or you're not."

"Well, I'm...not."

Rose gave a skeptical look, but let it drop, heading to the back toward the chatter and laughter.

Marriage? Grace stood still, trying to process the word, the concept, the very possibility.

Yes, she had feelings for Isaiah, but were they... forever feelings? She didn't understand them, but they were real.

Were her feelings for him...physical? Was it because she was so lonely? Was it because he was so awesome with Nikki Lou? And was this all disloyal to Nick? She just didn't know, and now wasn't the time to figure it out.

Sighing, she joined the others to find Dad already seated under two lighting umbrellas like he was literally on the beach.

"All right, now, let's try some more." Mel stood on a stepstool above Dad, two other cameras hanging around her neck. "Lift the book a few inches, Rex, so we can easily read the cover."

Dad obliged, throwing a victorious look at Kenzie's camera. "Rocksteady, am I not?"

"You're a beast, Grandpa," she agreed.

"Look serious," Mel called.

He did his best to wipe away his smile, frowning toward the camera.

"Not like you hate the book," Finn joked. "But you probably did. It looks...bad."

That cracked everyone up, including Dad, who looked toward the ceiling and laughed from his belly.

"And that," Mel said as she snapped away, "is the money shot."

"Well, it better be on the right," Dad said. "That's my good side."

"They're both good," Susannah chimed in, her eyes bright as she looked on.

"I love you, too, Susannah Wingate," he called, his words as clear as Grace could remember them since the stroke.

They took a few more pictures and repositioned Dad a couple of times, but like every other photo shoot Rose had managed for this calendar, it was over and done in no time. Just thinking about that made Grace's heart swell with love for her sister, who'd taken the reins on this project and saved Grace oodles of time, energy, and stress.

As they finished, Grace put her arm around Rose's waist and eased them both closer to Susannah, who leaned against a bookshelf, her gaze squarely on Rex, her smile crinkling her eyes.

"You look happy," Grace whispered.

"I am, honey," Susannah replied. "How can I not be? Look at him. Look at this family and this life. We've been blessed for forty years. In fact, our anniversary is coming up in November."

"Indeed it is!" Rose exclaimed. "What a milestone. What are you guys going to do?"

"I'm working on something but it's too soon to say. I have to be sure he's strong enough, but I'll let you know."

"Honestly, I'm in awe of you, Mom," Grace said, just as she heard a familiar deep voice from the front of the store and some very happy barking. "Oh, Isaiah's here!"

"Speaking of people she's in awe of," Rose teased.

"Rose!"

"Really?" Her mother's eyes widened to big blue saucers. "Grace, really? Are you—"

"No. Yes. I don't know." She dropped her head back. "Also, I hate this much attention on me and you know it."

"From your mother and sister?" Rose asked. "We just want to know, because we love you. And we want you to be as happy as we are. Right, Suze?"

Grace turned to her mother, who, once again, had misty eyes, although this time it was for a different reason. "Mom, what?"

"She's right. All a mother wants is for her child to be happy. You know that."

"I do, and...I am." But even as she said it, she heard the uncertainty in the two words.

They heard Isaiah laugh, then the low rumble of his voice as he talked to someone, and all the feelings rose up in Grace again.

"He's a good man," her mother whispered. "And he's doing a great job managing Wingate House."

Grace wasn't sure how to respond to that. Yes, Isaiah was a great guy. He was strong and faithful and steady and warm and...not Nick.

"I know," she said weakly.

"And he's crazy about you," Rose added. "And Nikki Lou."

"There's the man of the hour!" Isaiah's voice carried through the bookstore. "Hello, Mr. Wingate. You are looking dapper, sir. Not sure that photographer is going to like taking my picture after you."

The three of them exchanged a look.

"And your father really likes him," Mom added.

Grace sighed. Her father had *adored* Nick.

She just nodded with a sad smile. "We'll see what happens," she said, as vague as she could be just before she stepped away, turning the corner to see Isaiah taking the leash off Slinky, a Starbucks cup in his other hand.

Before he saw her, she took one second to ground herself and see him for the wonderful man he was.

"How did it go?" she asked. "Everything okay with Nikki Lou?"

"Easy as pie," he assured her. "Nikki Lou's tears dried up before we were off Wingate Way, and she was very happy to get to the 'place where she plays,' as she called Dr. Alberino's studio."

"Oh, that's good."

"And I stopped at Starbucks and got Slinky something called a puppuccino." He handed her the to-go cup with a flourish and a little bow. "And someone's favorite flat white espresso to get her through the day."

"Oh, thank you!" She took the cup and their fingers brushed, giving her a wee bit of a jolt and making her wonder if he felt the same thing.

He glanced around. "Looks like you're making progress on the photo shoot."

"We are," she told him. "And Rose has you up next. I hope you don't mind—I pulled a gorgeous leather-bound copy of the Bible for you. It should look downright, well, divine in pictures."

That made Isaiah laugh. "And I have March, right?"

"Rose said Easter's at the end of March next year," she told him, then glanced over her shoulder toward the noise and laughter, her conversation with Rose still fresh in her mind. When she turned back, he was studying her face.

"You doing okay?" Isaiah asked, always so intuitive about her feelings.

"I'm not sure," she admitted.

"Would you like to talk about it?"

She looked up at him, considering the question. "Yes," she said softly. "At some point, we should."

She could have sworn she saw that glimmer of trepidation in his eyes again. Probably because he knew his only flaw was that...he wasn't Nick.

And nothing was ever going to change that.

NIKKI LOU WAS sound asleep in her car seat by the time Grace pulled up to the small parking area behind the bookstore later that afternoon.

"I feel you, darling," Grace muttered as she parked and glanced in the rearview mirror to study her daughter's sweet, sleeping expression. "We had three photo shoots, way too many people, and a lot of confusion in my heart today."

She exhaled noisily, still struggling with the conversation she'd had with Rose. She could feel things getting more serious with Isaiah—everyone could—but she had to tell him that not only was she not ready now, she most likely would never be.

But even as she had the thought, something in her heart shifted.

Could she be ready? Now? Ever?

She mulled it over all day until the photo shoots were over and everyone left, leaving Grace barely enough time to hand things over to her manager and make this trek back and forth from Dr. Alberino's studio.

After parking, Grace opened the back door and unlatched Nikki's carseat belt, reaching in to try and lift her out without waking her.

"You need some help?"

She stilled, letting just the sound of Isaiah's voice send a thrill she didn't understand from head to toe.

"You do show up like an angel when I need you most," she said, easing out of the car to let him take over. "First coffee, now this."

"My guess is she's asleep and that makes her the weight of a sack of potatoes."

"Your guess is right."

In one smooth move, he lifted Nikki Lou from the seat. He tucked her against his shoulder and nodded to the back door, a private entrance that led directly upstairs to the apartment.

"Are you done at the inn?" she asked.

"For the time being. I wanted to swing by and see

how Nikki Lou did today, since I dropped her off. I felt invested in a great day."

Grace smiled, knowing he was officially concocting reasons for coming over here to see her. He didn't have to do that, but she liked that he cared.

He went ahead up the stairs, giving Grace an opportunity to look up at Nikki's sleeping expression, her head hanging over his broad shoulder. She turned her head from one side to the other, and her lashes fluttered as they neared the top.

From inside, Slinky barked happily at their arrival, and Grace braced for a noisy awakening. Her daughter's blue eyes opened and tried to focus, but all she did was stare at Grace for a few seconds. Her tiny hands fisted Isaiah's shirt and she shuddered a sleepy sigh.

"Zayah," she muttered, and Grace nearly fell backwards down the steps.

Well, her daughter had no issues with falling for this man, that much was certain.

Isaiah patted Nikki Lou's back and murmured something comforting, putting the child right back to sleep.

"You're truly a miracle worker," Grace whispered as she unlocked the back door.

"Hardly. Her room or the living room sofa? Where does the nap continue?"

"Just lay her down in the living room," Grace said. "I'll keep an eye on her while I get something ready for dinner."

"You want me to do that?" he asked as he walked through the kitchen, sidestepping the little dog, who jumped in greeting, taking Nikki Lou to the living room sofa. "She loves my Panko-crusted chicken and it's on Dr. A's approved list."

"Oh, Zayah," Grace sighed, grabbing a treat from the bowl and crouching down to pet the dog she was already used to having. "You've done so much for us."

"Never enough for you, Grace."

The words touched—and terrified—her. Silent, she watched him tenderly place Nikki Lou on the sofa and reach for her beloved pink blanket. As he covered her and adjusted the blinds to shade her face from the late afternoon sun, Grace could feel the lump in her throat growing by the second.

"Why are you so wonderful?" she asked on a raspy whisper, not even sure if he heard her and kind of hoping he didn't.

But he turned and smiled, the readjusted light now highlighting the strong features of his face and the spark in his dark eyes. "I take it that's a rhetorical question," he teased.

She smiled and shook her head, exhaustion pressing down hard enough that she buckled into one of the two chairs across from the sofa, watching Slinky leap onto the sofa and snuggle next to Nikki Lou.

"I guess," she agreed. "Because there really isn't an answer, which I think is the definition of a rhetorical question. But you are wonderful and I find myself wondering...why. But I think I know."

He looked at her expectantly, waiting for her to explain.

"God made you that way."

"Now we're talking my language." Smiling, he took a deep breath and exhaled it as he took the other chair, close enough that they could whisper and even hold hands. The thought made her heart stutter because...she wouldn't hate that.

But she should, right? She shouldn't be feeling these things. She swore to herself the day she accepted that trifold flag that lay over Nick's casket that she'd never ever feel anything for anyone else.

Her gaze shifted to that prized possession, next to Nick's framed picture.

"She looks so much like him," Isaiah said, making Grace realize he'd followed her gaze.

"So much," she agreed. "Just as stubborn and with the same weakness for sweets."

He reached his hand over to take hers, the move so natural she couldn't do anything but let him.

"You said you wanted to talk to me today. What's on your mind, Amazing Grace?"

For a few seconds, she couldn't speak. Frankly, she couldn't think beyond the fact that their fingers were touching and his hand was so warm and strong and dependable and, yeah, wonderful.

"Why have you never married, Isaiah?" The question tumbled out and she felt her cheeks warm for having asked it so bluntly, but she realized just how much she wanted to know.

"I haven't found the right person," he answered without hesitation. "I joined the military, did multiple tours, traveled the world, and then came back and took care of my mother until she passed. I'm only forty, you know. Not ancient." He gave a rumbly laugh and let go of her hand to swipe his bald head. "Don't be fooled by the dome. I'm still young."

She smiled at that, looking hard at his face and, yes, shaved head. On him, the look was commanding and attractive, one he carried off with ease.

"I know you are, but..." She realized she better have a darn good reason for having asked such a personal question. "You're so good with kids," she said, grateful when that popped into her head. "I'm surprised you haven't married and had a few of your own."

"I've certainly prayed for that," he confessed. "But the good Lord hasn't seen fit to answer that prayer...yet."

She didn't imagine the pause and hesitation on that last word, and it made her chest tighten.

"Was that what you wanted my opinion on, Grace? My marital status?"

She searched his face again, as much for the sheer pleasure of looking at him as the need to find the right words. With Isaiah, the right words were always...the honest ones.

But how honest could she be?

"In a way." She gnawed on her lower lip. "You're not like anyone I've ever met."

"Because everyone is unique," he replied, unfazed. "Kind of makes you in awe of God, doesn't it? What an imagination He has."

She nodded, but his point brought up another question. "Is that what you're looking for?" she asked. "A woman with a faith as strong as yours?"

He thought about it as some seconds ticked by, and she realized she was holding her breath. If he said yes, this was all moot. If he said no...

"No," he finally said.

She let out a noisy sigh, making him laugh softly.

"Don't be nervous, Grace. Just tell me what's on your mind."

She waited a beat, not even sure where to start. The feelings she had tumbling around in her stomach? The fear? The worry? The sense that she was being disloyal, all compounded by a longing to...be with him. To kiss him and hold him and be part of his life.

The feelings were *all* so real. They were all so...

She forced herself not to look at Nick's picture.

"Are you looking for someone to convert?" she asked, grabbing onto the question that floated around her consciousness.

"I'm not *looking* for anyone," he replied. "I'm waiting patiently for the person the Lord sends me, if and when He wants me to have someone." He leaned a little closer, keeping his voice low and his gaze direct. "I trust God's timing in everything, Grace. I trust His plans, which are flawless."

She looked away, the words slicing a bit.

"I know it doesn't always seem that way," he continued. "And it didn't seem that way many times in my life. Not when I lost my mother, not when I lost...my way."

"I can't imagine you lost," she said.

He tipped his head. "I have been, but my feet found the right path, with...light."

"What happened?"

She could see him swallow. "War happened, Grace. An ugly war, with brutal consequences. When comrades die in your arms, when children are..." He shook his head, silencing himself.

"And you think all that is God's flawless plan?"

He lifted a shoulder. "You know what I say: His ways are far greater than ours."

None of that made sense to her, not one bit. Why didn't his religion make any sense? Did it matter to their future that he had such a deep faith and hers was shattered?

Wait. Did they have a *future*?

Rose's voice echoed in her memory. *Marriage.*

"I'm sorry to probe into your personal life," she said instead. "I'm just curious."

"It's fine. I'm flattered you care."

"That's the problem," she admitted. "I do care."

She expected him to look surprised, but he just gave that slow, Southern smile that warmed her right down to her soul.

"I know you do," he said softly. "I also know that caring scares the life out of you. That's why I'm taking this very, very slowly."

"This..." She bit her lip. "What is this?"

"Well, it's nice, for one thing. It's a connection I haven't felt in a long time. It's hopeful and good and... and...I really like you."

She tried to breathe, the words making her light-headed. "You do?"

He laughed again. "Why does that surprise you?"

"Because I'm so...unavailable."

"Oh, believe me, I know. I tried to have coffee with you and you practically had me arrested."

She laughed at that, remembering how many attempts he'd made to talk to her...all to do a good deed and return Nick's wedding ring.

She reached for the heavy piece of gold that hung around her neck, realizing with a start that she hadn't even thought about that ring for hours. Maybe days. And that was wrong.

"It's still there," he said. "Did you think you lost it?"

"I thought...I think..." She squeezed the ring. "I feel like if I let this happen, I'm being disloyal to him. Even cheating on him."

Isaiah nodded. "I suppose you do. You took those vows for life, Grace, which is one of the things I like so much about you. One of many."

She closed her eyes. "Don't."

"Don't tell you how much I like you?"

She didn't answer, because she wanted to hear it, she needed to hear it, but...Nick.

Very slowly, he inched forward in the chair, coming off the seat completely and dropping to one knee in front of her. He still held one of her hands in his, and pinned her with his ebony gaze.

"I like your inner peace, Grace, even if you don't realize you have it. I like that you're quiet, that you listen

to everyone. I like that you love your daughter fero-
ciously, and that you'd do anything for your family. I like
that you feel loyal to your late husband, and that you care
what he thinks, even though he's gone. I like how careful
you are, how considerate, and how gentle."

Each word tapped at her heart, breaking down walls,
getting closer to her. Was she all those things? He seemed
to think so.

"All that said," he whispered, "I can wait for you to be
certain, and if the answer is no, you aren't interested, then
I will bow out and respect that, too." He lifted her hand
to his lips and pressed a kiss on her knuckles. "And, no,
I'm not trying to convert you. I can't speak for Jesus,
though. He may be using me and all I can do is let Him."

She stared at him, breathless, as all of it—every word,
his touch, even his sweet, sweet gaze—washed over her.

"Zayah," she whispered, taking her other hand and
placing it on his cheek. "I'm so..." She wanted to say
scared, but right then, right that moment, she wasn't
afraid of anything. Except maybe losing him.

Without finishing, she leaned forward to kiss him,
closing her eyes, letting more bricks fall, forgetting everything. Everything. Even—

"Mommy!"

They jerked apart, whipping around to see Nikki
Lou scrambling off the sofa, her eyes wild, her arms
extended, her mouth open to take a breath so she could
yell again. She looked half-asleep and fully ready for an
epic meltdown.

"Mommy! *Mommy!*"

Instantly, Grace launched toward her, snagging Nikki's little body and pulling her close, but it did nothing to stop the tantrum that vibrated through her body. Was it because she saw them kissing? Had a bad dream? Got put over the edge from the program?

Grace had no idea and it didn't matter. She had to... think. But it was hard when Nikki Lou squirmed and kicked and screamed loudly in Grace's ear.

"Honey, please, stop. Please—"

"No! No! Mommy!" She shook her head, then her whole body, then howled again, utterly out of control. Grace tried to think—what were all those calming techniques? Why couldn't she remember a single thing?

"Nikki Lou, please, you have to—"

"*Nooo*—"

Suddenly, sound filled the room. No, not sound. Music. A chord. A loud piano chord, making Grace look over to see Isaiah at the keyboard.

What was he—

"*Amazing Grace, how sweet the sound,*" he bellowed. "*That saved a wretch like me.*"

Nikki Lou froze, staring at him, blinking, stunned into silence.

"*I once was lost, but now I'm found...*" He closed his eyes and belted it out. "*Was blind, but now I see!*"

Nikki Lou broke free, mesmerized, taking one step toward the piano that she'd never seen anyone play.

"*'Twas Grace that taught my heart to fear...*"

"That's your name, Mommy," she whispered. "Grace."

"Yes," Grace whispered the word as relief rocked her. "That's…"

Isaiah kept singing as Nikki Lou walked closer, like he was the Pied Piper and she couldn't resist the call. Silent, fascinated, she reached the piano bench and, without missing a note or a word, Isaiah inched over and she climbed up next to him. She stared at his hands, watching them move, her jaw loose as she listened.

"You want to play, Nik?" he asked between verses. "Or do you want to sing?"

Chills exploded all over Grace as she stood and walked closer, as drawn to this moment as Nikki Lou had been. In her heart, she sensed something was about to change, something was about to give, something—something important—was about to happen.

"I want to play," Nikki Lou whispered, putting her tiny fingers on the keys. "I want to make that sound."

His large, dark-skinned hand covered her much smaller one as he guided her hand up an octave on the keyboard. "You make your fingers do what mine do. Press the same key I do, only up there, two octaves higher."

He looked up at Grace, holding her gaze for a second, both of them silently communicating without saying a word.

Nikki's fingers moved over the piano keys. Not banging like she usually did, but smooth, like Isaiah. He played three notes, she matched them. He played five, she matched again. He played what had to be a few bars of music, and she matched every one.

Grace reeled, trying to process what was happening

as Nikki continued to mimic his movements. Had he just found Nikki's *island of genius?*

"*And grace will lead me home,*" Isaiah sang, ending the verse with so much power, her knees nearly buckled.

She brought her fingers to her lips, remembering the kiss, her lips still warm. She lifted her gaze and met Nick's as his picture looked down at her from the shelf.

Oh, Nick, can I do this? Can I possibly fall in love again?

Nikki Lou let out a happy giggle, her eyes bright and clear. "Mommy!" she exclaimed. "I can do it."

"Yes, baby," she whispered. "Yes, you can."

Maybe...they both could.

Chapter Fifteen

Raina

The Sanctuary was magnificent, with a thoughtful design, magnificent light, and potential for days. In every way, the beachfront house was even better inside than Raina had imagined.

The owner wasn't bad, either, she thought as she spied Chase Madison on the phone in a spacious first-floor guest suite that only had a small single bed with a very old-fashioned chenille bedspread and a nightstand. The rest of the room looked like a rather hastily arranged workspace, with a simple Ikea desk and a chair.

He'd shown her around the downstairs, but had to take a call and suggested she roam the rest of the house, take pictures, and plan her listing strategy.

Blake would be here in a little while, coming in blind, since Raina had walked from her parents' house and didn't park a car out front. She felt a tad guilty for the entrapment, but Chase had assured her that this was an ideal solution for her inability to find Blake.

She meandered the spacious kitchen, which was

really top-notch, with a six-burner stove and massive prep island and a sunny eat-in area, all lined with French doors that led to the deck. As she went out there, she practiced what might be her opening salvo when she saw Blake.

"I know you don't think we want to talk to you..."

No, no. She didn't know that at all. Maybe *he* didn't want to talk to any Wingates. Okay. She took a breath and looked out at the horizon, digging for the heart of what she wanted to say to the young man.

"You're family, Blake. We're blood. I'm your aunt. That *matters*."

But did it matter to him? What had he said about reading an article featuring Raina in a real estate magazine, and then tracking her down? Why didn't she pay closer attention when he told her that convoluted story about what brought him to Amelia Island?

What brought him was Rex Wingate—the very *family* that Blake and his father had somehow uncovered. So maybe family *did* matter to him.

Which left one more question, and she pondered how to phrase that as she walked back inside and made her way to the front living area.

"Why did you run after saving me and never come back?" she asked, studying her own reflection in a hallway mirror. Clearly he had some issue with his father hitting Rex up for money, but enough to run away?

From the guest suite, he heard Chase's low voice and remembered this was still a house viewing for a listing, and she hadn't even been upstairs yet. So she slipped to the stairway, climbing up to the second floor, where there were three more bedrooms and a loft for games and gathering.

This house was much smaller than Dad and Suze's beach house, and not decorated with Susannah's impeccable design sense. But the layout was amazing, including the main suite behind a set of double doors.

Stepping through them, Raina put her hand on her chest as she took in the commanding view of the ocean through wide-open balcony doors that allowed the warm breeze to flutter her hair. There was a king-size four-poster with a sheer canopy, giving everything a tropical West Indies feel.

Her gaze slipped to a discarded T-shirt on a chair in the sitting area, a pair of large sneakers on the floor. She realized with a start that Chase must be sleeping in here, which gave her an unexpected quiver of...awareness. This was a private area and she should...

She swallowed. *Not* exploring the main suite would be far weirder than if she did. She wasn't touring in any capacity except as a real estate agent, who wouldn't be worth her salt if she didn't check out the full space.

She continued in, taking in a bay window where plush swivel chairs faced each other, then out to a smaller upper deck with an unobstructed and breathtaking ocean view.

Someone sleeping in that king bed would look straight out to the sunrise every morning. A longing hit Raina so hard she felt it in her gut.

Why did she feel this way? Why did she have such a visceral...

Oh. Of *course*. Raina felt home vibes. She wanted to live here. This didn't happen that often as a Realtor who toured homes for a living, but every once in a while, a house, she believed, would call out to a potential buyer and...well, claim ownership.

Then the house owned you as much as you owned the house.

Raina thought of that as a "home vibe" and had the happy opportunity to see it happen for a few of her clients when she showed them a property. But she'd never felt it herself.

Until now.

Oh, she'd wandered through the Coral Gables house and felt something like that, but only long after moving in and making the place her own. But she'd never walked into someone else's home and felt...claimed.

Good heavens, she ached to *live* here.

Taking a breath to tamp down the overwhelming feeling, she stepped into the ensuite bathroom, which was no less charming and welcoming. No sleek marble, no wet room with a standing tub, no modern tile choices. This bathroom had a shiplap ceiling and old school black and white hexagons on the floor.

There was a huge tub under a picture window overlooking the water. A perfect size for...two little toddlers who would splish-splash with a rubber ducky and giggle when she soaped up their hair into crazy styles.

She let out a whimper at the mental image, which came out of nowhere but really knocked her for a loop.

"You don't like the ensuite?" Chase's voice was close, just outside the bathroom.

"On the contrary," she said. "I love it. I love it so much I'm imagining myself..." No, she couldn't say that. "Selling the heck out of it," she finished.

She stepped out to find him on one of the chairs near the bay window, his long legs crossed at the ankles, his hands locked behind his head. The pose of a man totally comfortable in his own skin, with nothing to prove and the slightest smile of amusement lifting his lips.

"Please do sell it," he said. "The market is rock-solid, so I'm hoping to have an offer as soon as possible."

"You will." She took a few steps, sitting across from him in the other chair. "In fact, the market is so solid, I'm surprised you don't want to just hang on to it as a rental. This stunning home could be occupied year-round."

He shrugged. "I want to sell it. The hotel I'm building will be finished soon and I won't have to be here for long stretches."

"Where do you live? I mean, when you're not here."

He shrugged, as if the question didn't apply to him. "I have a place in New York that I guess is officially home. But I own properties all over the country, all vacation rentals, so I stay at my own places when I can."

"You sell when the market's strong and buy when it's soft," she assumed, knowing someone in his business could make a killing like that. It was like flipping, only the houses were rented and all expenses covered, especially if they were in highly desirable tourist destinations.

"Usually. This one?" Once again, he lifted a shoulder, seeming to be purposely vague. "I won't need to be here much longer."

She looked around, her gaze flickering over the bed and the view of the ocean. "This is a very special home," she said softly. "There's a lovely...vibe."

He smiled as if she'd said something he really liked, then studied her, his gaze direct and unnerving. "You want to buy it, don't you?"

She laughed, not surprised she couldn't hide her reaction. The right house could do that to a person. "I'm just not in the financial position to buy a house like this, at least not now. But if I could..." She inhaled and let out her breath with the biggest smile. "I'd pretty much say I died and went to heaven."

His eyes danced as he regarded her like she amused him. "Did you see the rooms down the hall? Perfect for a nursery...or two."

She sighed at the thought.

"Walking distance from their grandparents? The beach for a backyard? That guest suite downstairs has its own entrance, and did you see there's a laundry upstairs?"

She dropped her head back with a frustrated grunt. "Stop. You're killing me."

He laughed. "I hate to see someone want something so much and not get it."

"Well, I do and I can't. Not now, anyway."

He looked at her for a second, quiet, then his smile widened with genuine warmth. "You must be pretty stoked to be having twins."

"Stoked?" She laughed, not even knowing where to begin. "I'm over—overwhelmed, over the moon, overcome with emotion, and every other 'over' I could be, including tired, but that's improved now."

"I'm happy for you, Raina," he said, his voice low and real. "You deserve that."

"Thank you," she said, truly sensing the sentiment was real, not just a platitude. "Do you have kids?" she asked, remembering the two divorces but no mention of children.

He shook his head. "Nope. Just…a thriving business, though that's hardly a substitute." He flipped his hand to look at his phone. "It's Go Time, Raina."

"Blake's here?"

He nodded and stood, offering his hand to her. "You look a little nervous. You want some backup or would you like to talk to him alone?"

"Oh…" She looked at his hand. It would be rude not to…take it. She let their fingers brush for a second as she stood, then released the touch. "I guess I'll talk to him alone, if you don't mind."

He nodded as the doorbell rang. "You can answer the door," he said. "I'll be outside on the back deck to give you privacy."

Giving him a grateful smile, she walked downstairs, steadying herself as he went out to the deck. After Chase left, she walked to the front of the house, said one more silent prayer, and pulled the door open.

Instantly, the smile Blake wore disappeared, along with the color in his face when he hissed in a breath.

"Seriously, Raina?" He took a step backwards, but she reached for him.

"Please. Please, don't run off again, Blake."

He stared at her, giving her a chance to really look at him for the first time since she'd learned they were related. Was it her imagination that his hair was the same caramel color as that of her sister, Sadie? His hazel eyes the same as Tori's? And that was a Wingate nose if she'd ever seen one.

"I didn't poach the listing," he said, as the color returned to his cheeks—which had that distinct cheekbone structure that had made three previous generations of Wingate men so handsome. "The owner told me—"

"No, no," she insisted. "I don't care about the listing. I..." She let out a breath it felt like she'd been holding since the doorbell rang. "I just want to talk to you."

Silent, he waited, but she could practically feel how badly he wanted to bolt. Why? Why did he want to run away from family?

She'd start with the easy stuff.

Putting a hand on her stomach, she offered a slight smile. "First of all, I wanted to say thank you. I can't even put into words...you saved these babies, Blake."

He started to respond, then froze, blinking and giving his head a shake. "Babies? With an S?"

"I'm having twins."

"Oh...wow. That's...great." He swallowed as if he had to work not to beam at her. That made sense, considering he was a naturally enthusiastic—sometimes to a fault—person. "I'm glad to hear that. But I'll...um..." He took that step backwards. "Let you manage this listing."

"Blake, please don't leave. We have so much to say to each other. I know...who you are."

His eyes flickered, then closed.

"We found a picture of your father as a baby when we cleaned out Doreen Parrish's apartment at our inn. We put it all together. Doreen had my father's baby fifty-five years ago, and that baby is your father, Bradley Young."

He started to respond then shut his mouth, a question in his eyes.

"He's also my half-brother. So, you're my nephew." She reached a hand toward him. "I'm your aunt, Blake. But I guess you knew that all along, didn't you?"

He inhaled so deeply it made his nostrils quiver but still didn't take her hand.

"What did Rex say when you told him?" he asked quietly.

"We haven't, because—"

"Then don't. Please, save me the horror of having yet another man in my life recoil in disgust when he finds out—"

"Stop!" She refused to let him finish that. "You surely know Rex Wingate better than that, Blake. You worked for him."

"Not long enough to know."

"You worked for me."

His shoulders sagged and suddenly he looked very young to Raina. He might be twenty-six or -seven, but he was a boy, really. A boy who so desperately needed a family. Why was he fighting this?

"I don't work for you anymore, Raina," he said, "so I shouldn't be at this client listing. Good luck with the babies and the business."

He pivoted and started to walk but she charged forward and snagged his arm. "Please, Blake. Why are you running? Why did you disappear?"

He almost rolled his eyes. "As if you don't know."

"I *don't* know," she insisted. "But if you can't give the family a chance to get to know you—as one of us—then you haven't been studying the Wingates as well as you think you have."

His eyes shuttered as he rooted for a response. "Raina, I'm sure you and your sisters are cool. Maybe even Susannah. But Rex is my *grandfather*. He's a generation older than my own father, who cannot handle the person I am. I should never have pursued the job."

"With Rex? Why not?"

"Because I may have been the one to lead my father straight to Rex. I found the connection first and told my dad, who was mad when I told him his biological parents' names. But when I left town and told him where I'd gone, he figured out I'd gone to find Rex."

"Which was a good thing," she insisted.

"No, because my scummy father realized he had a

wealthy biological father who might feel guilty enough to part with cash. And he was right."

"So that's how he found Rex, but you didn't encourage him to ask for that money, which apparently he really needed to save the family farm."

He snorted. "Not *that* much money. When he found out Rex had a stroke, he emptied an account that was supposed to be for an emergency. I didn't know any of that, of course, but when you told me and I realized that night what happened..." He let out a noisy sigh. "I only stayed long enough to help you out and then I just couldn't face any of you. I'm so ashamed that my father took advantage of Rex."

"*You* didn't take advantage of him, or any of us," she insisted. "Why would my father have an issue with you?"

He shot her a *get real* look. "Once he knows I'm the son of such a user, he'll hate me. Rex deserves better than to have his soft heart used by that...that...I don't know what to call my father except a monster."

Raina's heart folded at the words, which only made her like him more. "What Rex deserves, Blake, is a chance for you to look him in the eye and tell him you are his grandson," she said softly. "Will you do that?"

He squeezed his eyes shut and, after a moment, he swallowed and gave a harsh negative shake of the head. "No. And I am begging you not to, either."

"Why?"

"Because I don't want to kill anyone else."

She jerked back. "*What?*"

He closed his eyes on an unsteady breath. "I went to

see my grand...Doreen Parrish. I told her I was her long-lost grandson." He shuddered. "She had a heart attack that afternoon and died."

"Blake, you can't think—"

"Oh, yes, I can. I might as well have strangled her with my own two hands."

"A little dramatic, but I can see why you'd carry guilt," she conceded. "Don't. If she died of anything, it was because her heart was made of ice. That's not your fault."

"And you know what caused Rex's stroke! My father showing up, I'm sure. What could happen if he finds out I'm his grandson? I'm not going to be responsible for another stroke."

"You won't be," she said, wishing she could grab him by the shoulders and shake just a tiny bit of common sense into the kid. "Rex lives for family. He loves all of us and he'll love you, too. We all will! Why can't you give us that chance?"

"You really surprised me the most, Raina," he said, searching her face as if he were looking at her for the first time, too. "I expected you to be so...hardened. Edgy and businesslike. But you're quite sweet and noble and..." His voice cracked and he shook his head to fight the emotion. "I just can't... Too much risk. Goodbye, Raina."

As he walked away, a movement in Raina's peripheral vision caught her attention and she turned to see Chase coming around the side of the house.

"Everything okay?" he called.

Blake froze mid-step, looking at him. "Yes, thank you,

sir," he said. "Your listing is in great hands with Raina and Wingate Properties." With that, he turned and hustled toward his car.

Raina pressed her hand to her mouth to keep from calling out, and squeezed her whole body to stay rooted and not run after him. He couldn't leave! He couldn't miss this chance to have a family! She had to keep him here. But how?

And then she knew.

"Wait, Blake, please."

He kept walking.

"I'm not taking this listing. It's yours."

Then he stopped and slowly turned to her.

"I'm serious. This is your listing." She looked at Chase. "With my blessing, please give it to him. He'll do a great job, I'm sure. And it will be a terrific start for him. I want him to have it. Please."

"Raina, that's not—"

She held up her hand to stop Blake. "Please. Consider it my thank-you for...the babies." And, she thought, a way to keep him on this island and give her family a chance. "I'm backing out."

Without waiting for any response, she turned and darted through the front door, closing it so she didn't hear their discussion. Inside, she glanced in that hall mirror again, not surprised she was pale and her lower lip was trembling.

She grabbed her bag from the coffee table and hurried out the back doors to the beach. She just needed to get...well, not *home*. Her parents' house wasn't home, but...

She stole one more look at the precious cedar shake siding and the mullioned windows of a property that called her name.

Someone would be very happy in her house. Someone else, just not Raina and her babies.

Chapter Sixteen

Rose

Just as she pulled into the beach house's driveway, Rose caught a glimpse of Raina marching up the sand toward the house. Even from this distance, she could see something was wrong.

And that meant the meeting with Blake didn't go well.

She parked quickly and darted down the side of the house to head her off before she went inside.

"Hey, Raindrop!"

Raina paused and her shoulders sank in what looked like relief. They met on the dune behind the house, where Raina basically fell into Rose's outstretched arms.

For a moment, they didn't say anything, then Rose guided her to the side stairs that led up to the deck, and they stood under those in the shade while Raina unloaded everything that had happened.

With each statement, Rose's heart broke more.

"He doesn't even want to give Dad a chance?" Rose asked, not getting that.

Raina shook her head. "But I'm not willing to give up,

Rose. I'll give him some time, and hope that getting this listing keeps him around."

"But the house will sell fast."

"So fast," Raina agreed. "So, what are you doing here?"

"Treasure hunting," she said, lifting the necklace she'd taken to wearing. "I am biting the bullet and asking Dad if he knows where the other half of this is."

Raina lifted her brows. "You want backup?"

"So much." Rose put her arm around her. "You sure you're okay?"

"I'm fine. You sure you want to ask him about this?"

Rose sighed and leaned into her sister. "I do," she said. "I've given it a lot of thought, and I do believe that we've danced around the subject of our mother for forty-odd years. We all love Suze, that isn't up for discussion. But I need to know more about her, Raina. Don't you?"

She nodded slowly. "I understand the feeling, but..." She blew out a breath and looked over her shoulder. "One lost family member at a time."

"You want to skip this conversation?"

"No, I'll come with you. I want to gauge Dad's mood and think about the best way to go forward with the Blake situation."

"The timing is good," Rose said. "Suze is out and Dad should be finished with speech therapy any minute. I'm here to hang with him until Suze gets back."

Still arm-in-arm, they walked in on the lower level and immediately heard Dad laughing, giving them reason to share a happy look as they stepped through the slider into his domain of a remade family room, now a rehab center.

"Hey, Daddio," they said in unison, making him turn at the favored nickname.

"Well, there are my matching girls," he said, beaming at them or maybe proud of his clear speech. "Have you met the twins, Corbin?" he asked a man who was packing up a laptop.

The gentleman looked up from his task, beaming at them. "No, but I've heard of you. Part of Rex's therapy is to tell stories from the past. You two are some of his favorite topics."

They smiled at that, kissing their father hello, and making small talk until the therapist left. Then Dad made his way to his favorite chair—he still used a cane but sometimes Rose thought it might be a prop, now—and settled in for their visit.

"I knew Suze sent Rose over here to babysit, but I thought you'd be at work, Raina," Dad said, turning to her. "Everything good at Wingate? What's new? Any good listings?"

Rose saw Raina pale a bit. "It's all...you know. Same old-same old."

Dad started to frown, but Rose moved in to save her sister from having to give any details about the listing she'd just turned down.

"Can I talk to you about something before Suze gets home, Dad?" Rose interjected.

That got his attention. "Of course. Although I have no secrets from her." A smile pulled, still a little more natural on his right side than his left. "In fact, I have none at all anymore, which I'm happy about. None from any of you now that you know about my, uh, youthful indiscretion and the child I fathered."

"Dad, it's—"

"It's not fine, Raina," he said. "But it is what it is and I've made peace with it."

"That's good," Raina said softly, glancing at Rose. "Why don't you ask him about the necklace?"

"What necklace?" Dad looked from one to the other, intrigued.

Rose leaned forward. "Do you remember a lady—a girl back then—named Annabelle? She was friends with our mother, Charlotte, when they were teenagers."

He thought about that for a second, then made a face. "Maybe. She was a flirty thing that worked at the five-and-dime, if I recall."

"That's exactly who she was," Rose said.

"Hey, how 'bout that?" Dad scoffed, tapping his temple. "The old kidney's still working up there. Take that, ischemic stroke."

Rose gave a sad smile. "I'm sorry to say she passed away recently. She was Kitty Worthington's aunt."

"Sorry to hear that." He frowned at Rose. "Is this about the calendar? Do I have to reshoot or something?"

"No, Dad. It's about this necklace." She unlatched the chain around her neck and held it out. "Charlotte had the other half, with an *A* engraved on it, and I was wondering if you knew where it was."

He reached out and took the necklace, examining it

for a few seconds. "I've never seen anything like this in my life. Cheap, isn't it?"

"Sentimental value," Rose said.

He let it dangle, then shifted his dark gaze from the trinket to Rose. "Why does it matter?"

She drew back at the question, not sure how to take it or how to answer. "Because...it was our mother's."

"You want the other half, Raina? Not that I have it."

"I just want Rose to be happy, and this matters to her."

He nodded very slowly, letting the chain pool into his palm before he reached it out toward Rose. When she went to take it back, he snagged her hand and held it.

"Why does it matter, Rosie?" he asked again.

She searched his face, getting that old feeling that only Wingate girls knew...the sense that Dad was about to impart some wisdom, whether it was welcome or not.

"There comes a time," he said softly, "when you have to face your fears."

"My..." She shook her head. "I'm not afraid of anything, Dad, but I want—"

"But you are."

She glanced over her shoulder at Raina, so curious to see what she thought of this discussion. Her sister just lifted her brows and shrugged.

Dad chuckled. "Raina, do you know what Rose is afraid of?"

Raina leaned forward. "Not much, except maybe something happening to someone she loves."

"Everyone's afraid of that," Rose said, easing her

hand from Dad's without getting the necklace. "And I don't know what it has to do with an old junkie necklace from a craft fair in the 1960s."

"It has everything to do with it," he said, leaning back, looking a little too wise and so much like the Dad of old. "It all started one very sad day when you were first separated from your sister, then your mother."

Rose stared at him, then glanced at Raina again.

This time, she smiled. "Listen to him, Rosebud. A few months ago, he helped me deal with the guilt I felt because Charlotte died. And now, he's even speaking more clearly."

Rose didn't know if she meant his enunciation or his message, but she turned back to her father, not sure if she wanted to hear what he had to say. But she'd been a Wingate a long time, and Rex had never steered any of them wrong.

"What are you saying?" she asked.

"Remember, I've had a lot of time to sit in this room and think," he said. "And couldn't talk much for the better part of the first few months. So, I've been thinking about every one of you girls and the things that you face."

He opened his palm and looked at the necklace, quiet for a long time.

"You are afraid of being left, Rose."

She started to disagree, but then remembered kissing Gabe goodbye for his last shift. The low-key worry that always circled her heart when they parted, and the constant checking of his location on her phone—and her relief when he was at the station.

"I'm married to a firefighter," she said slowly, as much to herself as her father. "I think worrying about him is normal."

He lifted a shoulder. "I remember your worst meltdown as a little girl, far more serious than anything we've seen from our dear sweet Nikki Lou."

"What was it?" Rose asked, even though she wasn't sure she wanted to hear about it.

"The day they put you and Raina in different classrooms. Fifth grade? Maybe fourth? I can't remember, but Suze will. You wailed, you thrashed, you fought it and cried and threatened to never go to school a single day all year."

She laughed softly, the memory shockingly vivid. "I hated that they put us in different classes. Why would they do that?"

"Probably for your own good," Dad said. "You needed to learn to live life as a person, not a twin."

She turned to Raina, who had a bittersweet smile. "I remember it," she said. "I hate to tell you this, Rose, but I was glad of the change. I didn't want to be 'the twins' anymore."

Rose's heart hitched, but she laughed. "I guess I do hate to be abandoned."

"But once you realize it," Dad said, "you can deal with it. You shouldn't spiral into anxiety every time Gabe goes to work. Or look at your children and fear the day they'll leave the nest. Or go into a funk when Raina returns to Miami."

"I'm not going back, so there's one concern you can mark off your list," Raina said, trying to lighten the mood.

But the mood stayed heavy as Dad's words pressed on Rose's heart. "I do live with that fear," she said. "I never thought about it coming from birth."

He held out the necklace to her again. "Rosie, I've given you and your sisters all the jewelry, clothes, pictures, and mementos of Char. Sorry, but I don't have a necklace that would match this one."

"You have given us her things, but you never talk about *her*, Dad," Rose whispered. "I want to know what she was like. What made her tick. Why you married her and what kind of woman she was."

His eyes filled as he reached out both hands, the right toward Raina, but the left to Rose, and that one still shook a bit.

"Come here, my girls."

Without hesitation, they scooched next to him, on the floor, but close enough for him to reach down and put a hand on each of their shoulders.

"First of all, she was like no woman I'd ever met. So pretty it scared me to look right at her. What made her tick was...love and laughter. She was funny as heck—like Tori—and smart, like you, Raina, and so neat and organized like Maddie. But more than anything, she had the sunniest disposition." He looked down at Rose with tears in his eyes. "Just like you, dear Rose."

Rose closed her eyes and leaned closer, inhaling each word and memory, almost unable to get enough.

He talked about Charlotte until it was clear talking

was hard for him, then they both gave him teary, happy hugs and by the time Rose was on her way home, she felt like her whole world had shifted.

And when she walked into the house and saw Gabe sitting in the living room, staring straight ahead, with a beer in his hand—in the middle of the day?

Once more, she sensed a shift in the world that had, just this morning, been so steady.

"What's going on?" she asked, dropping her bag as she came closer to see the utter misery on his face. "Was there an accident? Did someone die? Did you get hurt at work?"

"Yeah, there was an accident," he said bitterly. "Jeremy accidentally got my promotion. I feel like I died. And, yeah, it hurt."

"Oh, Gabe." She dug into her repertoire of positivity, but right then, she couldn't think of a thing to make her husband feel better. "I'm sure you're devastated."

"Not as devastated as Chief Keating, 'cause he's down one man today and it's not going to be easy to replace me."

She gasped, shaking her head. "Excuse me?"

"I gave my notice, Rose."

"You...quit? Without even talking to me?"

"I don't need a second opinion. I was passed over for a promotion I deserved far more than Hutch, and I let my feelings be known." He took a slug of beer. "And now I'm going to figure out what I want to do with the rest of my life."

With four kids, the first less than three years from

college? With bills and life and medical insurance that he had as part of his job and she didn't? "And you didn't even consult me?"

"I'm sorry, babe. I just did what I had to do and counted on you being...well, being you. Please, Rose, I need you to support this decision." He regarded her, agony and confusion in his deep blue eyes. And Rose felt that old feeling of abandonment strangling her, like she... was losing him. "Of course," she said softly. "We'll figure it out."

At least she knew what her fears were now. But that didn't make them any easier to take.

Chapter Seventeen

Chloe

"Yikes," Hunter murmured as he pulled up to the mid-century modern ranch tucked in the arid, brown hills of Laurel Canyon. "Dumpy. I expected more."

Chloe threw him a look, suddenly remembering that few things were ever up to Hunter's standards. "I'm sure it's lovely inside."

"Well, it's as old as Woody himself and just as, uh, rustic." Hunter grinned at her exasperated expression. "Come on, Chloe. I'm kidding. It's Woody Renault's house! I expected to be impressed."

The home of the seventy-year-old film legend famous for his deadpan delivery and the ability to make an audience love a bad guy *was* a tad underwhelming but, whoa, loud. Even from the bottom of the driveway, where a valet took Hunter's keys, they could feel the music screaming from every open window.

Inside, it was insanely packed.

In fact, five minutes in and Chloe felt like she couldn't

breathe. Hunter, on the other hand, seemed energized by the crowd. He prowled like a lion from one end of the house to the other, smiling at strangers, nodding at celebrities, and generally looking like he completely belonged there.

"This is what I call a target-rich environment," Hunter whispered as they rounded a corner toward a sleek, contemporary kitchen. It was so loud, Chloe wasn't sure she heard him. Had he just quoted one of her father's favorite old movies, *Top Gun*?

"Is Tom Cruise here?" she asked.

"Nah, nah. I just mean…the beautiful people are out in droves. C'mon, let's go to the bar."

She peered around him at the crowded outdoor bar by the pool. "You go. I need to find my boss, who is close friends with Woody and expecting me to check in," she said.

He barely spared her a nod and zipped out toward the massive patio to join the bar crowd, while Chloe moved at a slower pace through the crowd again, scanning faces for her messy-haired producer, Rory Sutton, who had yet to say a word to her since the Coo Coo Cooper debacle.

But he hadn't taken her off this assignment, which she thought was a good sign, and she fully expected he'd have a lead—or a thread of one—when she found him. This time, she would not screw up.

"Wingate."

She spun at the sound of her name, spotting Rory standing next to none other than Woody himself, beckoning her over. Woody gave his signature goofy grin and ran his hand over thinning hair as he looked at her.

"Ah, the fresh meat from *A-List Access*," he said to her, extending a hand. "I'm Woody, but my friends call me Wood."

Rory laughed like that was hilarious. "Chloe Wingate, our latest hire."

She shook the offered hand and gave a tight smile, the one she used for men who looked at her exactly like he was. "Mr. Renault. An honor to meet you. Thank you for including me."

"Don't say honor," he quipped. "It makes me feel like a legend."

"Which you are."

"Another word for old," he said, dropping his gaze over her. "And when I look at a woman like you, I don't want to be old."

Too bad, you are, she thought with one more cool smile that she hoped sent a clear "back off" message to the old coot, who was almost the same age as her father. *Eww.*

She turned her attention to Rory, who'd stood back to observe the exchange.

"Did you have someone you wanted me to inter-view?" she asked.

"What am I?" Woody choked, clearly not getting the message. "Chopped liver?"

"You are the host," she said smoothly. "And far too busy to worry about media. Rory, you mentioned that I might chat with the stars of the new Hulu original series, *Immortal Agent?*"

He eyed her for a moment, then lifted his shoulder with disinterest. "Pia's at the bar. It's her job to hound these people. Go ask her."

"I'll do that," she said, shooting another smile to Woody. "And thank you again."

She slipped out before he could waylay her for whatever he wanted—certainly not an interview—and headed to the crowd around the patio bar. At least she'd checked in with her boss and done that duty.

Picking up snippets of conversation as she walked, she caught a glimpse of Hunter head to head and chatting seriously with a woman. She was older, maybe in her fifties, but Chloe had to give him props for not standing around waiting to be introduced to someone.

She was about to join him when she caught sight of Pia's long bangs and heavy eyeliner and knew she'd better go suck up to the woman, who was now Rory's assistant, to see if she had anyone in particular for Chloe to meet.

Pia was listening to a man talking so animatedly, he kept spilling his drink, so Chloe sort of hung back in the general direction of the young woman's gaze. If she looked up, Chloe could catch her eye.

No such luck. Chloe stood for at least five minutes, hot, uncomfortable, shifting from one leg to the other, brushing away imaginary strands of hair, wishing she were anywhere in the world other than Woody Renault's stupid party.

She glanced over at Hunter, hoping to snag him,

because he might be able to get Pia's attention, but now there were three women talking to Hunter, appearing fascinated by whatever he was telling them.

Probably about the Kardashian butt lift they all wanted.

She couldn't fault him for talking his business, but the exchange kind of gave her an ick factor she didn't like. He'd better not be selling plastic surgery to these people.

"Are you looking for me?" Pia's voice cut through her thoughts and brought her back to the present.

"Rory suggested I talk to you," she replied.

Pia said something to the man, then stepped closer to Chloe. "You might have missed it, but Beau Fitz came in with some Instagram influencer named Jacqueline A. Spoiler alert, Beau's still married to Gabrielle...what's-her-name."

Whatever it was, Chloe didn't know either. "Okay, so..."

"So go find out if he's getting a divorce and dating this new babe," Pia said with an air of impatience.

Chloe did her best not to make a face. Was this really news? Yes, on *A-List Access* it was.

"Will one of them give me an interview?" she asked.

"Do I look like a reporter?" Pia rolled her eyes. "That's your job and I already did half of it for you. Look, over there." She pointed to a couple talking in a small group, their arms around each other's waists, drinks in hand. The woman looked positively plastic from head to toe but Beau Fitz, a former child star from a sitcom, seemed to be unable to take his eyes off her.

"Go, get crackin'," Pia ordered like she was Rory Sutton herself.

Chloe nodded, took a breath, and walked over to join the small group, passing Hunter in the process.

"But isn't there a way to get the same thing without any downtime?" she heard one woman ask Hunter.

Chloe froze and threw him a look. Seriously?

He didn't even see her, because he was giving his card to another woman.

Okay, *okay*. She took a breath and moved on, because how could she blame him, but...

Was that why he'd wanted to come tonight? Were her Hollywood contacts the only reason he'd reached out to her in the first place? She glanced over her shoulder at him, just in time to catch him drawing an imaginary line down a woman's jawline.

Selling...a facelift. *Dang it all*, she realized with a thud. That *was* what he wanted from her—access to these women. He was on the bottom rung of the doctor ladder and probably had to drum up business.

Feeling all kinds of used, she made her way to the Influencer and the Has Been, chatted up both of them long enough to find out Has was indeed filing for divorce and his new girlfriend would be thrilled to do a segment on *A-List Access* next weekend talking about her new deal with Tarte Cosmetics.

Fine. A tart for Tarte. Probably not the story lead they'd let her use, though. Have to make the A-Listers look good, even if they were homewreckers.

With efficiency and very little emotional investment,

Chloe had a story lined up and would get the interview done in the next few days.

Now what?

She poked around the patio again, then looked for Hunter who was...oh, boy. Talking to Woody Renault and Rory Sutton. Making them laugh. Giving them a card.

Using her for admission into a club she didn't even want to be in.

Prickles of heat climbed up her spine and her throat tightened. All of a sudden, Chloe felt...like she was suffocating. Everything about this place was crowded and questionable and phony and she'd never fit less into an environment in her life.

"Chloe! Hey, babe, come on over." Hunter waved at her to join his little gang like he was the host of this party, not the movie star next to him. "I met your boss." He put a hand on Rory's shoulder. "Turns out we have a friend in common."

Planting a smile, Chloe walked toward them.

"And Rory's niece is looking for an in at my practice," he added as Chloe reached them.

"Oh, she's a doctor?" Chloe asked.

Rory snorted. "No, she's a freshman in college and wants a new nose. It's hard to get to any of the bigshots at this guy's group, but Hunter thinks he can help."

She managed not to slice him with a look. "That's nice," she said instead of what she was thinking, which wasn't so nice.

"So, you two..." Rory pointed from one to the other. "Married? Hooked up? Dating? What's the deal?"

"We're ex—"

"Friends," Hunter interjected. "Absolutely the best of friends, right, Chloe?"

Oh, brother. "The best," she agreed unenthusiastically.

"Have your niece call me, Rory," Hunter said, whipping out yet another business card. "Ask your star reporter here. Does anyone do a nose job like I do?"

"Did he do yours?" Woody asked.

She touched her nose. "Nope, mine came straight from the gene pool. Hunter, can I talk to you for a moment?"

His eyes flickered like he didn't like the interruption, but he excused himself and stepped away.

"Are you here just to drum up business?" she demanded.

"Uh, yeah." He looked like she'd asked the stupidest imaginable question.

"And is that the only reason?"

"I'm not here for the drinks." He held up an empty rocks glass. "Which are water and ice."

"I thought..." But she didn't have any words, because what did she think? That Hunter wanted to support her work and go to a party for *her*? That his interest in her job had anything to do with *her*? No, this man was always going to be at the top of his own agenda, and she should have known that.

"Chloe, I meant what I said."

"That we're the best of friends?"

"That this is a target-rich environment. Look, I won't last long at my practice if I don't bring in new clients. And there's nothing wrong with networking, babe."

She bristled at the endearment.

"That's what you're here to do," he continued. "And him, and her, and...whoa, that woman could use an upper eye bleph. Lower, too, if we're being honest."

She backed up, suddenly feeling like she might drown. "Hunter, I got my story lead. I'm going to get an Uber home."

"Okay," he said, without even a question as to why. "I'll text you."

Bad idea. Majorly bad idea bringing him. She pushed her way through the crowd, just making it to the door when a hand snagged her elbow and brought her to a halt.

"Where you going, Wingate?" The English accent sent a bolt of resentment through her, but she managed to stay cool and slide her elbow from Rory's grasp.

"Home."

"Not tonight you're not."

She took a step back. "No? Well, I'm not staying here."

"I just got a call from the studio. Brandon Monroe is...not ready for his live report in two hours. Apparently, he's high as a kite and making no sense. Someone has to go on the air and do *The Monroe Moment*."

She stared at him. "And..."

"And I need you to get your backside to the studio and do one minute live in his place."

And she stared at him some more. "On the topic of..."

"Whatever you scared up at this party, and I do not mean some slick plastic surgeon trying to change the world one boob job at a time. *Monroe Moment* is supposed to be a snapshot of America, through the lens of Hollywood."

What the heck did that even mean? She'd seen the segment once and it was lame.

"I didn't get much here, Rory," she confessed. "Just the former child star and the Instagram model he's cheating with."

Rory looked unimpressed. "Do better."

She choked softly. "Okay."

"Look, luv. Just get in your Uber, look out the window, and get inspired. Then do the *Monroe Moment* better than Monroe, and you can have the slot yourself. *The Wingate...Window.*"

She managed—somehow, it was *not* easy—not to roll her eyes.

He must have known it was ridiculous, because even he had to laugh. "Just get your pretty face in front of the camera, be charming, amusing, entertaining, and informative," Rory said. "Give the forty-five thousand losers who are stuck in their little worlds watching *A-List Access* something to take to bed tonight."

With that, he disappeared into the crowd, leaving Chloe with no idea what she was going to say live on national TV—okay, syndicated, but still—in less than two hours. Whatever she said, it would make or break her career in Hollywood.

At the moment, breaking it didn't seem like the worst thing she'd ever do.

No surprise, traffic was wretched, but that gave Chloe time to think and come up with...absolutely nothing. She shuddered out a sigh and grabbed her phone, looking to open her Notes app, because she'd jotted down story threads from the past few weeks.

Oh...she'd missed a text from Travis McCall.

"Look who we have here," she muttered as she opened the text. "Cute, cute Travis. I've missed you."

The note came with a picture of Travis similar to the one Rose had sent, complete with the hot firefighter T-shirt, a copy of Shakespeare's plays, and the sly smile of a man who had to know he was a grade-A snack.

But this version was much more polished and attached to a calendar showing the month of June, proclaiming him "A Midsummer Night's Dream."

She didn't know what surprised her more—how incredibly raw it made her feel to look at this man or how totally adorable the calendar had turned out.

She instantly texted back.

Well, I'll keep my calendar opened to that month all year! Is every month this awesome?

The response was so immediate, she almost laughed.

Travis McCall: *Chloe! It's been a minute. You like? And yes, Rose & co. did a great job. Talk?*

Should she? Chloe stared at the request and considered just how vulnerable she felt at that instant. Maybe it wasn't the best time to chat with him, since all she wanted to do was give up, run, and find her way into the arms of this sweet, sweet man.

She lifted her gaze to the bumper-to-bumper madhouse of the freeway. Cars as far as the eye could see, hills in the distance, homes on every square inch, and so many people. She was lost in L.A. Lost and alone and fighting for her own square inch and it was all so hard.

"I don't belong here," she whispered. "I don't want to be here."

"You know a better route?" the driver, a woman with short buzzed hair and a warm smile, asked.

"Not...home."

Except that dingy, bug-infested apartment in Northridge wasn't *home*.

"I thought I was taking you to an office in West Hollywood?"

"You are, thank you. It's fine. Take your route and I'll..." She looked at the phone. "I'll just make a call."

But if she made that call? It was going to change everything. Once she heard Travis's voice, once they laughed and talked and he heard how sad she was, they'd start things up and it would be *another* long-distance romance.

On a sigh, she forced herself to check email first—on

the off-chance Rory Sutton took her off the live assignment tonight—only to find an email Travis had just sent.

She clicked on it and read the message:

*You have to see the whole thing. It's a masterpiece.
(Not just June, LOL) Sad news about Gabe. Can't believe
he gave his notice. Really going to miss him. Not as much
as I miss you.*

xo

T

Gabe quit his job? Her heart leaped to her throat as
she realized life and family and all that was Wingate was
going on and she was nowhere near any of it. At least
when she lived in Jacksonville, she was less than an hour
away. But this? Three thousand miles?

She tapped the attached document he'd sent, which
was a digital version of The Year of Classics. One month
after another, one man after the next, each image was
perfection. It was such an original take on the "hot guys
reading" concept, showcasing the inside and outside of
the bookstore, making Fernandina Beach look like the
single most adorable small town in America.

Which, she fervently believed, it was.

By the time she got to December, which happened to
be Silas Struthers, the sweet older man who owned the
ice cream shop between Rose and Madeline's stores, she
was enchanted and homesick and sad. Silas was dressed
in flannel and sat in front of the fireplace in The Next
Chapter, which they'd decked out for Christmas, using
some of the Netflix movie leftovers.

He read *'Twas the Night Before Christmas*, and just

looking at the friend and neighbor she'd known for years made Chloe's heart ache. Rose had used the quote, "Merry Christmas to all and to all a good night!" for his month, and for some ungodly reason Chloe choked back a sob.

Over Silas! No, that's not what made her cry. She was homesick to the point of pain.

"We're almost there," the Uber driver assured her, clearly misinterpreting the tears. "Are you late? I'm taking surface streets to get you there in less than ten minutes, sweetie."

"It's fine, thank you." She swiped at a tear she didn't want to shed, flipping through the calendar again.

That was *home*, she thought glumly. These people and those places and that street and all the memories and hope and family and—

"Here you go," the driver said brightly. "And I don't know what's bugging you, sweetheart, but you want my advice?"

Chloe didn't, not at all, but she smiled and nodded.

"There's only one thing that matters in the end, kiddo."

Really? She got the failed philosophy major for an Uber driver? "What's that?" she asked as she gathered her bag and prepared to hustle inside and get this job done—whatever it was.

"Do what's right," the other woman said.

Chloe froze in the act of opening the car door, looking at her.

"What's right," the driver repeated. "If more people did that, this would be a better world."

"Amen, sister." On a sigh, Chloe climbed out and ran into the building, checking the time. She had a little more than an hour to craft a story, write notes, get visuals, and go live. At least she had decent hair and makeup from the party, so she could skip the salon.

All she had to do was...how had Rory described the live gig? *Give the forty-five thousand losers who are stuck in their little worlds watching* A-List Access *something to take to bed tonight.*

Suddenly, she had the answer. Exactly what any woman in America wanted to take to bed tonight. And in the process, she could do...what's right.

Chapter Eighteen

Grace

One by one, the dominoes fell on Grace that morning from the minute she woke up and found Nick's weirdo lamp lit in the living room to picking up the store phone to find twenty voicemails.

She ignored them all, but wondered if this early hour had her seeing things. Twenty messages? Just then, another message clicked in. Whatever was wrong, she didn't have time for it.

Nikki Lou had woken up in the middle of the night with a wretched head cold, making her upset and teary. Grace finally got her back to sleep exactly when it was time to get up, only Rose had Gabe's schedule wrong and she had to cover all the morning deliveries at the florist.

That meant Grace had to go alone to meet with Kitty today to present the final calendar and get the sign-off. But how could she? She couldn't leave Nikki and—

A tap on the front door got her attention and the sight of Isaiah outside gave her the official first smile of the day. Exactly the man she needed for help. And, if she knew

Isaiah, his help came with coffee. Except, didn't he have to supervise breakfast at the inn?

She hustled over and unlocked the door, greeted by his familiar, warm smile and a cup of her favorite flat white espresso.

"I don't know why or how you're here, but I am beyond grateful." Grace took the cup and glanced over his shoulder to see customers on the sidewalk who looked interested in coming into the store.

Not at nine in the morning, sorry. Behind her, she heard the phone on the main desk ringing again, but she ignored it, ushering him in.

"How were you able to leave the inn?" she asked.

"God put you on my heart this morning," he said simply, as though God routinely did things like that. But then, maybe He did for Isaiah. "I have the new house-keeper, you know? She's a gem in the kitchen and is covering breakfast." He frowned. "Are you okay?"

"Just frazzled. Nikki's got a cold—always the end of the world with her—but she's sound asleep now and I do not want to wake her and drag her out."

"Out where?"

"I have to go meet Kitty at the Riverfront Café to get final sign-off on the calendar," she told him. "And to make matters worse, Rose has a conflict and I have to do the deed on my own." She made a face. "Kitty scares me."

He laughed at that. "Not me. You want me to go for you? I can speak with authority as Mr. March."

"That won't fly, but thank you. Any chance you can stay here and keep an eye on Nikki? I have a monitor in case she wakes up. Slinky is with her, of course, and I did get him outside already." She reached under the front desk and pulled out a small speaker. "Or you can go hang in the apartment, since we don't officially open for over an hour. Whatever you like. I don't think this will take long, if you're willing."

He glanced at the monitor and around the store. "I can handle it. You go meet Kitty."

"Isaiah, how can I thank you?"

"First, drink your coffee."

She took a sip and moaned her gratitude.

Then he put his large, warm hand on her cheek, looking into her eyes. "Then say yes to a proper date with me."

"A...really?"

"Dinner, a movie, a walk along the water. Think we can get a sitter and arrange that?"

She nearly melted as a dozen emotions jumbled her insides. But not one of them was...doubt. Or fear. "I believe a date can be arranged, Mr. Kincaid."

He laughed and eased her closer. "We'll celebrate Kitty's approval of the calendar."

"God bless you." She put a hand on his shoulder for the pure pleasure of maintaining contact.

"You know what I'm going to say, right?" he asked.

"You'll say, 'He already has.'" She smiled at him, then inched back. "What did you mean when you said God put me on your heart?"

He lifted a shoulder. "I woke up thinking about you, which, I have to tell you, isn't unusual. But this morning,

I just had a sense that you needed...something. I prayed for you and God led me to one of my favorite scriptures, Philippians 4."

"There's something in your Bible about a single mom who can barely hold it together?"

"That's exactly what it is." At her look, he laughed. "It says, 'I can do all things through Christ, who strengthens me.' If that's not an inspirational scripture for someone who has to do the impossible, I don't know what is. Just keep saying it, Grace. 'I can do all things through Christ, who strengthens me.'"

"Well, if He can help me endure a meeting with Kitty Worthington, then He's a good God, indeed. Oh! Take a look at the final product." She slid a pile of calendars toward him, drinking her coffee while he looked through one. "Rose was so excited that she had twenty printed up. Hopefully, Kitty won't want a change."

"She won't. What time is your meeting?"

"Soon."

He gave her a nudge. "Run and don't worry about a thing here."

With a quick hug that she wished could last longer, she hurried out with her bag and one copy of the calendar, happily sipping her coffee on the way.

People still lingered outside the bookstore, but she'd let Isaiah handle early birds who were desperate to buy a book. She strode toward the café, her heart a thousand times lighter than just a few minutes ago.

What was that quote he'd shared?

She could do all things through...Isaiah, who... who...who... .

She slowed her step just before she reached the wharf and the café, sucking in a soft breath.

Who loved her.

He did, she realized. She could see it in his eyes, feel it in his touch, and knew it by his actions. That man loved her. She knew it like she knew her name, and...and...and she might just love him right back.

"You're late," Kitty said without getting up from the table near the window. "My time is valuable, too, Grace."

"Three minutes," she said on a laugh, so happy at that moment that not even Kitty's sour expression could dampen it. "Good morning to you, too, Kitty."

"Since you took the time to stop for coffee, just show me what you've got and it better be good." She reached for the calendar that Rose held back as she slid into the chair.

"It's better than good. I think it's amazing."

"What *I* think is what matters," Kitty said.

"Here you go." With a smile, Grace slid the calendar across the table then looked around for her niece, Kenzie, who usually worked breakfast with Tori. She didn't see any of the staff, but then Kitty made a clucking sound that stole her attention.

"What is it?" Grace asked.

"This is too..." She flipped to the next month. "I don't know."

"Too good? Too clever? Too perfect?" Grace scoffed. "Come on, Kitty. Even you have to see that this is a great calendar that promotes reading, our town, and twelve of Fernandina Beach's best men."

"There's going to be pushback." She flipped the page to October, where Gabe graced the top holding *The Adventures of Huckleberry Finn*. "Wasn't that book banned for racism or some such thing?"

Grace let out a sigh. "Kitty, please, you know this is good."

"I'm sorry. You're going to have to do at least half of these photo shoots again, and this time, use women. I've been thinking about this and maybe we shouldn't include only men. You know what this world is like. There could be so much...drama."

Was she serious?

"No," Grace said, sitting up straight, as if she'd just discovered her own backbone. And, whoa, that felt good. She could do all things. She *could*.

"Don't argue with me, Grace. You can't—"

"We can and we will," she said, staring Kitty down. "This is a work of art that will sell copies and we're not changing a thing. As a matter of fact, the first twenty are printed and we're going to sell—"

"Aunt Grace! Aunt Grace!" Kenzie's voice echoed through the restaurant as she came running closer, her phone extended. "Did you see Chloe's story? Did you?"

"I can't talk right now, Kenzie," she said, not wanting

to let this argument get derailed, because she was not going to lose. "Kitty, we are not—"

"But it's your calendar!" Kenzie exclaimed and pointed to the one in Kitty's hand. "It's a hit. It's a national hit, all because of Chloe."

"What?"

"Let me rewind so you can see it from the beginning. Chloe had one minute on air last night, and she did this amazing piece about the heart and soul of America being in small towns—where people still read classics—not Hollywood. She used all the images from your calendar."

As she flipped the phone around for them to see, Grace felt her jaw drop. "That was why I had so many voicemails this morning. And the people outside."

"What?" Kitty took the phone and scowled. "Who gave her permission to—"

"Listen!" Kenzie insisted.

Chloe's voice came through the small speaker, clear and bright and positive. "Just take a look at this precious calendar from the Local Business Organization in a tiny Florida town called Fernandina Beach."

Well, that shut Kitty up.

"There, they celebrate locals, not celebrities. The politics is all about how to help small businesses like this one, a little bookstore called The Next Chapter. Want to support it? Use that link on the screen and get your copy now. And when you do, remember that outside of Tinseltown, there are hundreds and hundreds of places like this, and people like"—she held up Mr. June—"this firefighter named Travis McCall, who is truly *A Midsummer Night's Dream*."

A small group had gathered around their table, all of them listening, cheering, and explaining to each other what they were watching.

As it unfolded, Kitty's face grew pale and her lips tight.

"I guess we're going to sell some calendars for the LBO," Grace said. "And then we'll—"

"Fire!" The single word echoed through the restaurant, punctuated by the bang of the front door.

"The bookstore's on fire!" someone screamed.

For a split second, Grace thought she was in a dream. A nightmare. This couldn't be real. She could almost feel herself describing the dream…

We were watching Kenzie's phone in the café and Chloe was promoting the calendar and someone yelled—
"Fire!"

With this shout, everyone moved, including Grace, who felt like she was slogging through Jell-O as she leaped to her feet and made her way to the door.

Nikki. Nikki Lou. Nikki. Nikki Lou.

Her daughter's name pounded in her head like her feet on the cobblestones as she ran as fast as she could the one block to the bookstore.

Nikki. Nikki Lou. Nikki. Nikki Lou.

She was there in a matter of seconds, looking up to see smoke billowing from the massive picture window in the living room. She could hear shouts around her and a siren in the distance, the chaos around her fading as she stared in abject horror.

"My daughter is in there! My daughter!" she screamed, working her way through the crowd to get to the front. "Nikki Lou is in there! Let me through! I have to get my daughter!"

"Fire department's on the way," some man said, snagging her arm.

"Is your kid alone?" someone else asked.

"No, no, but...she's up there."

She stood in shock, hands to her head as she saw the first bright orange flame flash in the upstairs front window.

"Nikki!" she screamed, and suddenly she was surrounded. Tori and Kenzie grabbed her from either side, and Madeline rushed toward them, breathless as they all tried to envelope her with supportive arms.

But she thrashed against them. "Nikki's in there! Help her! We have to help her!"

Rose ran from the flower shop, arms outstretched. "They're on the way! Gabe is on the truck and they're on the way. Less than a minute!"

Her baby could die in a minute. And Isaiah! Had he gone upstairs? Had he been trapped downstairs? Where was he?

She scanned the crowd, looked at the front door, which was wide open.

Where was Isaiah?

"I was in the store!" Pam Dunbath bounded toward

Grace. "I was there to buy a calendar when we smelled the smoke and Isaiah hollered for everyone to leave!"

Grace stared at her, too shocked to react to any of that.

"Why were you inside?" Madeline asked. "The store's not open yet."

"Isaiah let us in for the calendar! People were lining up..."

Her words faded out as Grace broke free and tried to get closer. The people and their stories didn't matter. Nothing mattered. Nothing but—

"Look!" someone yelled, the word nearly lost in the scream of the siren as the firetrucks barreled down Wingate Way.

Something made Grace look up, but not at the truck. Straight up to the balcony covered in smoke. And there, suddenly, she could see Isaiah holding Nikki Lou, talking to her as he brought her closer to the railing.

Alive. *Alive.* They were both alive. Grace called out but no sound came, or it was utterly drowned out by everything else. She reached both arms in the air, but so did a lot of other people, gathered under the overhang below the balcony.

"We got her! Let her go! We got her!"

In his arms, Nikki Lou writhed and clung to his shoulders as he brought her to the edge and she must have realized she was going down into waiting arms.

He took one hand and held her face, speaking to her. He said something. She said something. He talked again, and then she did, then they were both talking, staring into each other's eyes as more smoke wafted around them.

What were they talking about?

"Nikki Lou!" Grace cried out, awash in helpless fear as seconds ticked by at a glacial speed.

Isaiah finally lifted Nikki Lou higher and held her over the railing, looking down at the crowd, his mouth still moving—and so was Nikki's. Grace could feel someone guiding her back and away, but she had no capacity to do anything but watch the drama unfold.

Nikki Lou's mouth never stopped moving as she nodded and Isaiah set her on the roof below just as three firefighters bolted to the front, yelling orders and demanding space.

"Come on down, Nik!" Gabe's voice rang out the loudest and even from where she stood, Grace could see her baby's face light in recognition.

"Gabe's got her," Rose said. "She's fine, she's fine."

Rose, Tori, Kenzie, Madeline, and now Raina all seemed to hold her as Nikki Lou scrambled down the roof and finally landed in her Uncle Gabe's waiting arms. Instantly, he swung around as Rose cried out his name.

Holding Nikki Lou, he rushed toward Grace, as if he instinctively understood that the mother and daughter had to be reunited.

Grace ran to meet him, wrapping her arms around both of them the minute they met.

"She's good, she's good," Gabe assured her as he did the handoff.

"Oh, Nikki!" Grace sobbed, holding her close,

hearing her little voice reciting something over and over. "Nikki Lou!" She eased back to look at her baby, whose eyes were squeezed shut, her mouth still moving. "Nikki?"

Finally, she opened her eyes. "I can do all things through Christ, who strengthens me," she murmured. "I can do all things through Christ, who strengthens me. I can do all things—"

"Oh, my darling, yes."

As if she finally realized she was safe, Nikki Lou's whole body collapsed in exhaustion as she dropped her head on Grace's shoulder.

"Zayah taught me, Mommy. He told me to say the words so I could get on the roof, Mommy," she whispered. "He did, he did."

On another painful sob, Grace could feel herself practically melting to the ground, but the drop was eased by the many arms that held her.

"Where's Isaiah?" she called out as she looked up and realized how much she needed him that moment. "Didn't he come down..."

Rose lowered herself close to Grace. "He went back inside," she whispered.

"Why?"

Rose glanced at Nikki, whose face was turned the other way. "The dog," she mouthed.

Slinky! Grace gasped, sitting up.

"Gabe's gone in," Rose said. "He'll save them both."

Grace just stared at her sister, both of them frozen in fear.

Chapter Nineteen

Rose

Of course Gabe ran into the burning building on his last day as a firefighter, because...he was Gabe.

But that didn't make Rose feel any better. Still, she couldn't think about that. Grace and Nikki Lou needed every ounce of support and love Rose could muster.

Medics surrounded them, easing Grace to her feet and taking charge.

"Let's get your little girl checked out, ma'am," Brady, a good friend of Gabe's, ushered Grace and Nikki Lou away. "Come this way."

Rose started to walk with them, but then turned toward the bookstore, catching a glimpse of the hoses opening up and the sea of firefighters moving in choreographed madness, all under the direction of Chief Keating and Lieutenant—no, *Captain*—Hutchinson.

Was Gabe already upstairs? Had he found—

"I'll go with her," Madeline said, hugging Rose. "You stay. He'll be out any minute, I'm sure."

Rose thanked her and walked toward the crowd of

onlookers, the lucky people who didn't have a person they loved inside that building.

"He's going to be fine."

Rose turned and blinked at Raina, who she hadn't realized had been with her the whole time.

"It's his last day," Rose whispered.

"What?" Raina sucked in a breath. "What do you mean?"

"He's quitting." Rose stabbed her hands through her hair and pulled it back as she stared at the building and gauged the power and direction of the smoke. "It's starting to let up, can you tell?"

Raina turned from Rose to the bookstore, her eyes narrowing. "There's an awful lot of smoke up there. But then, you're a firefighter's wife, so you'd know."

"I *was* a firefighter's wife."

"Rose, he's quitting his job? Why? Why didn't you tell me?"

She groaned. "I kept hoping he'd change his mind," she admitted. "He got passed over for a promotion and it's left a gaping wound and he just doesn't know what he wants to do with the rest of his life. And if he doesn't get out here soon, I'm going to be sure that isn't very long," she added in a strained voice.

"Gabe?" Raina choked. "Not sure...oh, God, him, too? What is wrong with these men?"

Rose nearly crumbled at the question, which encapsulated everything she felt in just a few short words. "Is he like...like Trey and Jack?" Rose asked. "My perfect husband?"

Raina put an arm around her. "First of all, he's nothing like Trey or Jack, but no one is perfect, not even your angel Gabriel."

"There he is!" someone hollered, making them both search the crowd. "And he's got the dog!"

Rose's heart soared but it dropped instantly when she spotted Isaiah lumbering out of the front door, holding Slinky. His clothes looked tattered and covered in soot, but he appeared to be fine, just coughing.

"Where's Nikki Lou?" he bellowed. "Grace? Nikki?"

"Oh, wow," Rose exclaimed. "They're his first thought."

Torn between going to him and waiting for Gabe to appear, Rose watched the big man and tiny dog power through the crowd toward the ambulance. She heard Nikki Lou scream with joy, barely held back by a medic as she reached out her arms and called for Slinky.

Isaiah delivered the dog, gave Nikki Lou a hug, then turned to Grace and folded her in his arms.

"Oh," Raina practically whimpered.

"He loves her," Rose whispered, everything else forgotten for a moment. "Look at how he's holding her. He loves her."

"And speaking of love." Tori joined them, pointing toward the bookstore.

Rose turned, just in time to see Gabe emerge from the same front door, his arms laden with...what was he holding?

"He got Nick's flag!" Tori said. "He saved it."

With weak knees and a pounding heart, Rose ran

closer, knowing that she couldn't throw her arms around her angel Gabriel like she wanted, not when he was in the middle of a fire. But she was close enough to catch his gaze as he handed another firefighter the flag, a picture, Nikki Lou's beloved blanket, and what looked like Grace's wedding album.

In that split second, she remembered the boy she saw across the cafeteria at fifteen, the man who waited at the front of the church, the father who'd held each of their four children moments after birth, and the husband she loved with her entire heart and soul.

She hadn't married a firefighter. She'd married Gabriel D'Angelo, and the man he was would never change, regardless of his job.

With peace in her heart, she headed to her family, all gathered around Grace.

"A LAMP?" Rex's voice broke through the hushed discussion going on throughout Rose's house, where she'd insisted the family and some friends wait together for an official report hours after the last flame had been extinguished.

Isaiah, who'd been talking to Rex, threw an apologetic look at Grace. "It had a short and I think that's where the fire started," he said. "I'm not an investigator, obviously, I'm just basing that on...what I saw."

Grace just gave a sad sigh—one of hundreds she'd let out in the past few hours— stroking Nikki Lou's hair. The poor little thing had fallen asleep an hour earlier, holding her precious blanket. Slinky, who'd hidden under Grace's bed when the fire broke out, snoozed on the floor, just as worn out.

"What lamp?" Rex demanded, inching forward in his chair and leaning on the cane that had become an extension of him.

"Nick's honey bee lamp," Grace said softly. "It's been flickering and Isaiah offered to fix it, but..." She let out a moan.

"We don't know that's what caused it." Rose breezed into the room with a tray of cold drinks, knowing this conversation wasn't going to help Grace at all. "And even if it was Nick's lamp, you can't blame yourself, hon."

Grace closed her eyes and shuddered. "Watch me."

"No." Isaiah stepped away from Rex to get closer to Grace, crouching down next to her. He put one hand on hers and the other on Slinky's head. "No guilt, no second-guessing, Grace," he said softly. "No lives were lost and Gabe saved your dearest possessions. I couldn't get that darn piano out or I would have, just because Nik loves it so much."

Grace took his hand and brought it to her lips, pressing a kiss on his knuckles. "How can I ever thank you?"

"You just did."

Rose couldn't help smiling at the exchange, which was so personal and real. Everyone in the room was silent, and no doubt thinking the same thing—including her father, who cleared his throat and got everyone's attention.

"Isaiah, we owe you a monumental debt of gratitude," Rex said, his voice thick with emotion. "I shudder to think what could have—"

"No, no, sir." He looked around at the group, the sisters and all the cousins, and Susannah, and then his gaze settled on Rex. "I would do anything for Grace and Nikki Lou, sir, anything at all." He lifted their still-joined hands to his heart, then turned to Grace. "You know that, don't you?"

She nodded, her eyes misty. "I am so grateful we found you."

Once again, the room was quiet as the sea of change rolling through the Wingate family seemed almost too sacred to break with a comment or even a lighthearted joke. Grace had found love again and today, although it was hard to see it, they'd been blessed.

The sudden sound of the front door opening pulled all their attention as Gabe's footsteps and voice in conversation echoed in the hall. A second later, he and Jeremy Hutchinson stood in the entrance to the den.

"Hey, all," Gabe said, going straight to Rose's waiting arms.

As they hugged, she closed her eyes and said a silent prayer, happier than ever that he was home.

He said hello to the others, did a sweeping introduction of Captain Hutchinson, in case anyone didn't know him, and took one of the tall glasses of water Rose offered both of them.

"First off," Gabe said, lifting the glass. "Isaiah? Hat's off, big man. You acted fast, saved my niece's life, and because of your measured response, we were there in time to manage the fire with minimal damage."

A huge group sigh rolled through the room as Gabe nodded to Jeremy. "You can take it from there, sir."

Jeremy, a tall, fair-haired, and serious man stepped forward. "The official investigation will be finished in a few days," he said. "Our initial guess is that there was an electrical short somewhere in the living room."

Rose's heart dropped. It *had* been that hideous, but sentimental, lamp. From the look on Grace's face, she knew it, but Isaiah put a strong arm around her shoulders as if he could somehow replace the guilt on them with his love. Rose believed he could.

"The good news is that building is Fernandina Beach strong, which means it is brick from the foundation to the roof, and, in my unofficial opinion, structurally sound. That will be confirmed by an inspector when we finish our investigation. I know it's a Wingate property and you all have your heart in it, so I'm happy to say, from the outside, you'll barely be able to tell there was a fire."

"But...inside?" Grace asked.

"The fire was contained to the second floor, and the front of the building. Living room, kitchen, part of the hall bath, all gone. The two back bedrooms were spared fire and heat. However, the real enemy of a house fire is water, and there is a *lot* of water damage." He grimaced. "I'm afraid most of your books are lost. Maybe not all, but water poured into the store, so..." He nodded. "I hope you have insurance."

"Every inch of that building is insured," Rex said, looking at Grace. "And Wingate Properties will rebuild it exactly as you want it."

"Thanks, Dad." She managed a smile.

"It's a time-consuming process," the captain said. "But once the inspections are finished, and the building is cleared, you can take a contractor in there and get started."

"We know plenty of contractors," Raina chimed in. "And we will all help you, Grace."

After Jeremy finished the preliminary report and left, the mood felt lighter. The Next Chapter wasn't lost...but would certainly be getting a massive renovation inside.

"You can rebuild," Rose said with her brightest smile. "And it can be exactly what you want."

"Until then..." Susannah, holding Nikki Lou's feet in her lap, leaned over to reach her hand toward Grace. "Why don't you two move into the third-floor apartment at the inn? There's a tiny bit of renovation that we could do around you, but we've already ordered some new furniture, so it's a perfect place for you and Nik to live until your own home is complete. We'll make it wonderful as a temporary place to stay."

Everyone reacted to that with a cheer and support, but Grace gazed at Suze with teary eyes. "Are you sure, Mom? It could be months, and I know you wanted to rent that out as part of the inn."

"Nonsense," Rex said, putting an end to any discussion. "You will live there as long as you need to live there."

"But tonight, you'll stay here," Rose insisted. "And we'll get the apartment ready for you to move in ASAP. We'll make it easy and fun for Nikki Lou, too."

"Thank you," Grace whispered. "Thank you, all." Then she let her head fall back as though the drama of the day had wiped her out.

In fact, they all felt that way and in less than an hour, everyone had left.

An hour or so after that, Rose came out of the bathroom to find Gabe on the bed, his laptop open as he clicked some keys.

"Filing a report?" she asked.

He looked up, his expression a little...guilty? Maybe just surprised. "No report for me. I'm done, remember? Today was my last day."

She sighed at that. "Of course. Talk about going out with a bang, huh?"

He lifted a shoulder. "It was a day in the life of a firefighter and medic."

"Will you miss it?" she asked, searching his face.

Before he answered, a tap on their bedroom door pulled her away.

"Rose?" Grace called. "Sorry to bother you, but I—"

Immediately, she went to the door, her concern only for her sister. "No problem. What's up?"

Grace looked past her at the bedroom. "Privacy?"

"Of course." She walked into the hall and closed the door. "Everything okay in the guest room? Nikki Lou asleep? Does Slinky need to go out? We won't have the alarm on, so—"

Grace made a face. "I started my period and don't have a thing."

"Oh!" Rose laughed softly at the simple request. "Hang tight."

She darted into her bedroom, where Gabe was back on the computer, typing away. She got what she needed from the bathroom and stepped out again to give the box to Grace, who leaned against the wall with her eyes closed.

"Oh, baby," Rose said, giving her a hug. "Mother Nature sure makes her presence known on the worst days, huh?"

Grace managed a smile and Rose walked with her down the hall toward the guest room. "Well, it wasn't the worst day of my life."

Rose's heart dropped. Poor Grace had been through a *lot* in this life. "No, that's true. No lives were lost."

"And Isaiah..." Grace bit her lip. "I think he's..."

Rose waited for her to finish, uncertain and hopeful.

"He's...perfect," she finally said. "And I'm falling in love with him."

"Grace!" She bit back a squeal, nudging them both away from the girls' bedroom door so they didn't wake them. "That's amazing!"

"Well, I have you to thank, Rose. You made me go on five dates with him. How did you know?"

Rose shrugged. "Mostly because he looks at you like..."

"Like Gabe looks at you."

"Like he cares very deeply for you, and for Nikki Lou." Rose gave her a squeeze. "Just keep your heart wide open, Gracie girl. That man is as good as they come."

"I will," she said, her eyes filling as she looked at Rose. "I've always looked up to you. Always admired your spirit and your marriage and the kind of mother you are."

"Thank you, sweetie. The love is mutual."

Grace reached her arms around Rose and squeezed, the two of them silent as they wallowed in sisterly love.

"Now, go be with your wonderful husband." Grace added a kiss on Rose's cheek. "He saved so many memories for me that no other firefighter would have known. The flag and Nick's picture and did you know he found our wedding album that was on the bookshelf? Please tell him again how grateful I am."

"I will. Get some rest, sweet Grace."

"I will," Grace agreed. "I know that we'll get through the next few months, no matter what they bring."

Holding on to those words, needing them as much as her sister did, Rose tiptoed back to her room. When she opened the door, Gabe was still looking at his laptop, a huge grin on his face. He looked up at her, immediately closed the screen, and looked like he was working to wipe that smile away.

"All good with Grace?"

She nodded, searching his face, so curious what he'd been working on but weirdly...afraid to ask. What was going on? What was he smiling about?

Of all the nightmares Rose had about losing Gabe, not one included not trusting him. But what was he hiding on that laptop?

She stared at him for a beat, then shot into the bathroom again, only a little surprised that her heart was hammering. She rinsed her face with cool water, slathered some lotion on trembling hands, then made a decision.

She would not ask. She would not beg. This was Gabriel D'Angelo, for heaven's sake. They had no secrets, no distance, and no issues.

Coming back into the room, she slid under the covers. Immediately, he turned on his side and propped his head on his hand, staring at her.

"What?" she asked.

"I need a reason to look at my wife?"

"None at all." She looked right back, oddly mystified by his expression. "You okay?"

"Very much so," he said. "In fact, I'm great. I'm...so great." He gave a mysterious little laugh. "I'm ready."

"For...what?"

"For what's next."

What *was* next? Rose knew that was four kids who needed everything and, right around the corner, the first of four college degrees they would have to pay for. She tamped down the thought and nodded.

"Any ideas about what's next?" she asked, still feeling tentative, which was just unnerving. This was Gabe. They talked about anything and everything. Was he *hiding* something from her?

He swallowed and turned over, rolling toward the laptop he'd set on the nightstand. "Well, as a matter of fact...I just found out what's next."

Unexpected chills rose on her skin. "You did? You got another job?"

"More or less."

"Oh!" She put her hand to her mouth and gasped. "When were you going to tell me?"

"When I thought..." He sat up and slowly opened the laptop. "You could handle it."

She glanced at the screen, which looked like his email. "What do I have to handle?"

For a long time, he didn't say anything, but looked at her. "Babe, do you trust me?" he finally asked.

"With my entire heart and soul, Gabe, but you're scaring me."

He didn't smile. "Don't be scared, but be...open."

"To...what?"

"Change," he said simply. "A new normal and a slightly different life for a short period of time."

She wanted to curl her lip, but didn't. She wasn't a huge fan of change, but she did trust him. And it certainly didn't sound like he'd been cheating on her or doing anything to break her heart.

"Oookay..." She wiped damp palms on the comforter. "What is this change and different life?" Did she even want to know? She liked her life. A lot.

"It's my dream, Rose," he whispered. "You know, sometimes someone comes into your life and they...make you see that you still have dreams. And those dreams need to be nurtured, or you die inside."

She balled the comforter in her fist. "Someone came into your life?" Her voice rose with uncertainty. "Someone I should...worry about?"

He chuckled. "Only if you think I'm gonna leave you for Travis."

"Travis?" She sat up, utterly confused.

"Yep. That young man blew into my life and I didn't even want a probie to train, but..." He shook his head. "He taught me as much as I taught him."

"What did he teach you, Gabe?" Even as she asked, she wasn't sure she wanted to know.

"No regrets."

She stared at him, frowning. "What do you regret, honey? What would you do differently if you could?"

He slowly exhaled and looked at her, his eyes expectant, like she should know the answer. She didn't. Did he regret marrying her? Having four kids? Living here or... what? Rooting through the history of his life, all she could come up with was...

"Medical school?" she guessed.

A little bit of color faded from his cheeks as he closed his eyes in a nod. "Bingo."

Before she could form the next question, he tapped the keyboard and a document flashed as he turned the laptop to her.

Congratulations. You have been accepted into the fall program of the University of Miami Leonard M. Miller School of Medicine.

"Medical school," she repeated, only this wasn't a question. This was...impossible.

"Hear me out," he said quickly, reaching for her hands the way he did when he wanted her undivided attention. "They accepted my credits for five semesters, Rose, and offered me a pretty impressive scholarship. That cuts out more than two years. I only have to be down there for three semesters, maybe four, then I will move heaven and Earth to get residency at a hospital in Jacksonville. While I'm down there, I can work part-time as an EMT and with what we have in savings, we are perfectly fine, I promise."

"*Miami?*" She could hardly say the word. "I lost Raina to Miami for sixteen years and now she's back and we have four kids and my business and the family and... and...and *Miami,* Gabe?"

He stayed quiet while she ranted. Then he squeezed her hands and brought them to his lips.

"If you can believe this, UNF wouldn't accept the old credits and that's the school I attended. Trust me, I tried to do this locally. Same with UCF. I got into University of Florida, but no scholarship money and they only accepted foundational credits. Honestly, I tried Miami on a lark, because it was always my dream med school, and wham! Turns out they are trying to find older students who have life experience. They wooed me, to be honest."

She tried to breathe, and failed. "You've been applying to medical schools all this time? I thought...you told me everything." The crack in her perfect marriage seemed gaping and impossible to comprehend.

"It started on a whim and I didn't want to worry you. You do worry so much, Rose."

"And now my fears have come true."

He gave her a look. "You worried I'd be killed, not become a doctor."

She conceded that with a sigh. "I worried we'd be separated."

"Briefly, temporarily," he insisted. "I could be finished with med school and residency and practicing right here on Amelia Island well before I'm fifty. I'll have twenty years to pursue what I've wanted since I was a child."

She nodded, listening, knowing all this was true but...*Does everyone get to have their dreams come true?* Well, she did, but...she wasn't asking to leave for almost two years.

"I would come home every chance I can, every month for sure. You know I couldn't stand to be away. I already talked to the dean, and they said I might be able to do a semester or two from up here, and only go down for labs and such."

"Every...*month?*"

"Rosie, honey, I know it sounds awful for the immediate future."

"And the distant future," she added.

"I get that," he said. And I will turn it down if you feel that has to be the decision. But, I'm scared that if I don't accept this, then I'm...I'm...I'm going to regret it." He squeezed her hands. "It's a blip in our long, long life together, and I will do everything I can to make it go smoothly. But I want to do this, Rose. I need to do this. Only if you agree."

Silent, she leaned back, but held on to his strong, warm hands, wanting so badly to accept this but deep down, she ached to wake up and find out this entire day had been a bad, bad dream.

But that wasn't happening. This was.

She closed her eyes, silent, trying to corral thoughts that were wildly out of control. On a slow breath, she let her heart go where it had to go...to the promises she'd once made in St. Peter's...vows to Gabe, to God, and in front of everyone she loved. She'd sworn to love him through sickness, health, rich, poor, good times, bad, and...all the other stuff.

Like this.

"Rosie? Say something."

She swallowed and it hurt so much, she couldn't say anything.

"Rose." He pulled her closer. "Please, can we talk about it?"

But he hadn't talked to her. He'd talked to...*the dean.*

"If you don't want this, then I swear, I won't—"

She held up a hand to silence him. "Gimme a second," she managed. "I need a second."

He nodded, waiting. His hands were damp, too, and she swore she could feel his pulse pounding in her hands, the blood pumping from his beautiful, tender, caring heart.

The heart he'd given her and their children. The best

heart God ever made. The heart that belonged to her. The heart...that would make a very good doctor.

The best.

One word, and he'd change his mind. One insistent, "There's no way we're doing this, Gabe," and he'd back off, give up his dreams, and figure out a different path.

Who was she to take his dreams away? She was his wife, that's who. And she loved him more than any person, place, or thing on the Earth.

"Yes," she finally whispered, the word nothing more than a breath.

"Yes?" He gripped her harder. "You think we can do this?"

She opened her eyes, instantly lost in his. "Yes, Gabe. You should have your dreams and we can make it work. I know we can—"

He cut her off with a hard, full on the mouth kiss, wrapping her in his arms with a murmur of relief and gratitude.

"Oh, my Rosie, sweet, sweet Rosie. I love you so much. I love you so much. You're the best thing that—"

She laughed softly at his desperation. "I love you, too, my angel Gabriel..." She eased back and looked at him. "Dr. Angel Gabriel, that is."

His eyes closed as he inhaled the words like a man who needed them more than anything. "Thank you, Rosie. I love you."

With that, they reached for each other and shared the longest, deepest, truest kiss she could remember.

As they parted, another thought floated in her mind. "My dad says my deepest fear is abandonment."

"I am not abandoning you," he promised. "I'm making an unexpected change to our lives that will be temporary and brief."

She smiled. "You know who you sound like? Me, the eternal optimist."

He put a hand on her cheek and gazed into her eyes, silent for a long time. Then he just kissed her and trailed his lips over her throat, heat building as it always did.

How was she going to do this? How lonely would she be? What was about to happen to her and the family and...

She just closed her eyes and let him erase every single doubt, silence every question, and calm every fear. In Gabe's arms, under his touch and spell, all she could feel was hope. And love.

Chapter Twenty

Raina

"That's my cell," Raina said, backing away from Dani's desk. "Can you finish revising those...stippies?"

Dani snorted. "Did you just say 'stippies'?"

"It's what Blake called the stipulations in a contract." Raina shook her head. "I miss that little goofball."

"No word?"

Raina shrugged as she walked to her office. "He's had the Chase Madison listing for two weeks now and the place hasn't sold, but we knew sometimes it takes a little time to find the right buyer for a house that special. I think he's holding the open house this week."

She pushed the problem out of her head and picked up her cell, groaning at the sight of a new problem—Jack Wallace.

"This is never good," she muttered, tapping her screen and speaker to give a perfunctory, "Hey."

"You'll sound happier in a minute." Jack's familiar voice came through the phone. "Are you sitting down, Rain?"

She bristled at the use of the nickname he didn't get to call her anymore. "I don't need to be. What's up?"

"Berkshire Hathaway made an offer on W&W. They beat RE/MAX by a lot."

Hissing in a soft breath, she rounded the desk to her chair. He was right; she did need to sit down.

"That's...interesting," she said, sounding far more cavalier than she felt at the idea of selling the company they'd built together. He'd been shopping it, trying to get a better offer?

So like Jack.

"Interesting is an understatement. It's...lucrative. Extremely lucrative for both of us. You want to know the number?"

"Sure." She picked up a pen. "What is it?"

As he said the figure, her hand froze in the act of writing it. "Oh...that's, um, good."

"Are you kidding? It's great!"

Why was he so happy about dissolving this business and this marriage and this life? She swallowed against a lump in her throat as she finished the last zero.

"Obviously, that's not the final number," he said. "We can negotiate, we'll have to pay some costs, discuss what to do with this building, pay a zillion lawyers, etcetera. But in the end, we'll each have a mountain of money."

A mountain of money.

Not exactly what she wanted from her sixteen-year marriage to a man she'd loved or the business she'd hoped to hand over to her children.

At the thought of her children, one of them moved,

and she put her hand on her belly, getting bigger now that she was past the halfway mark. The children, she remembered, that he wanted to relinquish.

"I think we should jump on this, Rain, and get the ball moving. That way the deal can be closed before the holidays, and then we can sign the divorce papers early next year."

Early next year, she thought. When the babies would be born.

"Yes," she said softly, feeling zero desire to fight, negotiate, or even discuss this issue. "That sounds good."

"Yeah? You agree? Want me to accept?"

She could have sworn he sounded a little disappointed, but then, Jack loved going to the mat on any contract.

"You can." She turned to her computer and tapped the screen, something brewing in her heart that she couldn't quite capture. "Just let me take a look at the final offer."

Because Jack was terrible at getting rid of...stippies.

She closed her eyes for a second, concentrating on whatever it was tapping at her heart right now. What was happening inside her? She needed...she wanted...she had to have...

That house. The Sanctuary. With the sale of her business, that beautiful beachfront haven was within reach. She clicked a few keys into the active listing page, whimpering a little when a picture taken from the main bedroom through the open doors to the balcony and ocean beyond came up on the screen.

Everything in her ached.

"If the offer's solid, we might even get this zipped up sooner," Jack said. "We could close as soon as two months, maybe three. Wouldn't that be great?"

Two months, maybe three?

All those days and nights, deals and deadlines, decisions, inside jokes, trips, and dinner dates. Making love on the stairs one night after getting their first eight-figure listing because they just couldn't take the time to get to the bedroom. Laughing when they closed a deal. Crying when they lost one.

Now, it could be over in two months, maybe three.

And their marriage, over when they flipped the calendar to the next year. The babies that didn't happen, the renovations that did. The memories and feelings and days and nights they'd shared together. All that...*life*.

Tears stung as she tried—and failed miserably—to swallow.

Her marriage, for all intents and purposes, had come to an end. She glanced at the sparkling wedding band and solitaire she had never taken off and let out a soft grunt, the rings suddenly feeling heavy and awkward.

"Sounds good, Jack," she said. "Let's move on it. Hey, I gotta go." She hated how thick her voice was. "And, what can I say? Job well done."

"Thanks, Rain. I think this is the best possible outcome."

Well, at this point, it was the *only* possible outcome.

"Yep. We'll talk." She barely heard his goodbye when she tapped the red button, squinted at the computer for one word—*available*—which danced in front of her face like the best possible consolation prize.

It took her exactly three seconds to concoct the plan.

"Dani! Hey, Dani!"

She was in the doorway in a flash. "What's up, Raina?"

"I have an idea," she announced, slowly standing. "But you might have to do something just outside the bounds of completely and totally ethical."

"Putting on my rule-bending gloves," she said, miming the act of tugging on a glove. "What can I do? Forge a signature? Fake a phone call? Change a...stippie?"

She laughed. "Call Blake, pretend to be an out-of-town agent with a buyer who saw Chase Madison's beach house and wants to make an offer—full asking price. Tell him to meet the buyer tonight, at seven."

"Raina! You got a buyer?"

Raina inhaled and grinned, suddenly feeling so light she might float away. "Yeah. You're looking at her."

And that very moment, the weight of unhappiness, of a cheating husband and a profound sadness just...lifted.

CHASE ONLY LOOKED SLIGHTLY surprised when he stepped out on his deck and met Raina's gaze.

Slightly amused, too, and really darn attractive in khaki shorts and a black T-shirt.

"Brought the A-team, did you?" he asked, still only looking at her and not the crew assembled behind her.

"Absolutely. Meet my sisters Madeline, Rose, Grace, and Tori, and my niece, Kenzie, and nephew, Finn. Fam, this is Chase Madison, owner of this gorgeous house that is about to be mine."

They greeted him with handshakes and hellos, some small talk and joking about the size of their family.

Then he gestured toward the open sliding French doors, inviting them into the house. Raina held back, looking up at him, prepared to offer a full explanation.

"You're buying it." It wasn't a question, and he looked nothing short of pleased. "And you brought your family to persuade Blake to become part of the pack."

"Am I that transparent? Yes and yes. I assume you're fine with that. It's really not a ploy this time, I *am* buying this house."

He studied her face for a moment, taking time to look deep into her eyes and give her the feeling that he was searching her soul. "You belong here, Raina. I felt it after you left. And you're right. The house has a good vibe."

"I felt it, too."

"Then I'll sell it to you," he said. "I'll take off for a bit while you work out the offer logistics with Blake. Will you need me to negotiate?"

"Not likely." She lifted a shoulder. "Unless I need to go over asking."

His eyes flickered with a hint of a smile. "Not a penny."

"But I'd like it furnished," she added quickly. "I'll

want to move in immediately after a short close, because I've invaded my parents' house for far too long. I'll pay cash, but that could take...two months, maybe three." She swallowed at the phrase, which sounded hopeful now, not sad.

"We can work a cash deal," he said.

"Well, I'd like to arrange a short-term mortgage until..." She swallowed, hating the words. "Until my divorce is final early next year."

He held her gaze again, long enough for her stomach to feel something that wasn't a baby kicking.

"Only if I have permission to visit." He waited a beat, then added, "To see what you've done with the place."

"Permission...granted."

"Thank you." He slipped into a smile that was a little like the sun coming out on a cloudy day. Bright and welcoming and she just wanted to bask in it.

A second later, he headed down the back steps toward the sand, leaving her standing on the deck, feeling a little warmer than she should for an evening at the beach.

"This place is the bomb, Aunt Raina!" Kenzie came bounding out. "That upstairs suite is insane. You can lay in bed and look at the ocean."

She glanced over her shoulder and took a look at Chase Madison walking toward the sand, a sudden—and unwelcome—image hovering around the corners of her imagination.

He'd slept in that bed. He'd awakened to that view.

Well, she'd change the sheets and forget about him.

"I know, right, Kenz? You better come and stay with me over here." She wrapped an arm around her niece, taking her inside to join the others. "Okay, you guys," Raina called, gathering them all in the kitchen from the various rooms they were touring.

After a chorus of how beautiful the house was, Raina clapped her hands to make a little speech.

"Let's not ambush Blake when he shows," she said. "Let's just somehow demonstrate...love, support, and family. I'm not sure how, but I trust you all."

Before they could answer, the doorbell rang and they all stood silent and stunned for a moment, like a group of people waiting to scream, "Surprise!" at a birthday party.

Only this wasn't a party, and he wasn't going to be thrilled. But Raina had to try. She had to show him what they were made of. And she had to have this house...but that would be the easy part. The owner just said yes.

"Who wants to answer the door?" she asked.

Six hands went up like a bunch of kids on a playground, wanting to be picked first.

"Oh, let's see. Madeline, you're the oldest and probably should do the honors."

"I'd love to."

Raina followed her, then slipped into the living room so she could stay out of sight but still hear the exchange. Only she wasn't sure she could hear anything, her pulse was pounding so noisily. Just as she rounded the corner, she nearly burst out laughing when Tori, Kenzie, Finn, Rose, and Grace followed Madeline to the door.

"What are you doing?" she asked in a harsh whisper.

Tori stuck her tongue out defiantly, Rose shrugged, Grace laughed, Finn pointed at the door, and Kenzie—God bless her—had put her phone away for once. Still, it felt very much like an ambush.

"Hello," Madeline said when she opened the door. "Blake Youngblood? I'm—"

"Madeline Wingate," he said, the tightness in his voice like a knife to Raina's heart. "I know who you are."

"Then you might know my sister, Tori. And her kids, Finn and Kenzie. That's Rose and Grace."

Raina could hear the breath he exhaled. "Where is she?" he asked. "Where's Raina?"

"I'm right here," she said, stepping out from the protection of the living room wall to meet an angry gaze. "And I'm here to buy the house."

"You can't just...excuse me?" He inched back, eyes wide. "How far are you going to take this, Raina?"

"Far," she said simply. "I'm making a full asking price offer and I brought my family to see the wonderful house I'm buying."

"And meet our nephew," Madeline added.

"And my cousin," Finn said, extending his hand. "Hey, man. I'm Finn, but you can call me Finnie. I don't hate it."

Blake stared at him, slowly lifting his hand to shake, because what else could he do? "Hey."

"And I'm Kenzie, your other cousin. There are more of us cousins. Rose has four kids and Grace has little Nikki Lou, but Raina told us not to overwhelm you."

"Too late," he said softly.

Rose stepped forward, extending her arms, tears in her eyes. "Hello, Blake. I'm Aunt Rose and you are..." She inhaled as though words escaped her. "Dear Blake."

He gave a soft laugh at the description and surrendered to a hug he couldn't avoid. "Hi, Rose."

"And I'm Grace."

His eyes flickered from one to the other. "Grace, I heard about the bookstore fire," he said. "I'm so sorry."

Raina's heart shifted in her chest at the sincerity in the comment.

"Thank you," Grace said. "I think I recall seeing you in the store in the past. You like...legal thrillers, right? I put a new one aside for you, hoping you'd come back. I can reorder it for you, even though we're closed. I knew your name, but I didn't know you were...*our* Blake."

He might have swayed, like he didn't trust himself not to overreact to this.

"And we've met," Tori interjected, reaching out for a handshake. "When you worked for Raina and the movie people were here. So nice to see you again."

He shook her hand, too, letting out a sigh as though he simply couldn't fight this...Wingate tsunami.

"I really do want to buy the house," Raina assured him. "It wasn't a ploy."

He lifted one "get real" brow, making them laugh.

"Okay, slight ploy," she said. "But I really, really want—"

"I know what you want," he said, backing up as though he were a little afraid of the full power of them. "I know what you all *think* you want."

"Not what we think!" Rose insisted. "We know."

Madeline pressed her hands together at her chin and gazed at him. "We're family, Blake. There's just never enough of that, in my opinion."

He smiled at her for a moment, then closed his eyes. "I'm overwhelmed," he admitted.

"We didn't mean to—"

"In a good way," he promised, holding up a hand to stop any arguments. "I'd like to...I need some...I just can't..."

"Take your time."

"Relax and get to know us."

"There's no agenda!"

"We're not going anywhere."

He laughed softly at the avalanche of kindness rolling over him, then reached into his messenger bag.

"I have an offer form here," he said, pulling out a document and handing it to Raina. "Obviously, you know how to complete this. When you do, just leave it here and I'll go over it with my client, Mr. Madison. We'll be in touch."

Raina took the document, fighting the urge to grab his hand and hold him. "No weird stippies I should look for?" she teased, praying a little humor would soften him.

He smiled. "Just the usual. Now, ladies and gentleman, if you will kindly excuse me. I have some...some thinking to do."

With a simple nod, he turned and left, and they all stood in dead silence, stunned by the anticlimactic ending to their plan.

"So, I think that went—"

"If you say *well*, Rose..." Raina ground out.

"He didn't run screaming out the door," Finn said. "He seems like a cool guy."

"He *is* a cool guy," Raina said, looking from one to the other. "And you are a cool family that he should want to be part of." She shook her head, glancing at the offer form. "I think it is clear we should leave, though. I'm going to fill this out and take a walk. Maybe Chase will call me if Blake doesn't."

They shared a few hugs and goodbyes, then left Raina alone in the house with the contract to buy it.

As disappointed as she was over Blake's reaction, she couldn't be more excited about buying this place. Chase was right. She *belonged* here.

It was easy enough to complete the offer. Even though she wanted to linger and look and wait for Blake to come back, she left by way of the back deck again, not taking even one more cursory tour.

There was no sign of Chase or Blake, or any of her family, so she headed back down the beach to her parents' house, a cocktail of emotions swirling in her.

She looked out at the water, which was calm today, letting the summer sun warm her from head to toe as she took a little life inventory on this monumental day.

In just a few months, she'd moved here, left her cheating husband, survived half a pregnancy with two babies inside her, sold her business, and now, bought her dream house.

No, she hadn't fixed this broken relationship with her

long-lost nephew, and Raina—despite all the changes in her life—still lived to fix anything that was broken. She needed to let go of that, allow Blake to take charge of the relationship and simply revel in the progress she made every single day on Amelia Island.

She was fixing herself, and wasn't that the most important thing?

Maybe, maybe not. She hadn't come here to fix herself—heck, she didn't know she was "broken" when she left Miami—she'd come here for Dad.

The thought of him made her slow her step as she reached the beach house. Instead of taking the stairs up to the main level, she crossed the dune by foot, following a path that led to the downstairs patio and Dad's little rehab kingdom.

All she wanted to do was talk to her favorite man on Earth. She walked across the patio, noticing that the sliders were open, but there was no sign of Dad sitting outside and getting air like he usually did after PT.

Maybe it was time to tell him about Blake. Then, maybe she'd pull out her biggest gun and have Rex talk to Blake directly. Maybe she'd gone about this all wrong. Her father just might be the secret weapon she needed to convince Blake to be part of their family. Because, face it, Rex didn't raise quitters.

She paused at the sound of a man's voice coming from inside, not wanting to interrupt his rehab, checking her watch to gauge the best time to drop in on him and—

"Well, it did take me a while to get here, sir, and I'm sorry for that."

Wait a second! That was Blake! He was here? Talking to Rex?

She put a hand over her mouth to keep from crying out, taking one silent step closer to the sliders, but still hidden by the sheers that Susannah had drawn to the side of the doors.

"No matter, Blake. None at all. Good to see you."

"You look great, Mr. Wingate. As healthy and hardy as I remember."

"Call me Rex, son. And take a seat. I'm healthy enough. Are you prepared to tell me where the heck you've been and why you didn't come around to claim your crown for saving my grandbabies? Raina's having twins. Did you know?"

She took a breath and saw the figures move on the other side of the drapes, knowing where her father sat, and picturing Blake across from him.

Should she walk in? Should she facilitate the discussion and break the news? Should she *fix* this relationship?

No, Raina. Just listen.

"I'd heard that," Blake said, his voice deep with respect and tension she could feel fifteen feet away.

Fighting the urge to go in and help her nephew, she fisted her hands and let him handle the conversation the way he wanted to. She owed him that.

"I understand you've left the company," Rex said. "I'm sorry to hear that."

"I struck out on my own, sir."

"That's why you left? Why you couldn't be bothered to come and see me?"

She could practically hear Blake shifting with discomfort in his seat.

Now? Should she help him now?

"Sir, I haven't come, because I've been keeping a secret from you."

Nope. Not now.

"I don't like secrets," her father said, making her suddenly wonder if this news could be bad for his heart or head.

No, it could only be good. She hoped.

"I know that, Mr...er, Rex. But I kept my secret none-theless."

"If you think I'm going to be all shocked and old school when you tell me you're gay, you're wrong. Although I am disappointed that you have so little faith in me."

"Sir?"

"It's Rex, son, and I knew at your first interview. I don't give a flying hoot!"

Raina bit her lip to keep from laughing at the total Rex comment.

"Well, that's...that's good to hear, Rex," Blake said. "But that's not what I came to tell you."

She heard him inhale slowly and imagined Blake rooting for the right words. *Just say it, dear nephew. Just say it and see how loved you are.*

"Rex, you should know that Brad Young is my father."

Then...silence. She didn't move, waiting for Rex's reaction, waiting for him to erupt with emotion, to fling a thousand questions and maybe a few choice words. But then...

"And that means, sir, that I'm your grandson."

Then...nothing. A long, endless, painful silence. She waited and waited, feeling her whole body take a few steps to the left so she could see. She had to know. She had to—

"Please, sir. Rex. Oh, no! Don't cry. Please."

"You're...my...grandson?" Dad asked in a ragged voice.

"And I may not be what or who you want for—"

"Get over here, son! I can't stand like I used to!"

Rex struggled to get up, but Blake launched from his seat in an instant, closing the space between them and helping her father to his feet.

She backed away behind the drape again, putting her hand over her mouth to stay quiet and let these two men, this grandfather and grandson, hold each other for the first time.

"Grandson!" She heard Rex pat Blake's back. "Holy moly, boy! Your face screams Wingate! How the heck did I miss that?"

"You see what you think you see, Rex."

"That's Grandpa Rex to you, and all I see, all I can see when I look at you, is the grandson I already love." His voice cracked and he covered it by clearing his throat. "Susannah!" he called in a gravelly voice. "Suze! Where are you?"

"I'm right here, Rex. What's the matter?" Susannah's voice floated down from upstairs and seconds later Raina saw her dart into the room. "Oh, hello, Blake! We'd given up on you!"

"Not all of you haven't," he said on a half laugh, half sigh. "I know you're out there, Raina, so come on in and join the fun."

She snorted and stepped into the room.

"Raina!" Dad exclaimed. "Did you know this young man, our assistant, your savior, is my grandson? Did you know—"

"Yes," she whispered. "I knew."

Blake took the hug she offered. She held him in her arms, her heart as full as it had been for a long, long time.

"Oh, Aunt Raina."

She kissed him on the cheek, laughing at the title. "Welcome to the Wingate family, Blake."

Chapter Twenty-one

Chloe

Rory Sutton hadn't fired Chloe for the calendar story, which was a shame. She'd hoped to go out in a blaze of glory. Oh, he'd given her grief for the lightweight reporting, told her not to mess up again, then sent her on a wild goose chase. This one was to find out if there was any truth to the rumors that Gwyneth Paltrow didn't use her own products but instead slathered banana peel on her face every night.

Chloe gave her two weeks' notice the next day and the big fat jerk made her work the days, which included one more on-air appearance with none other than her pal Coo Coo Cooper, slobbering over his "return to roots" album, with no mention of his quiet separation from Lacey Britton.

During those two weeks, she hadn't told anyone in her family, or Hunter—she ignored his texts—that she would be driving back to Amelia Island for good when her prison time in L.A. was over.

Truth was, it was so darn hard to admit yet another failure.

"I can't seem to finish anything," she muttered, throwing a look at her sweet pupper, curled on the passenger seat. "It's true, Bugaboo. I messed up my engagement and ruined my own wedding."

Lady Bug's eyes fluttered, probably in agreement.

"Then I ran off to L.A. and struck out so hard, it hurts to even think about it."

The dog gave a sad sigh.

"And now I'm coming home, darn near thirty years old, and a complete and total loser."

Instantly, Lady Bug sat up, gave a shake, then climbed over the console into Chloe's lap, giving her arm a quick lick with her bubble gum tongue.

It just about folded Chloe's heart in half.

"Oh, baby," she crooned, taking a hand off the steering wheel to pet her sweet angel. "You're the only thing I've ever stuck with from beginning to end. Do you know that? Through it all, you, sweet Lady Bug, have been my constant. How can I ever thank you?"

She nestled into a ball on Chloe's lap, basking in the attention. Also thrilled to be out of the hellhole in Northridge.

"I'll figure out my next step, Bug," Chloe continued. "I don't know what it's going to be, but you will be there. I'll never leave you alone again for long, lonely days, I promise. I just don't know what I can do with the rest of my life."

Lady Bug looked up at her with eyes full of...longing.

"Well, yeah, there is Travis," Chloe agreed on a laugh.

He was the only person who knew she was on her way home—and it *was* home—and he was pretty darn excited about the decision. He promised to keep her secret if he saw any of the Wingates, and begged her to time her arrival so he was off duty and could give her a proper hello.

She checked the clock as she left Yulee, knowing they were about a half hour from downtown Fernandina Beach, and more than an hour from the end of his shift.

But it was Sunday afternoon, and that meant she had a very good chance of finding most, if not all, of her family at her parents' beach house, where she'd go first.

Her whole body vibrated with happiness when she saw the VFW branch, cruised past Shuckers, and finally crossed the bridge to Amelia Island.

"We're home, Bugaboo!"

Lady Bug, who'd crawled back to the passenger seat, just lifted one brow, her expression a total dog version of *I'll believe it when I see it.* She got that. It had been a long road trip.

"Trust me, Lady B. You'll be at your happy place on the beach in no time, surrounded by a giggle-gaggle of Wingates and all the people you love." Tears stung her lids. "I've missed them all so much."

She kept the tears at bay until she flew down Fletcher and finally reached the beach house, only to see...an empty driveway. Where was Rose's family, and Grace and Nikki Lou? Where was Madeline's car? Raina wasn't here and there was no sign of Tori's SUV parked in front of the bungalow. Where *were* they all?

Well, surely Mom and Dad were here, and their cars were in the garage.

She used the code to get in the front door of the beach house, only to find...no one.

"Where are they all?" she asked no one in utter exasperation as Lady Bug tore through the house, barking for attention she wasn't getting. Some surprise.

As she was headed back to her car—the one that had just traveled 2,400 miles across Interstate 10 to get home and be showered in Wingate love—her phone buzzed with a call from Travis. She couldn't deny the fact that merely seeing his name on her screen gave her a slight thrill.

"Hey, there," she said as she tapped the speaker button. "I got here early and the beach house is empty."

"You're here? In Fernandina?"

"I went to my parents' house but everyone is gone."

"They're at the inn," he told her. "I talked to Gabe and he said there's some Wingate gathering there. Something to do with Isaiah and Grace."

She squeezed her eyes and stifled a grunt, frustrated to be left out and aching to be with them.

"Then I'm on my way there," she told him. "Come over after your shift."

He chuckled. "I will. And Chloe?"

"Yeah?" She pulled open the car door for Lady Bug to jump in.

"You're not leaving again," he said simply.

She smiled into the phone and felt the chills that defied the late afternoon sunshine. "I'm not planning on it, although...I have zero idea what I'm going to do with my life."

"Oh, I have ideas."

The chills only intensified. "I mean work. Not sure I can go back to the café as the world's worst waitress and I don't even know where I'm going to live." She curled her fingers in Lady Bug's fur. "All I know is this dog is going to be with me every minute."

He chuckled. "Then she better get used to me."

That made her smile, and when they said goodbye, she turned on the ignition and felt the blast of cool air from the vents, strong enough to make her close her eyes and let joy wash over her.

Nope, she had no idea what she was going to do on Amelia Island, other than *stay put*.

Not fifteen minutes later, she pulled onto Wingate Way and spotted *all* the vehicles that had been missing at the beach house in the lot behind the inn. Not a place they usually gathered, but Grace and Nikki Lou had moved into Doreen's old apartment on the third floor, so maybe everyone was here to paint or bring in furniture.

Whatever, her FOMO was blinding. No more missing out on anything.

She grabbed an open spot on the street and scooped up Lady Bug, practically running through the gate and down the path that led to the front door of the old Victorian. Her heart pounding in anticipation, she crossed the porch and opened the main door, not entirely sure what to expect.

Nothing. No one. The silence of an inn when most of

the guests were likely in town shopping or eating. Where was—

She slowed her step at the sound of music. Was someone...playing a piano in the library? There'd never been a piano at the inn.

She walked through the living room, following the sound, which included a chord now. Wasn't that a song from church? *Amazing Grace?*

She rounded the corner to the double doors that led to one of the prettiest rooms in the inn, a charming library with one stained-glass window, two walls of shelves, and...oh, wow. *That* was new, she thought, gazing at one very ornate and antique-looking upright piano in front of the window that faced the garden.

There, Nikki Lou was seated on the bench, playing the piano. Wait...*what?*

All around little Nikki Lou, captivated and enthralled, the Wingate family watched, their backs to Chloe, so they had no idea she'd joined them.

Still holding Lady Bug, who hadn't so much as whimpered, she stayed stone still and took in the scene.

Behind Nikki Lou, Grace and Isaiah stood looking on, occasionally sharing glances with each other, giving off proud parent vibes. They held hands and beamed as the three-year-old's tiny fingers hit the right chords and notes with precision and a remarkable amount of emotion.

A dachshund—that had to be the infamous Slinky—snoozed under the piano bench, doing double duty as Nikki Lou's footstool. He looked up at them, showing a bit of interest, then dropped his head as if he couldn't leave his post.

Her parents were next to Grace, grinning. Well, Mom was grinning. Dad kept wiping his eyes, but they were obviously happy tears. Tori stood with her kids and Dr. Hottypants, who had one protective hand on Tori's shoulder and the other on Finn's. Kenzie had her phone up, recording the moment and proving that some things *never* change.

Rose and Gabe and their kids were there, too, all fascinated by the show. Raina and Madeline flanked a young man Chloe had seen in the Wingate Properties offices in the past. That was Blake, she knew, her nephew, though he was not much younger than she was.

In the profile view, it was easy to see that Raina's pregnancy was showing for sure now, with one hand on her stomach in the classic "pregnant lady" pose.

"Now, sing, Zayah!" Nikki Lou called as she dragged her hands over the keys and started the whole song again.

"*Amazing Grace, how sweet the sound...*" As he belted out the words, everyone's gaze shifted from Nikki Lou to Isaiah. "*That saved a wretch like me.*" With his next breath, he raised his hands and flicked his fingers, inviting everyone to sing.

They sort of laughed and looked at each other, no one diving in to sing the next verse with Isaiah. But Nikki Lou kept playing as if she didn't know how to stop, so Chloe took a few steps forward and cleared her throat to sing words she wasn't sure of, but they felt right.

"*I once was lost, but now I'm found...*"

They turned, shrieked, hooted, and came at her with open arms, and Nikki Lou just kept playing like nothing could stop her, not even Chloe's surprise entrance.

As Chloe buried herself in various embraces and greetings, each one warmer and more precious than the next, Isaiah picked up the rest of the verse and filled the room with his booming baritone.

It wasn't until Nikki Lou finished the song—and she went three more verses—that Chloe had a chance to have a proper, but not nearly as musical, hello. She finally let Lady Bug go, everyone laughing as the little dog went straight for Slinky and they sniffed each other.

"When did we get a piano in here?" she asked as the excitement settled down.

"Zayah surprised me!" Nikki Lou announced, spinning around on the bench like a virtuoso pro, and gazing up at Isaiah with adoring eyes.

He tilted his head in that cloak of humility he wore so well. "It was at my mother's church," he explained. "I heard they were going to get rid of it, so I arranged to get it here. Not the baby grand, but—"

"That one burned," Nikki Lou stated with the sweet simplicity of a child. "Now I have this piano!"

"And you play beautifully," Chloe said, smiling at her and all the others in the room. "I guess you guys have some questions," she added on a laugh. "I'll make the long story short for you. I hated that job. I hated that city. And I hated being away from you. I'm home for good."

"That's my girl," Rex said, giving her another hug as all the others reacted.

"Really? I know how you feel about quitters, Dad."

"You also know how I feel about being far away and making dumb decisions," he fired back, proving that he was well on his way to a full and complete recovery to the man who never minced his words or held back his opinion. "No more goodbyes, Chloe Wingate."

"No more, Dad. I'm here to stay. Jobless and homeless, but here to stay."

"You can stay with us!" Rose said, reaching for her. "Your room is empty and our house is..." She glanced at Gabe. "Going to be a little emptier, as you know."

"You're more than welcome to live with us, whether I'm there or not," Gabe added, giving her a hug. "I'm happy you're back, kid. And I know someone else who's going to be even happier."

She just smiled.

"Or you can stay in the beach house guest suite when I close on my house," Raina said. "That's less than two weeks from now."

"I could do that," she agreed, not a hundred percent thrilled with the idea of living with her parents or even with Rose. She had hoped for another solution. "You guys are not in the bungalow for too much longer, right, Tori? Not that I'm rushing you back to Boston, so..."

Tori gave a quick look to Justin, then her kids, all of them weirdly quiet for a beat.

"Do you have news?" Raina demanded.

"I do," Tori said, taking Justin's hand. "I was saving this until after Nikki Lou's recital, so your timing is perfect, Chloe." She glanced at Justin, then her kids, who all nodded as if they were ready for whatever she was going to announce. "We just found out yesterday and discussed it as a fam...as a group."

But something told Chloe it was only a matter of time until this foursome was a family.

"Well?" Dad asked.

"I'll tell them, Mom," Finn said. "That whole trip in the RV with my dad, so I could play baseball? Turns out it wasn't for me at all, it was a tryout for Dad to coach college-level ball. He got a job at some school in North Carolina."

The entire room reacted with a gasp as Tori held up her hand. "He has asked if I'd consider a change in the custody agreement so the kids would live there in the summers and holidays, and in Boston with me the rest of the time."

"Uh, that would be a no," Kenzie said with the perfect eyeroll of a sixteen-year-old girl. Finn looked a little pained, but gave a tight smile to Justin, who returned it. The non-verbal communication was so strong, it nearly took Chloe's breath away.

"Are you going to do that?" Mom asked Tori. "Is that what you want?"

Tori blew out a breath. "I've decided to fight him for full custody and the three of us are moving here. They'll visit, but this will be their permanent home. Lawyer is hired, hearings are scheduled."

Raina let out a little scream and Rose launched forward to hug her.

"And to answer your question, Chloe, you can have

the bungalow, because the kids are going to come with me to Boston until the holidays. They'll do one semester in their school while I sell the house, transfer my business to my two sous chefs, and hopefully iron something out with the lawyers without going to court. We hope to be back in the new year, and I'll run the Riverfront Café for good."

"And before you ask," Kenzie added, "I'm cool with splitting my junior year. I just want to live here, and for my mom to be happy."

"We both do," Finn said.

"I think you all know how I feel," Justin chimed in, sliding a warm look at the other three. "In fact, while Tori and the kids are up in Boston, I'll be buying a house here."

"I can help with that," Raina cracked, making them laugh.

"As long as it's big enough for..." He held Tori's gaze. "A family."

Chloe just about melted, and a few of them gave in to *awws*, but Tori held up her hands, laughing self-consciously.

"One major life change at a time," she said.

Chloe pressed her hands to her chest as all those life changes rolled over her, taking in the sheer happiness of everyone in the room. This family so totally deserved to be together.

She turned to Blake. "And welcome to you, finally out of—"

"Don't say 'the closet,'" he joked.

"—hiding," she finished, laughing as she stepped to him for their first hug. "I heard you've not only joined the family but you're back at Wingate Properties."

He gave a shrug, but his eyes danced with happiness. "Raina *had* to hire me as an agent or else I'd beat the pants off her as competition."

"And you're okay?" Chloe asked, turning to Grace, who'd been quiet the whole time. "Going to rebuild?"

She nodded, still holding Isaiah's hand. "Yes, we are. In fact, I'm meeting the contractor this week. Insurance is covering almost everything, but the calendar sales have been through the roof, thanks to you. Kitty kindly offered to give all the proceeds of this year's fundraiser to The Next Chapter, so we're able to do even more, and get it done faster, than we'd hoped."

"And I have a new piano!" Nikki Lou announced, making them all cheer and laugh.

As they all started talking again, Rose slid even closer to Chloe.

"I know you have options," she said softly. "But if the bungalow seems too small, I would so love to have you live with us, Chloe."

She searched her sister's face, which for once didn't look like the expression of a woman whose life was perfect. There was some strain around Rose's brown eyes, with the hint of shadows under them.

"Let me think about it," Chloe said, hugging Rose.

"And here's someone who can help you," she whispered.

On a breath, Chloe turned, knowing exactly who had just walked in.

She let that breath out as she met Travis's green eyes and slightly uncertain smile. The world tilted a little, and time stood still, but there was nothing but hope in her heart as she held her hands out and beckoned him closer.

She heard the others greet him, picked up a joke Gabe made, and knew that all eyes were on them, but none of that mattered. She'd missed him deeply, and standing in the midst of her family holding this man in her arms felt utterly and completely *right*.

After a long hug, he finally drew back and looked at her, more handsome and adorable than she remembered. At his feet, Lady Bug barked desperately, clawing at his khaki uniform pants without a morsel of shame.

"So," he said, leaning down and gathering the tiny dog in his big hands but never taking his eyes off Chloe. "Is it over?"

"My short side trip to Los Angeles? My searching for my happiness when it was right here all along? My television career? Yes, Travis, they are all over."

He shook his head. "I meant that stupid man hiatus you were on."

"Oh, that?" She laughed, petting Lady Bug's head as the little pupper nestled into Travis's nestle-worthy chest. "Yes. It has officially ended."

"Hallelujah." With Lady Bug between them, he leaned over and kissed her right on the mouth, nearly making her knees buckle.

Oh, yes. The hiatus was over. And up next? She had no idea, but something told her it was going to be great. And, best of all, no goodbyes.

Chapter Twenty-two

Raina

Final *walkthrough and closing.*

Oh, how Raina loved the sound of those four happy words. Everything was official, like a stamp that said: *something new and amazing and different is about to begin.*

Raina couldn't wait for her new and amazing life in The Sanctuary, a house name she intended to keep.

She fairly hummed as she meandered through the rooms, certain this *would* be her sanctuary—a private world just for her and, soon, her babies. Here, she would become a new woman and a first-time mother. Here, she would shake off the past and look to the future. Here, she was ready to face life without a husband, a partner, or a man.

Upstairs, she tiptoed into her favorite room, glancing around to see the primary suite looked very much like it had the last time she'd been here, minus any sign of Chase Madison sleeping in the four-poster bed.

He'd left all the furniture, as they'd agreed, and the bed was even made with a cool sage comforter. She'd replace that, already planning a fat shopping spree for finishings that would reflect her taste and fresh start.

She did have to do the short mortgage until the sale of W&W went through, but she was comfortable with the arrangement that she'd worked out with Chase. A few signatures on the papers that Blake was bringing over and this beautiful oasis would be hers.

She stepped out onto the balcony, looking at the deep blue water and frothy waves hitting the sand. Every morning, every night, she'd be here, alone until—

"Raina! Raina!"

"Up here, Rose!" she called.

"Oh, my gosh, brace yourself, Raindrop!"

The nickname made her smile, like everything else that day. "I'm braced, Rosebud. What's up?"

"This!" Rose rushed into the room, holding something out. "Look what Grace found tucked into a loose brick behind the back shelves of the bookstore!"

Raina knew instantly what was hanging at the end of the silver chain. "Charlotte's necklace," she whispered, chills tiptoeing up her spine. "Let me see."

Rose came closer, her eyes damp as she held out the tin half-heart that matched the one she'd worn since Annabelle Greene had died. She held it next to the one on her neck, the two halves fitting perfectly to form a complete heart.

Taking the bauble, which was tarnished and slightly dented, Raina looked at the scripted letter *A*, then turned it over to read, "*Never*."

"Never apart," Rose said, wiping a tear. "That's what their necklaces joined to say."

"That's so sweet, Rose."

"You want to have it?" Rose asked. "I can wear one and you can wear the other."

Raina considered the offer for a moment, but looked into her sister's brown eyes and knew the answer.

"You wear them both," she said. "Make the heart complete, and keep the words 'never apart' on your heart, Rose. You're going to need that in the months ahead."

Rose's shoulders collapsed in a rare display of a negative slump. "Years, you mean."

"Barely two," Raina reminded her. "He'll be home a lot, and now I live right here. Plenty of room in that bed if you need a sister on a dark and stormy night."

Rose gave her a look. "I'll probably take you up on that, and bring a few kids. And, come January, that bed will be filled with mama and *her* two babies."

The very idea gave Raina a shiver. "I know, right? I'm so happy I got this place, Rose. It feels so right, my new home, and I just cannot wait to nest and grow and make it all mine!"

Just then, they heard an outburst of laughter from downstairs. "Blake must be here. He and Dani are hilarious together."

"So that's working out?" Rose asked.

"Better than I dreamed and so much fun. She's my right hand on admin, he's my left on listings and sales."

"Which is ideal, because you're going to need both hands soon." Rose gave Raina's tummy a rub.

Raina gave her a happy hug. "I'll need your help, and, also, I'm here for you, Rosebud. Now, put that necklace on and let it serve as a symbol that you and Gabe are never *really* apart."

Rose wrinkled her nose and reached under her hair to unclip the chain she wore, then slid the new imperfect but beautiful heart on it to join the other. "There. Never apart. Except when we are."

She turned and lifted her hair so Raina could latch the chain. "You're going to do great, Rose. You have your wonderful kids, your also wonderful sisters, plus Suze and Dad. Your business is thriving and pretty soon, you'll have a new niece and nephew or two of each."

"Why don't you find out?"

She shrugged and gave her belly another rub. "I want to be surprised. Life is surprising me a lot lately, and I mostly like it."

Raina laughed. "You took my positive pills and I..."

"You are Rose Wingate D'Angelo, the happiest, brightest light in the bunch and, I think we've confirmed, the most like our precious mother."

Rose clasped the necklace charms again. "You're so right, Raindrop."

"Right and—"

"Hello? Raina? Are you up there?"

They both turned at the sound of Chase's voice at the bottom of the stairs.

Raina sucked in a breath, her eyes widening. "What is he doing here?"

"Um, the closing?" Rose frowned. "Isn't the seller always at the closing?"

She shook her head. "He was supposed to go to Europe and was going to sign virtually. There's no reason for him to be here today, unless..."

"Unless what?"

Unless this was too good to be true and he was backing out of the sale. "Unless I'm about to get one of those surprises I claim to like so much."

"Like what? Could he change his mind? That's impossible, isn't it?"

"Nothing is impossible," Raina said dryly, knowing that stranger things had happened in real estate transactions. "It would cost him, but he could."

"He won't," Rose assured her, back to her old self. "There has to be another reason he's here. Maybe to say good luck or get something."

Raina considered that, nodding. "Maybe he has a housewarming gift."

"He could *be* the housewarming gift," Rose teased, making Raina's eyes flash. "What? I've seen the man. It doesn't hurt to look at him."

"Stop."

Rose's brow just lifted as Chase came to the top of the stairs, his sizeable frame filling the doorway to the bedroom.

"Can I talk to you for a minute?" he asked.

Oh, that couldn't be good.

"She's all yours," Rose said brightly, sailing past him. "Congrats on closing today."

He just gave a smile that made Raina's heart drop with a thud to the ground.

"You're backing out," she said, knowing there could be no other reason for that really, really serious look on his face.

She fought the urge to howl when he didn't answer instantly. Instead, she let out a soft whimper, swallowing the most bitter taste of disappointment she could remember in a long, long time.

He only made it worse when he sighed and tipped his head to the two chairs in the bay window. "Can we talk?"

"No." She let her head fall back with a moan. "I can't lose this house."

"Will you hear me out, or do you prefer to assume you know everything I'm going to say?"

She peeked out from under her lashes. "Don't give me hope, Chase."

"I'm giving you...an option. Please?" He gestured toward the chairs, so she followed him, sinking down with a sigh.

"What is it? Better offer? Pulling it from the market? You met your dream girl and want to live here with her?"

A flicker of amusement crossed his strong features. "I want to live here...with you."

"*Excuse me?*"

He leaned forward, bracing his elbows on his knees. "I need to stay a little longer for, uh, personal reasons."

"Can't you stay at your hotel?"

"It's not officially open and it will be full from day one, so no. I need..." He cleared his throat. "A little more time to work something out. So, I could either renege on the deal—"

She swore under her breath.

"*Or...*" he added pointedly. "I could rent from you."

She let out a breath, considering what a hassle that would be. Of course, the owner wanting to close but stay in the house and rent wasn't unheard of in real estate. But it meant that Raina couldn't move in, couldn't nest and get a nursery ready for the babies, which was a huge disappointment.

"How long?" she asked.

"I honestly don't know how long..." He gave a pained expression. "Six months at the most."

Six? She was having these babies in four! She closed her eyes in frustration. "I guess I could postpone moving in..."

"No, no. That's not what I'm suggesting," he said quickly. "I'll rent the guest suite downstairs, which is self-contained and has its own entrance. I'll pay enough to cover that mortgage you had to get, then you can just flip it to a cash sale whenever you're ready. The house is yours, completely. All I'm asking for is that one room and, well, use of the kitchen."

Oh, that was different. Certainly not ideal, though.

"It's a great deal for you," he added.

Live with him? As her roommate in the guest suite on the first floor? Seeing him every morning and night, when she was in her PJs and clay mask, when she came in from the beach, when she was...lonely—er, *alone*—at night?

"I don't know if I'd call that...great."

He laughed. "What would you call it?"

She'd call it insane. Inconvenient. Intrusive. And...*intimate*. That last thought brought a rare flush to her cheeks.

"I'd call it...not what I expected."

"I know, I know," he agreed. "I understand you want to settle in on your own, find your footing after your divorce, and have these babies."

"I doubt you understand *that*."

He smiled and tipped his head in concession. "Look, I don't want to break this contract. I know you love and want this house. You belong here. Would you just consider this arrangement and make my life easier for a while? I am taking that trip to Europe, so I'll be gone for a bit at the outset."

She stared at him, everything in her wanting to say no. But he'd so unselfishly helped her reconnect with Blake. He didn't have to do that, or give Blake the listing to help her out.

Not to mention that if this sale fell through, *anything* could happen. She'd been in this business long enough to know that if she didn't close today, she might never get her Sanctuary. But if he moved in, at least she'd have the contract signed and sealed and the house would legally be in her name.

"Just think about it this way," he said. "Your mortgage gets paid, you get the main suite, the run of the house, everything."

"But share the kitchen."

He shrugged. "You won't hate that once you've tasted

my homemade pasta. Remember?" He tapped his chest. "Half Sicilian."

"So you're making me an offer I can't refuse."

He laughed at that, a rumble from his chest that sounded warm and friendly and not at all threatening. How bad could it be?

"Okay," she whispered, surrendering to change, but not complete disappointment.

He extended his hand. "We have a deal?"

"We have a deal." She took his hand and they stood at exactly the same time.

"This could be fun, Raina."

She eased her fingers free from his touch. "It could be...something."

Yes, it certainly could be something. Soon enough, she'd find out...*what*.

∼

DON'T MISS The Florist on Amelia Island, the next book in the Seven Sisters series!

Change is certainly in the air on Amelia Island. With Gabe gone for weeks at a stretch, Rose's unwavering enthusiasm is tested in ways she never expected. Chloe finds the courage to try one more career path, with help from the most unexpected source...Lady Bug. The sisters team up to surprise Susannah and Rex on their fortieth wedding anniversary, and Raina settles into her new beachfront nest. As she brings her marriage to an end and cruises ever closer to motherhood, there's only one unexpected complication in her life...a new roommate who isn't at all the man she thought he was.

When the clouds roll over the florist on Amelia Island, the Wingate women learn over and over again that the bond between seven sisters is as strong as steel, as gentle as an ocean breeze, and as lasting as their family legacy.

Visit www.hopeholloway.com for release dates, covers, and sneak peeks into the series!

The Beach House on Amelia Island - Book 1
The Café on Amelia Island - Book 2
The Bookstore on Amelia Island - Book 3
The Florist on Amelia Island - Book 4
The Chocolate Shop on Amelia Island - Book 5
The Dressmaker on Amelia Island - Book 6
The Inn on Amelia Island - Book 7

Love Hope Holloway's books? If you haven't read her first two series, you're in for a treat! Chock full of family feels and beachy Florida settings, these sagas are for lovers of riveting and inspirational sagas about sisters, secrets, romance, mothers, and daughters...and the moments that make life worth living.

These series are complete, and available in e-book (also in Kindle Unlimited), paperback, and audio.

The Coconut Key Series

Set in the heart of the Florida Keys, these seven delightful novels will make you laugh out loud, wipe a happy tear, and believe in all the hope and happiness of a second chance at life.

A Secret in the Keys – Book 1
A Reunion in the Keys – Book 2
A Season in the Keys – Book 3
A Haven in the Keys – Book 4
A Return to the Keys – Book 5
A Wedding in the Keys – Book 6
A Promise in the Keys – Book 7

The Shellseeker Beach Series

Come to Shellseeker Beach and fall in love with a "found family" of unforgettable characters who face life's challenges with humor, heart, and hope.

About the Author

Hope Holloway is the author of charming, heartwarming women's fiction featuring unforgettable families and friends, and the emotional challenges they conquer. After more than twenty years in marketing, she launched a new career as an author of beach reads and feel-good fiction. A mother of two adult children, Hope and her husband of thirty years live in Florida. When not writing, she can be found walking the beach with her two rescue dogs, who beg her to include animals in every book. Visit her site at www.hopeholloway.com.

Made in the USA
Columbia, SC
08 August 2023

21400641R00207